LOOKS LIKE LOVE

LOOKS LIKE LOVE

An Eros & Co. Novel

KERRI KEBERLY

Medusa tucked an errant serpent behind her ear. The writhing coils were already hard enough to tame in the humidity of the Underworld.

Sitting in front of the Collector of Souls this hellish Monday morning, they were acting downright unhinged. In fact, one had the nerve to interrupt her by springing up and striking another with a hiss.

She really thought the girls had more self-control. Then again, when had her little danger noodles ever behaved?

"Cool it, ladies." She separated the tangled offenders before continuing on with her conversation. "See, Your Hotness? Even my snakes are restless. We need to blow off some steam. I'm telling you, there is only so much reality television the girls and I can take. I need a vacation, and what better place for a little 'me time' than in the mortal world?"

Hades lifted a dark brow at her, his red eyes glowing like banked embers. Had she referred to him as "Your Hotness" again?

Oops.

She just couldn't get used to the official titles they were supposed to use down here now. She'd been working for

Hades pretty much since Almighty Douche had given him cart blanche to run "everything below" as he saw fit.

Yeah, right. It hadn't taken long before the "as he saw fit" part was given a caveat. Now that Almighty Douche—sorry, Zeus—was strongly encouraging his brother to run the Underworld and its inhabitants more like Life Industries up on Mount Olympus, they were suddenly supposed to start being all formal and shit?

Not happening.

"For the last time, Medusa. You're dead. You cannot walk among the living without special permission." Hades leaned back in his massive chair, fashioned from skulls of the damned. It was respectfully done, of course, with the whole thing elegantly encased in gold and the seat tastefully fitted with a silken black cushion.

Living trapped under the thumb of his brother turned him into a diabolical fiend sometimes, but he wasn't a complete demon.

"You're lucky you even got your head back," continued Hades. "You do know Athena refused to hand it over at first, right?"

"Right," agreed Medusa. "But only because you've reminded me literally a thousand times. Look, no one has more first-hand experience with how big of a know-it-all bitch Athena is than me, but Hades, I've been cooped up down here for ages. I mean, I like being Head Monster and all, but, and I don't mean this in a bad way, some of the freaks you've got down here just aren't pulling their weight. All they do is sit around while snapping bones and eating raw flesh rolls." Medusa shuddered. "I hate raw flesh rolls. They taste like a dirty fish tank. I think it's the seaweed wrap."

"How long are we talking?" asked Hades.

"A mortal year," she replied. Might as well go big.

"A full year? As in three hundred and sixty-five days?" His eyes went wide, and his mouth dropped open.

She bit a dry, cracked lip and nodded.

Hades tilted his head. He was thinking, and Medusa didn't know if that was good or bad. He suddenly snapped his mouth shut before folding his arms as he crossed an ankle over one knee.

"Okay. Out with it," he said. "What's the real reason you want to mingle with the human meat bags?"

Medusa shifted her eyes toward the throne room ceiling with a sigh. She surveyed the sparkling stalactites, listening to the hissing coming from somewhere around the back of her head. After fixing her gaze back on Hades, she went for broke.

"I'm bored. There, I said it. I'm a strong, independent gorgon, but I still want to get gussied up and paint the town black every once in a while, you know? And who can I do that with, huh? Cyclops? No thanks. He's tall, dark and relatively handsome, but he's dumber than a city full of Trojans."

As if to prove her point, a ground-shaking bellow came from the break room. "Stupid machine. Give Cyclops wakey juice. Now!" Two loud booms followed the outburst, and Medusa rolled her eyes. That slobbering idiot was going to crack the granite countertop in half again.

"You have to press the START button, Clops," shouted Medusa in the direction of the break room. She maneuvered her office chair made of rickety old bones across the rocky, uneven floor.

The wheeled femurs rattled and shook, and when the giant's hunched back came into view, she waited until she heard the one-eyed son of Gaia mumble "Oh yeah" before tilting her head at Hades.

Hades stretched his lips into a grimace. "Touché. What about Achilles, then? He's smart," he suggested, turning a palm up as if the answer were that simple.

"Are you kidding me?" snorted Medusa, scooting her chair

back to its original position in front of his throne. "He only has eyes for Patroclus."

Hades studied her for a moment before narrowing his gaze. "So that's it. You want to bring one down here before its time, don't you? You want your own meat bag to terrorize."

"What? No . . ." A nervous laugh bobbed in her throat. That's exactly what she planned to do. Except, she didn't want to terrorize it, necessarily. She just wanted it to adore her, send her flowers, feed her chocolates . . . worship her like there was no tomorrow. "Maybe I just want a little rest and relaxation, okay? What's wrong with wanting some carbs and a frozen margarita every once in a while?"

Now it was Hades' turn to tilt his head. Not to be outdone, he upped the ante by adding an accusatory raised brow into the mix.

Medusa pinched the thick ridge that served as the bridge of her nose, or what resembled a nose, anyway. She'd worked for the Collector of Souls for a long time, he knew her well enough to know she was lying through her rotten, chipped teeth.

"Oh, all right. Yes. I want to find a meat bag to do my bidding."

Hades slapped his thigh. "I knew it!"

"So what? That's not the *entire* reason I want a vacation. I need a break from wiping everyone's ass around here. For Fates' sake, Clops can't even figure out how to get his "wakey juice," and it's been like that every single morning for an eternity. Can I help it if my dream vacation just happens to involve easy-to-manipulate meat bags who would worship the very ground I walk on? Come on, Hades, I deserve this."

"Trust me, I get it," he replied. "But we're not supposed to bring any more souls down here before their time. The Fates will have my ass if I let you mess with protocol like that. Besides, we're full. When's the last time you watched the news? Murder, hate crimes, human trafficking, they're at an all-time high. You've got celebrities buying their kids' way into prestigious universities, movie producers preying on innocent women, leaders of nations being absolute pieces of . . . Shit, don't even get me started, Duce."

Medusa flushed, her scales turning a darker shade of green than normal. Her chance at companionship, even if it would have been forced, was slipping through her gnarled, claw-like fingers.

Time to do what she did best. Prey on his insecurities.

"You know what, Hades? I've been an absolute pillar of the monster community for centuries. I've helped build the reputation of this realm of yours from day one. I've fueled countless nightmares. I've been the source material for horror stories *and* films," she said, ticking off her accomplishments. "Don't *you* get *me* started on how much general terror I've caused, and that's based on the stone thing alone. See this rat's nest of snakes?" She pointed at her head. "And the fangs? *Hello*, can you say Halloween costume inspiration? Have I not been instrumental when it comes to instilling fear into the hearts of man?"

A deafening screech from an incoming harpy nearly drowned out Hades' heavy sigh. The winged creature flew into the throne room shortly after, unleashing another eerie cry as it swooped and darted between the columns. With a gust of wind, it landed in a crouch in front of the dais on which Hades' desk sat.

The harpy retracted its wings as it bowed its feathered head. Its yellow-eyed gaze flicked toward Medusa before the half bird, half woman turned back to Hades. Without further ado, it held out a pink envelope in one of its talons.

"A message from Queen Persephone, Collector," croaked the harpy.

Hades took the letter with bright eyes and eager hands, bringing it to his nose and inhaling deeply.

Medusa held in a groan, pursing her lips as she patiently waited for Hades to finish blissing out. Persephone sent a memo near the end of every summer, giving him the date of her return to the Underworld for the winter months. She always perfumed it with a heavy dose of spring flowers.

Must be nice to have someone to send you notes like that. Someone who didn't think you were an ugly monster.

Hades tucked the envelope between the arm of the throne and his thigh. Presumably, so he could open it later, in private. "Thank you, Aello."

"Collector." The harpy nodded before spreading her wings with a snap and launching into the air again. She signaled her departure with another ear-splitting scream.

Hades slapped the arms of his throne with his palms. "So. Where were we?"

Medusa pursed her lips. He really couldn't wait to open that letter, could he? So annoying. But maybe she could make its arrival, and the resulting lift in his mood, however small, work to her advantage. "You were about to approve my vacation days."

Hades huffed, clearly hoping she'd forgotten. "Right. Well, I don't know that I can afford to let the beasts of the Underworld go unsupervised for that long."

"I'm sure one of the Furies can keep them in line."

She was about to suggest which Fury would be most fit to fill her shoes when the atmosphere to her left began to shift. A moment later Hermes stepped out of a pocket of swirling air and into view. "Knock, knock."

In addition to being the messenger of the gods, Hermes was also a psychopomp, which meant he could cross over into all sorts of boundaries, including Hades' Realm. Being patron of travelers, it had just seemed a natural fit for him to escort souls into the Underworld.

Well, as far as the Styx, anyway. That's when Charon, the

ferryman tasked with collecting payment before bringing souls over to be sorted, took over.

The real baddies went to Tartarus, the lowest, and most torturous, circle of Hades' Realm, so they usually tried to make a break for it. Hermes had a real knack for putting souls at ease on the trip down, minimizing the number of freak-outs, which is why Hades had requested him for the job. It had been the rare instance one of his petitions had been granted with very little argument from Olympus.

"Hermes! What a pleasant surprise," said Hades, his delight the conversation had been cut short yet again obvious.

Medusa leaned back in her chair, crossing her legs and folding her arms, resigned to wait out the latest interruption. She didn't mind this one, necessarily.

Hades was right, it was always a pleasant surprise to see Hermes. He was a god, sure, but he didn't take himself as seriously as most of the others did, and it was why everyone down here liked him, even her.

But, judging by the size of the envelope in his hand, Hermes wasn't there to shoot the shit. He was there to deliver a message, and messages from Olympus usually put Hades in a terrible mood.

So much for getting those vacation days approved.

CHAPTER TWO

ermes gave them both a nod. "Hello, Hades. What's up, Medusa?"

Medusa nodded back, appreciating Hermes' dark skin and his bright sea-green eyes, which still sparkled even in the dim light of the Underworld. But despite the easy-going twinkling in his eyes, the expression on his face was drawn and serious. Whatever new decree Zeus The Douche had for Hades now wouldn't bode well for vacay.

Hermes held out the delivery to Hades without a word. Yep. She might as well just get back to wiping asses.

Hades blew out a breath before leaning forward. "How does Zeus want to boss me around now?" He snatched the envelope from Hermes' outstretched hand. "His holier-than-thou bullshit is really getting old. You know that, right?"

"I know," agreed Hermes, "but the big guy is still kicking, so we've all got to—"

"*We* don't have to do shit. I didn't even want this gig, yet he put me in charge down here. You know what? I've got half a mind to give it back. Let him get a taste of what it's like to run all nine circles at the same time." Hades mumbled the last part as he tore open the envelope.

Medusa stiffened, anxious to hear all the ways the message was sure to stop what little progress she'd made with her vacation dead in its tracks.

"Oh, for Fates' sake. Is he serious?" The envelope and its contents went up in flames before Hades tossed the ashes to the floor. "He thinks *that* will help boost Olympus's image?"

"What's going on?" asked Medusa, unfolding her arms. If she wasn't already dead, her curiosity would be absolutely killing her.

"Besides the fact that my brother is apparently an idiot?" A cynical laugh burst from Hades' throat. "And here I thought he was just a pompous asshole."

"Relax, man." Hermes lifted a hand in a calming gesture. "I'm sure there's a work-around. The last thing you want to do is go off half-cocked and say something you'll regret."

Hades forcefully brushed away the ashes that had fallen into his lap. "I'm not a *man*, Hermes. I'm the King of the Underworld, the Collector of Souls, ruler over the nine circles of hell, which, may I remind you, were left to me to run *as I see fit*. But we all know how hard it is for my brother to keep his hands out of the cookie jar, don't we? Selfish bastard."

Medusa swallowed hard. She hadn't seen Hades this upset in a while, and he must be royally pissed because he never used air quotes.

Also, he was performing horribly at providing context.

"Is this something I can help with?" she asked.

Hades' glowing gaze landed on her. It pulsed in perfect time with the heavy rise and fall of his chest. Thankfully, the longer he thought about her question, the more his breathing slowed, and the scowl on his face loosened.

"There might be."

That's right, Your Hotness. Talk it out. "Okay, then let's hear it."

"Suppose I do approve your request for time off. You'll

need a mortal shell. And where does one go about getting one of those? Who must one ask?"

"I have a feeling I know where this is going," interjected Hermes. "And I don't think it's—"

Hades flipped up his hand, cutting Hermes short.

"My dear brother. That's who."

Medusa shook her head, thoroughly confused. It was no secret the Collector of Souls had poor communication skills, but he was making zero sense right now.

"Whoa, whoa, whoa," said Medusa. "Back up. What does this have to do with my vacation time? I'm a monster, not a mind reader. Start from the beginning. What did Zeus's message say?"

Hades' eyes fired up again, and a crimson flush shot up his neck like a thermometer, rising past his mouth, which was screwed shut, until it hit his hairline.

Since her boss was obviously useless at the moment, Medusa turned her attention toward the messenger for answers. "Hermes?"

"There's a soul whose fate is nearing its end," he explained. "It's got a year or so left before it's due to expire."

"Yeah, so? Why is that Hades' problem?"

"Because this mortal's soul is questionable. Meaning, he could go either way—good or bad. What makes it Hades' problem is that Zeus's publicist has talked him into doing a complete overhaul on the Olympians tarnished reputations, so . . ."

Medusa chuckled. Good luck with that. Excluding Hermes, the Olympians were the biggest bunch of A-holes in the Greek pantheon.

"So, he doesn't want any soul that has even the slightest potential to be bad anywhere near Olympus."

"Which means he's pawning souls off on me," blurted Hades. "Even though the Underworld is at capacity. We can't find room for the ones that *do* belong down here."

Now the pieces were starting to fit. Once Zeus got his giant mitts on an inch, he didn't waste time taking the whole damn mile.

"But it's just one soul, right? Are we really that full?"

She'd been asking either one of them, but Hades answered. "For now, but you know what happens when Zeus gets a bug up his ass. Before you know it, he'll be diverting millions of souls to the Underworld, just to clean up the reputations of those ungrateful dicks. We are literally bursting at the seams. If I let him get away with one, he'll decree a mandatory detour for the rest of them and this whole place will blow. Either that or we start recycling souls . . . and that's getting into the Fates' territory. So not going there. Ugh." Hades shook his head, and a pad of paper and pen materialized in Medusa's lap. "Here, write this down."

Medusa gritted her teeth. Really? He was going to use her, Head Monster of the Underworld, as his personal assistant right now? Despite her irritation, she picked up the pen so she could take down every word Hades dictated.

I, Hades, King of the Underworld, Collector of Souls, and official Ruler of Death, hereby refuse the admittance of the soul named within the memo sent via the messenger, Hermes.

Yep. That was exactly what he was going to do, treat her like a secretary.

And she was going to let him. She'd learned from experience it was better to stand back during one of his flare-ups. Trying to stop it was about as successful as stopping dynamite from exploding after it's been lit.

I feel it undermines the authority expressly granted to me, and directly interferes with my right to rule "everything below," also referred to as "the nether," "Tartarus," and/or "Hades'

*Realm," as a separate entity from "everything above," the
realm also commonly referred to as "Mount Olympus."*

Hades stopped to wiggle a finger at Hermes. "Don't go anywhere. I need you to take this to Olympus ASAP."
Hermes, ever patient and always affable, nodded.

However, being the fair and reasonable ruler that I am . . .

"Make sure fair and reasonable are in all caps," directed Hades.
Medusa rolled her eyes. "Got it."

*. . . and having held jurisdiction over said realm for eons,
without incident, I reject this preposterous suggestion that I
blindly take on the aforementioned soul without due process.
As such, I return this proposal with conditions of my own. No
further negotiations shall be accepted, and any remaining
points of contention shall be mediated by the Fates.*

*1. The soul in question shall undergo a thorough assessment of
quality (good vs. bad), which shall be the final determination
regarding to which realm it belongs.*

*2. The assessment shall be done by an associate of my choosing,
as the good reputation of yours (the Olympians) cannot be
trusted.*

*3. You agree to this or I hand over the keys to Tartarus effective
immediately.*

Eagerly awaiting your reply,
Hades

Medusa began to fold the letter. True to form, Hades was

throwing fuel onto the fire, which never went well for any of them.

"Wait, wait, wait," continued Hades. "Add this, too . . . P.S. Good luck trying to repair your reputation while running this hell hole, bro."

Medusa shook her head before scratching out the post-script and then handed the letter to Hermes.

"You sure you want to do this?" asked Hermes.

Hades answered by lifting his neatly trimmed goatee in defiance.

"All righty, then. Be right back." Hermes parted the air like a curtain and disappeared.

Medusa stared at Hades, regretting she hadn't gone with her original plan to call in sick that morning. "Let me guess, I'm the associate of your choosing."

"Oh, don't get your snakes in a bunch, Duce. It's perfect. My brother gets his balls busted, you get your vacation, and I kill two birds with one... wait for it... stone."

Medusa held in a grumble while Hades laughed at his own stupid joke.

He was right, though. He should absolutely push back on The Douche, or else the Underworld would be undergoing a complete rebrand before they knew it.

Besides, even if Hades had approved her vacation days before this trash fire had erupted, she still would have had to beg Zeus for a mortal shell. The king of d-bags granting her one of those, even for such a relatively short time-period, was about as likely as him keeping his pecker in his pants for one whole decade.

A smile played at the corner of her lips. She was beginning to see the beauty of Hades' plan. This way, she wouldn't have to explain why she needed a mortal shell, and Hades would have insurance he'd win this round in his never-ending battle to keep his brother's hands off his tar pits. Keeping the Underworld a Zeus-free zone was good for everyone, especially her. Being Hades' right-hand monster, if he was happy, she was happy, and winning a fight with Zeus would definitely make Hades happy. Not having him bored and in her snakes all the time always made her job so much easier.

Medusa glanced at the pink envelope still wedged between Hades' thigh and his throne. He was already caressing its edges impatiently, and she knew he would tear it open the first moment alone he got. Pushing back on his brother's ridiculous demands had undoubtedly jacked up his testosterone.

Poor Persephone. No one saw her for the first few weeks when she returned. After this, it would probably be a solid month and a half.

Medusa bit the inside of her cheek. At least someone would be getting laid, so maybe lucky was a better word. If she spent one more immortal night alone, drinking merlot and binge-watching Lucifer for the twelve hundredth time, she was going to frigging lose it.

Assessing one soul while she was on vacation shouldn't be too hard, right? And it was certainly better than trudging back to her thankless job managing the hubs of Hell every day.

An explosion of thunder rumbled from somewhere far above the throne room, violent enough to shake both the ground and Medusa from her thoughts.

Hades' message had been received.

The lights flickered, the electrical current longing to join forces with the lightning bolts that had undoubtedly accompanied the rage-thunder above ground. A few seconds later the air rippled, and Hermes popped his head through the part he'd made in the space-time continuum.

"Life Industries tomorrow morning, 9:00 a.m. sharp. There should be a mortal shell waiting for whomever you send."

hen the elevator doors slid open, a gods-awful light slashed across Medusa's face, forcing her to shield her eyes.

"Seriously?" she snarled as she stepped into the atrium of Mount Olympus, hand still planted on her forehead while her slitted pupils adjusted to the harsh light. The Underworld was scarce on sunlight, but damn, the glare up here was freaking ridiculous.

Her scowl widened as she made her way across the atrium toward the imposing corporate headquarters of the gods, wincing as she took in her surroundings. Life Industries, along with the other shops and buildings located in the sprawling divine complex, had been built with enough glittering granite and gleaming marble to give a gorgon one helluva migraine for *at least* a century.

And was the water pouring from the massive fountain in its courtyard really that dazzling? It looked as though the copper nymphs huddling in the center were dumping an endless stream of diamonds from their urns. Knowing the gods and goddesses, and their fondness for luxury and love of excess, they probably were.

Hades' wrath, even the air was over the top; so crisp and clean and delicious she pulled it into her lungs in huge, greedy gulps without thinking.

Until she caught herself and stopped.

Speaking of fresh, she bent her head slightly, cocking a shoulder up for a quick sniff to check and see if the au de toilette of the Underworld had clung to her as strongly as she suspected.

Yep, she stank of ash and brimstone.

What had she thought she'd smell like? Roses? She was a monster for Fates' sake, and an infamously gruesome one at that. Olympus would just have to deal with a little rankness. They were lucky she didn't reek of terror and rot that morning.

She straightened, pulling her shoulders back, and was just about to take a step when she heard whispering, accompanied by low, smug laughter.

Determined not to give whomever it was the satisfaction of looking their way, Medusa tried to ignore it, focusing instead on the irritatingly cheerful chirping of songbirds bouncing around the atrium. She would have much rather it had been the flapping of bat wings, which was ten times more soothing in her opinion, but she wasn't at home, now was she?

"What is *she* doing *here*?"

Chirp!

"Shouldn't she be turning people to stone somewhere?"

Chirp! Chirp!

"Gods, she's so *ugly*."

Chirp! Chirp! Chirp!

Medusa's head spun, twisting on her shoulders until it stopped in the direction of the three Graces who stood staring at her. She fixed a narrowed gaze on them and proceeded to pin them in place with dagger eyes.

One wore an expression of horror, but the other two

donned defiant looks of open hostility along with their diaphanous dresses. Medusa couldn't detect an ounce of grace among them. And wasn't that ironic, since grace was kind of their thing?

Clearly, they were shocked that such a wretched creature had slinked up from the Underworld and had the audacity to set foot on their precious mountain.

They were probably scared, and Medusa could understand that. She could even sympathize, she really could. Scaring the shit out of people came with the territory, but the looks of contempt—not sympathy, not pity, but pure, unadulterated disdain—distorting their rosy-cheeked, Rubenesque faces, pushed Medusa into the red zone faster than a siren could lure a sailor to his death.

Fuck you, bitches. I don't need your approval.

Medusa's nostrils flared when her forked tongue shot out of her mouth and flickered. Her snakes, having her back as always, hissed while she unleashed a monstrous growl. The Graces shrieked, groping for one another as if it would make the big, bad monster go away. Well, it didn't, and to prove it, Medusa took a step in their direction. They squealed again, bouncing into each other before scattering every which way.

Feeling better, and thoroughly satisfied at the way they'd tripped over their rather outdated gauzy dresses, Medusa flipped her snakes over her shoulder and continued on toward the giant doors of Almighty Douche's headquarters.

If she couldn't be beautiful, damn right she'd be ugly.

Her lips curled into a wicked grin at the thought of the Graces running home to wherever it was they lived to change their undergarments. They deserved it. They didn't even know her—hadn't even *tried* to get to know her—yet they'd decided she wasn't worthy of an ounce of the grace and humility they were supposedly known for.

A small twinge of guilt came on the heels of her delight, urging Medusa to pick up the pace in an attempt to leave the feeling behind. Even though she'd gotten the last laugh, her run-in with the Graces had pulled an old longing to the surface. One she tried to keep buried. She'd had friends once. Friends and family who'd adored her. And she missed them.

Praise Hades, no one ever heard what was really going on inside her head. Or knew that her stone-cold heart sometimes still hoped for a different outcome, just once.

She took the wide stone steps two at a time, despite being a touch nervous her still shaking limbs might give out.

Monsters had a reputation for reveling in their horribleness. And she mostly did, but it was hard sometimes, especially since she hadn't had a choice in the matter of becoming a monster. She hadn't been born this way . . . she'd been cursed.

Medusa sucked in a few deep breaths as she crossed over the porch, and by the time she reached the gilded doors of Life Industries, she'd managed to clear the thought from her mind. The doors opened easily, and she found herself surrounded by more polished and shining fixtures than necessary. The whole light and airy thing bordered on cliche at this point, to be honest, but she plastered on a smile and headed toward the front desk.

The receptionist paled when she looked up to see Medusa coming straight for her.

"Good morning," said Medusa. "I have a meeting with Zeus at nine. Hades sent me."

"Name, please?"

What. The. Fuck. Seriously? Medusa tilted her head at the goddess of dunces, apparently.

"Sorry. Yes, I know who you are," said the receptionist with a nervous laugh. "I'm just not used to monsters being on the mountain. One moment, please. I'll see if Zeus is ready for you."

The nameplate perched on top of the ledge surrounding the receptionist's desk read *Leto*. Medusa could tell she was a goddess by the way she glowed, and her name sounded familiar. If Medusa remembered right, Leto was one of Zeus's wives. She just wasn't sure where in the line-up this particular goddess had been—earlier or later. Medusa racked her brain trying to recall while the goddess uttered a series of "uh-huhs" and "okays" into the phone.

When Leto finally hung up, she looked as though she were about to shit bricks again.

"Is there a problem?" asked Medusa. So help her Hades, if she didn't get the mortal shell she was promised, this whole damn mountain was going to learn a new meaning for the term "frightening."

"I'm afraid Zeus can't meet with you this morning."

"*Hades* worked it out with D—Zeus. I'm just here to pick up the mortal shell they agreed would be issued to an associate of the Collector's choosing. That associate is me. I have the green light to conduct official business on . . . You know what? Just tell him it will only take a few minutes and I'll be off his precious mountain."

Leto clicked her tongue. "I'm so sorry, Medusa. He told me to tell you you'd have to meet with Athena for the mortal shell."

Medusa clenched her jaw. Son of a gods-damned satyr fucker. This was precisely why everyone in the Underworld called him the Almighty Douche. The imperious bastard always found a way to go back on his word. How had he known Hades would send her, anyway? She supposed it was no secret that her and the Collector of Souls were tight. He wasn't going to send Cyclops, that was for damn sure.

And if making an educated guess Hades would send her had been the case, Zeus knew full well pinning Athena down wasn't going to be easy, not with her schedule, and definitely not with the bad blood between her and Medusa.

He may be an unscrupulous bastard, but he sure was clever like a fox.

"Fine. Fuck it. I'll meet with Athena, then." After a beat of silence, Medusa smoothed down a snake, wondering if her outburst had worked for or against her. Another beat passed, so she added, "In the meantime, where's the nearest rest area?"

Leto pointed behind her and off to the side. "Just through that stone arch, darling."

"Thank you," said Medusa. "I'm going to go powder my nose while you get Athena on the horn."

Medusa turned on her heels, trying not to break out into a run. How humiliating. First Zeus refused to meet with her, a lowly monster, and then she'd referred to the bump on her face as a nose. Anyone with retinas could see it was more of a snout.

When she was inside the privacy of the rest area, she exhaled loudly as she sank into a cushioned chair. Her head jerked from side-to-side and back-and-forth as her most headstrong snakes struck out at the air and each other.

She gripped the arms of the chair. "Get a hold of yourselves, ladies. We can do this, all right? We get in, we get what we came for, kick rocks, and then it's margaritas on the beach at sunset with hot mortal meat bags. Won't that be nice?"

The promise of alcohol-fueled trysts on Earth seemed to do the trick, and the violent lashing settled into a subdued wiggling across her back and shoulders.

Medusa peered at the ornately framed mirror hanging on the wall across from her and sighed. She brought a man-hand to her face, poking a pointy nail at the rough ridges of her scales. Her skin used to be flawless. Now it was a putrid green, pocked and pitted. Her gaze dropped to the thin, cracked lips that used to be full and luscious, and the memory of once being beautiful stabbed at her chest.

She forced her gaze to meet the reflection's eyes. She was not going there. No way. What she was going to do was get that gods-damned mortal shell from someone on this mountain because she deserved it.

"Stop being such a coward," she scolded the monster in the mirror.

She'd do whatever it took to get to Earth, where she could finally take a break from being friendless, lover-less, and totally under-appreciated.

Dwelling on the fact that she had been unceremoniously stripped of her former beauty hadn't done her any good before, and it wasn't going to do her any good now. Oh, she'd tried pleading her case in the beginning, but it had only led to several bouts of sore, bloodied knuckles from pounding on the stony and unyielding walls of Athena's temple, begging the goddess to listen.

Did it make her angry that Athena had refused to hear her side of the story? That she chose to ignore what that insidious bastard Poseidon had done? Absolutely. Was Medusa able to do anything about being turned into a hideous monster? Nope. Not when the goddess of stubborn asses thought she knew what had gone down and lost her shit, blaming Medusa instead of Poseidon for what happened inside her precious little temple. The harder Medusa had tried to explain that she in no way had given consent to the god's dastardly act, the more Athena had refused to listen, turning Medusa into a gorgon and leaving her with no other option but to embrace her freshly cursed ugliness.

Over time, Medusa forgot she'd once had a heart, soft and forgiving, and she had gradually let the emptiness take over, until the memories of her mortal life had faded away and she was left cold as stone.

Pun very much intended.

Instead of crying over the mortality she'd lost, she'd decided to live her eternal life as a monster to the fullest. Once her mind was made up, she channeled all her rage into being the best damn Head Monster the Collector of Souls ever had. She'd made the best of an unfair situation and had become one of the most ruthless monsters in the Underworld. A real hard-ass bitch.

Not hard enough, apparently, since a tiny part of her still held out hope that people might see her as something other than a monster . . .

Medusa scoffed. Done with feeling sorry for herself, she banished the annoying thoughts and stood. She smoothed her scales back into place before heading out of the rest area. Whatever her past, she was a monster now, and monsters didn't care about shit. They were tough as harpy talons, and they didn't give a satyr's ass whether they were liked, or if Graces thought what they lacked in beauty they made up for in personality. And they for damned sure didn't whine about potentially having a one-on-one with the goddess who'd turned them into a frigging nightmare.

Medusa stalked toward Leto's desk with renewed determination. When she tapped her claws on the ledge, Leto's worried look intensified.

"Um, Athena didn't answer, so I, uh . . . I called . . ."

Medusa's eyes, normally gaping-hole black, flashed a you-better-be-worried red as she balled her man-hands into fists.

She was getting ready to spew a string of curses when the god of love, all dimpled-cheeked and golden-haired, rushed into the lobby.

edusa's gaze went right to the rather large appendages on the god's back. Not her type, as she preferred skeletal and leathery, but she had to admit, he did have an impressive set of wings.

"I called Eros," finished Leto, her teeth trapping her bottom lip.

"Good morning, Medusa," greeted the god of love. "Leto says Zeus couldn't make his meeting with you this morning. Anything I can help you with?"

"Well," said Medusa, folding her arms. "Unless you have the authority to issue a mortal shell to a monster who's supposed to start a very important off-site project in less than 24-hrs, then no, I don't see how you can help."

Eros gave Leto a look that screamed, *"You're right . . . She is scary as hell."*

"Well, creating lasting love is my main thing, but I can also create the illusion of beauty, if need be. Forgive me if I'm being rude, but I'm assuming that's what your meeting was about? Signing out a pleasing mortal shell, to enable you to work out in the field?"

Medusa nodded. That about summed it up, all except the

work part. She supposed making her assessment could qualify as official Underworld business, technically, but after she got that out of the way she'd be free to engage in as much debauchery as she felt necessary. If she couldn't get her hands on a mortal shell, she'd need some serious magic to hide her ugly. She couldn't go on vacation without it.

It looked like Eros was her best option at this point.

"Are you confident your illusion will hold, matchmaker?"

"Ever heard of the saying beauty is in the eye of the beholder?"

Medusa shrugged. "I don't recall. Why?"

Eros jerked a thumb toward his chest. "Because I'm the guy that makes it happen. It's not permanent, but it should be strong enough to get you through a long-term project. You're pre-approved for a leave of absence to conduct official Olympus-related business, right?"

"I'll be conducting Underworld business, but yes, the vaca—project has been approved by Hades . . ." She tacked on a little white lie for good measure. "And Zeus."

"Perfect. Why don't you come back to my office and we can get the paperwork started? We'll just need your signature to move forward."

Disarmed at both Leto's determination to help her, even though the goddess was clearly nervous a monster was in their midst, and Eros's willingness to work with her, knowing full well she could be scary as hell, Medusa lowered her guard. It felt as though her heart might have warmed for a second . . .

Nah. It was probably just indigestion.

"Okay, then. Lead the way, matchmaker."

The god of love gave her a warm smile before beckoning her to follow him. Medusa tried not to seem too obvious gawking at the extravagant surroundings as they made their way to his office.

The shiny gold fixtures, the sparkling crystal chandeliers,

the plush carpets, they sparked something deep within her, and those embers of longing she'd thought she'd long since smothered began to smolder again.

She could hardly wait to get her claws on that mortal shell —or magic—or whatever it was Eros was going to give her.

Nervous anticipation bubbled in her belly as she thought about the *real* reason why she needed some time off. She was low-key looking for a soul to steal. Even though she had tried to pretend loneliness hadn't been part of why she wanted a break, Hades had seen right through her.

As far as Eros knew, she was conducting business. She crossed her claws he wouldn't ask too many questions. If he figured it out, it might be more than his big heart could handle and he might rescind his offer.

The majority of her vacation would be spent getting into as much trouble as she could find, but some of that time needed to be dedicated to attracting as much attention as possible.

She'd skipped her favorite episode of Lucifer last night to do some research on how to do just that. After spending a few hours that somehow felt like only mere minutes on the human trapping called Youtube, she'd decided that becoming an "influencer" was the way to go. If everything worked out, come this time tomorrow, she'd be sipping on the finest champagne Earth had to offer while setting up various social media accounts.

She wouldn't be just any influencer either; she would become *the* influencer. How absolutely perfect was it that the way she was going to achieve her instant celebrity was by becoming the world's newest model slash beauty guru slash fashion designer slash overnight sensation.

Move over Jeffree Star, here comes Medusa.

Oh yes, her brand of beauty would knock it out of the park. Snakes on everything. Jewelry, accessories, clothing. Her look would be dark, brooding . . . Dangerous. Don't forget unapproachable, because mortals? Totally desperate for things they couldn't have.

A shiver of excitement shimmied its way up Medusa's spine. She'd rake in the sponsorships and have money to burn on her own crystal chandeliers in no time. The fact that the dude she was supposed to be assessing resided in the exact location she'd decided would make the perfect vacation spot was the icing on the cake. No, the cherry on top of the whipped cream. Tomorrow she'd begin her adoration-fest in one of the most beauty conscious places in the world.

Los Angeles, California.

When they finally reached Eros's office, Medusa took a small step backward when he turned and motioned toward the door. "Ladies first."

Medusa narrowed her eyes at him, not quite knowing what to make of his . . . niceness.

A chestnut-haired goddess with gossamer wings sat behind a desk that looked like it had been the centerpiece of *the* Louis the XIV's drawing room at Versailles.

"Hello, there. I'm Psyche, goddess of the soul, personification of spirit, wife of Eros." She stood, hurrying around the desk toward Medusa. "But who cares about all that. It's so nice to meet you."

Brace yourselves, ladies. I think she's coming in for a—

Psyche hugged Medusa before she could finish her thought, and naturally, not used to being so warmly embraced, Medusa froze.

"Wow, you really are made of stone—ouch!" Psyche took a step back, the fangs of one of Medusa's snakes embedded into her bare shoulder.

"Shit. Sorry." Medusa bent her head forward in order to dislodge the serpent with as little discomfort to the goddess as possible.

"No need to apologize," replied Psyche, accepting the tissue Eros had conjured so she could apply pressure to the puncture wounds, which were already starting to heal. "I suppose I deserved it, huh?"

"Yeah, monsters aren't really the touchy-feely type," replied Medusa.

Eros motioned to a chair. "Well, let's get you set up, shall we? There's a pretty important detail we need to discuss."

Medusa glanced down at the paperwork as she took a seat. They better lay it all out on the table now, because if they thought she was going to read that much fine print they were crazy. She had followers to amass and meat bags to seduce, so just tell her where to sign.

"I'll get right to the point," started Eros. "Without an actual mortal shell to temporarily turn you human, you can't go down unless the curse is lifted. We can't have you turning people to stone."

"So, you're telling me you *can't* help me, then?"

"I didn't say that. What I *am* saying is that we may have to ask Athena to lift the curse. How long did you say you'd be off-site?"

"Three hundred and sixty-five days."

"Yeah. I think it's best to get buy-in from Athena."

"Good luck with that," sulked Medusa.

Her pulse jumped a second later when Eros picked up the phone and began to dial. *Sweet siren's deadly song, matchmaker, don't you dare say anything about me sitting in your office, or I swear to Hades . . .*

"Hey Athena, Eros here. I'm great, how are you? Say, I've got a mandate from both Hades and Zeus regarding a special project Medusa will be working on, and I was wondering if you could do me a huge favor? Yeah, I'd just need her curse lifted for a year is all." Eros moved the receiver away from his ear.

Medusa frowned, curious what he was up to when Athena's voice exploded from the other end of the phone, "A

YEAR? ARE YOU FUCKING CRAZY, MATCHMAKER? THAT BITCH DEFILED MY TEMPLE!"

"Well, I just don't believe *that* at all," murmured Psyche, shaking her head and sending Eros a skeptical look.

"Athena, I know you're still upset, but everyone knows you can't trust Poseidon as far as you can throw him. Have you considered that perhaps . . ." Eros looked at Medusa with sympathetic eyes before steering his conversation with the goddess of know-it-alls back toward its original direction. "This request is coming from the top down. I'd be happy to take it up with Zeus if you'd like, but I don't think he'd be too thrilled, seeing as he's swamped with all this reputation stuff, you know?"

Medusa bit back a growl when Eros winked at her.

"Look, what better way to help him out?" he continued. "Prove to him that at least one of his Olympians is doing something right. You have to admit, it's a pretty solid strategy."

Medusa grinned. What a clever Cupid. Using Athena's gigantic head against her. Pressing that button of constant need to prove how smart she was. How *brilliant* she thought she was when it came to outsmarting everyone else.

Talk about thirsty.

"FINE. I'LL SUSPEND THE CURSE, BUT YOU MAKE SURE SHE KNOWS I'M NOT DOING THIS FOR HER. I'M STILL SUPER PISSED."

Clearly.

Impressed, Medusa lifted her brows at Eros after he hung up the phone.

"That went well. Don't you think?" said Psyche, fluttering to the other side of the room on her butterfly wings. She swung open the French doors of an armoire turned shelving unit and plucked out an ancient-looking clay jar from inside.

Medusa's gaze bounced around the office, landing on an industrial cooler full of flowers, then a sales counter. She rolled her eyes when it finally hit her that Eros and Psyche's office was set up like a flower shop. Gods and goddesses were so . . . weird.

Eros cleared his throat, pointing at a little "X" at the bottom of the paperwork. "If you could sign and date this line right here, please."

Medusa bit down on her bottom lip as she picked up the plumed pen that had appeared on the desk. Practically biting through it was the only way she knew how to stop a string of excited giggles from escaping. She scrawled her signature and date on the dotted line while Psyche handed the jar to Eros. He gave it a shake, the contents giving off the scratchy sound of sand.

"What's in there?" asked Medusa.

"Powdered beauty," explained Psyche, taking the seat Eros had vacated in order to come around the desk and stand in front of Medusa.

"Total real deal, my friend," said Eros. "Sea foam sourced straight from the severed genitals of Uranus."

"Gross," protested Medusa. Was he really going to use genital foam on her? Wait, what if he wanted her to swallow some of that shit?

"I know, but I can't make the illusion work without it. Don't worry, it's freeze-dried. I ground it into the strongest beauty powder imaginable myself. My mother, Aphrodite, was born from it, you know, and she's the most beautiful goddess in existence. Now, close your eyes."

Eros dipped a fluffy pink makeup pouf that had appeared in his other hand into the jar.

"Most beautiful according to whom?" snorted Medusa. "Paris? How'd that work out?"

Eros shook his head, giving her an *I'm-not-mad-just-disap-pointed* look as he waited for her to do as he'd asked without commentary.

"What? It was a joke," she said, knowing full well that

bringing up the beauty contest between goddesses which had resulted in a grudge that Hera still held against his mother Aphrodite—and by proxy, him—to this day might not have been as funny as she'd intended.

She couldn't help herself, though. He was such an easy target.

Eros stared at her, one eyebrow arched and meaning business. She sighed, but closed her eyes as instructed. A second later, the pouf smacked her in the face, harder than necessary in her opinion.

Upon impact, the powder turned into a fine mist. Surprised by the sensation, Medusa gasped, and briny droplets of sea water infiltrated her nose and mouth. She began to cough. A small hand patted her gently on the back, but Medusa still startled when she heard the goddess's voice inside her head.

That's it. Keep your eyes closed for just a little bit longer . . .

Foam popped and fizzled on her skin. It didn't burn or anything, but it felt as though her face might bubble right off her skull. She wanted to open her eyes in the worst way, but she wanted the magic to have time to do its job more, so she forced her lids to remain closed.

After an agonizing thirty more seconds, she heard Eros finally say, "Aaand, we're done."

Medusa's eyes popped open. She blinked a few times before her gaze went straight to her hands, which, to her delight, were now clad in skin and not scales. She held them up in amazement, inspecting long, slender fingers. When she looked at Eros, he was holding a hand-held mirror out to her.

She hadn't expected her heart to lodge in her throat like this, and when she tried to swallow the lump forming there, it was difficult. She'd been hideous for so frigging long. She took the looking-glass, and with trembling fingers turned the mirror towards her face.

"Holy shit," she whispered.

Her snakes had transformed into spirals cascading down her back and over her shoulders. She stared at her reflection with striking hazel eyes, and she smiled with full lips at her strong nose, perfect and free of bumps and ridges. Her high cheekbones were covered in flawless skin once again.

And damn, were her eyebrows on point or what?

"You like?" asked Eros.

Medusa's mouth opened and closed a few times before she managed any words. "I hardly know what to say except . . . I'm gorgeous."

Eros laughed. "How about you just promise not to break too many hearts while you're on Earth, okay?"

"Sure thing," lied Medusa, running a fingertip over her smooth, unblemished skin.

She was going on vacation, and she intended to live her temporary life to the fullest. She was going to trash anything and everything she could, hearts included.

CHAPTER FIVE

*H*eart pounding, Medusa stepped through the portal gripping the handles of her Snake Head bag. She couldn't wait for everyone to start scratching each other's eyes out just to get their hands on one, which was why, even though she'd had to go through a lot of crap to get here, she was excited to officially be on vacation.

Unfortunately, when she discovered she stood in the cramped stall of a toilet at LAX, her smile vanished along with her excitement, and her nose wrinkled at the slew of grimy fingerprints on the stainless-steel door in front of her.

Having never used a portal before, she hadn't known what to expect. She knew all entrances and exits into the mortal world needed to be discreet, but damn, His Douche-y-ness really made sure to drive home the point that if you weren't one of his precious gods or goddesses, you should expect to be dumped out into a place where humans unloaded their waste. She was an abomination in disguise, so yeah, she supposed she should have known.

Still didn't make it right, though.

Medusa pushed open the door with a manicured finger, taking care to find a spot not covered in visible human filth, and headed straight toward the mirror. As she checked to make sure her mortal shell hadn't been knocked askew, a female meat bag, quite advanced in age, proceeded to purse her lips and shake her head while scrubbing her hands under running water. When Medusa turned to leave the restroom without performing the same hand-washing ritual, the woman added in a huff.

"And we wonder why everyone is so sick," the woman said under her breath.

A shot of adrenaline spiked through Medusa, hot and prickly, and that same sense of not belonging she'd had up on the mountain, when the Graces said needlessly cruel things to her—about her—wound its way up from the pit of her stomach, gripped her chest, and settled in her jaw, which was now clenched.

Please stop talking. Please stop talking. Please. Stop. Talking.

If the woman stopped now, Medusa could let it go.

But the woman kept talking.

"Girls like you can take selfies all day long but can't even be bothered to wash your hands. It's disgusting! I bet your parents are really proud." The woman let out a sardonic laugh. "At least *my* generation knew how to raise kids the right way."

A growl rose in Medusa's throat, along with several choice insults regarding the woman's unsolicited opinion about her upbringing. She knew some humans had a penchant for being self-righteous, but she hadn't expected to encounter one with such a raging case of entitlement so soon.

She kept her mouth shut. The best course of action for this situation was to play the part and be on her way. She refused to let anything make the underwhelming start to what was supposed to be her epic vacation more of a shitty experience than it was already turning out to be.

Medusa stuck a hand under the soap dispenser, keeping

her eyes on the woman and smiling sweetly as she then rinsed off the small mound of foam in her palm under the faucet. No scrubbing, and zero effs given.

Still staring at the woman, whose eyes had gone wide and mouth had dropped open, Medusa flicked the fingers of her elegant new hand. Water droplets showered the meat bag's face as Medusa chirped, "Have a nice day."

She didn't wait around for the woman's reaction, but she did hear horrified sputtering as she turned and walked toward the exit and had to suppress a laugh. She'd come to Earth for a little fun, and a lot of rest and relaxation. No high-handed, dowdy-ass meat bag was going to ruin her good time, or her Zen.

The loud clicking of stilettos on tile instead of a wispy slithering as she walked out of the restroom lightened her mood. She rummaged through the bag on her arm as she walked, and when she found what she was looking for—an expensive pair of sunnies—she slipped them on so she could size-up the meat bags as inconspicuously as possible.

A twenty-something with way too much makeup plastered on her face holding a tiny dog captive inside a sparkly pink bag rushed past, nearly plowing straight into Medusa.

"Ugh," scoffed the young woman when Medusa didn't move out of her way.

Medusa narrowed her eyes and waited for the hissing to start. When the girls didn't respond, her hand automatically flew to her . . . that's right, she had hair now.

"Jesus Christ, lady. *Move.*"

A satisfied smile curled Medusa's lips when the young woman went on to confess, "Sick bag, though," as she stepped around Medusa, the tiny dog barking in agreement. Or in desperation to be rescued, who knew.

Medusa continued on, immediately spying a male meat bag with a rather alluring physique up ahead. His backside was easy on the eyes, especially in those snug-fitting designer jeans, and, according to the generous amount of swagger he was putting into his stride, he knew it.

Target number one.

Low whistles came from the waiting areas as she sauntered past gate after gate, following the tantalizing male human. She licked her lips, all the blatant appreciation making it hard to keep a devious smile off her face.

That's right, ladies and gentlemen. I have arrived.

Sure, there were matters like accommodations and wardrobe to contend with, but all the delicious attention was too good not to gobble up. Yet, hungry for the spotlight as she was, she decided what she could really use was a drink. Besides, she wasn't here to do the chasing.

After veering off into the first place that looked like it served alcohol, she headed straight toward the bar and settled onto a stool next to the only other patron present.

The man didn't look at her, even when she cleared her throat to get the bartender's attention. Even more irritating? The bartender, a tall, slender female with shiny hair who had perfected the cat-eye, was obviously ignoring her as well.

Medusa didn't need eyeliner to accentuate her eyes. She didn't even need makeup, to be honest. It was no wonder the bartender was jealous. She probably wasn't used to being the ugliest woman in the room.

When the bartender continued to wash and sanitize glasses, Medusa cleared her throat again, louder, careful not to let the growl waiting on standby in her throat slip out.

After a heavy sigh, the bartender finally spoke. "What can I get you?"

Oh, Hades, no. She was not going to get away with that attitude.

"You're the expert," snapped Medusa. "What do you recommend?"

Relax. Have fun. Be nice . . .

The bartender tossed the towel next to the sink located under the bar. "One strawberry daiquiri coming right up."

The man sitting next to Medusa snorted into his whiskey tumbler. "Too many calories. Try vodka tonic, hold the tonic."

The bartender laughed through her nose and nodded. "Totally."

"Excuse me?" said Medusa, turning on her barstool to better address the asshole daring to assume she preferred sugary-sweet girly drinks to a nice stiff one, even though a frozen daiquiri had actually sounded delightful.

"And what's that? Whiskey?" She tipped her head toward the glass of amber liquid sitting on the bar in front of him. "Oh, how original. I bet you think you're a real fucking connoisseur, too."

So much for relaxing . . . or being nice.

The man turned his head, fixing a green-eyed gaze and a smirk on her. The moment he did, everything went still. Limbs, breath, ass cheeks. All clenched tight. Everything except her heart. Of course, that shit still worked, pounding in her chest like a jackhammer.

She was pissed, yeah, but that's not why she'd gone deer in headlights. She knew this guy. Well, she didn't *know* him, but she knew *of* him.

He was the one. The meat bag she was supposed to assess. She had a picture of him in her bag right now, in fact, and judging by her interaction with him so far, she had a feeling her job wouldn't be that hard. What luck.

Medusa rolled her eyes, which turned into an intense stare directed toward the bartender. "And how's that acting career going?"

Medusa had just taken a guess, but the way the woman responded by pressing her lips together confirmed she was indeed a struggling actress. One who was now thinking very carefully about the next thing that came out of her mouth.

Good. She must have thought Medusa would just take her

judgmental shit. Apparently, so did the clown sitting next to her.

Well, they'd been wrong.

"I'll have a glass of Cristal Gold Medallion," said Medusa, cold as ice. "Unless, of course, you don't have any at this . . ." She turned up her nose as she glanced around the sufficient but definitely not anywhere close to classy airport bar. "Fine establishment."

The man raised a brow before returning to his whiskey.

Medusa flipped a lock of hair over her shoulder. *That's right, buddy. Look away.*

Screw being nice. Any more trouble from this arrogant bastard and his bar wench sidekick, it was going to be Stonesville for the both of them.

Shit, wait. Eros had talked Athena into putting the brakes on the curse, which meant her stone-making days were temporarily over. She'd been effectively rendered a plain, old meat bag, incapable of turning unworthy assholes to stone for at least three hundred and sixty-five days.

Thank Hades she could still shut them up with a razor-sharp tongue.

"We don't have Cristal," mumbled the bartender, unhappy she had to bow out of their catfight because they didn't serve top-shelf champagne.

"I'll have what he's having, then."

The man snickered. "Damn, you're determined, aren't you?"

Since he wasn't looking at her, Medusa surveyed his jaw, and the sexy-as-hell stubble lining it. She swallowed. "Determined to do what, exactly?"

"Get my attention."

A laugh burst out of Medusa. It had been accompanied by a weird little dip in her stomach, so she took a sip of the whiskey the bartender had begrudgingly poured for her to burn away the fluttering. "Trust me, I don't need your attention."

What she did need, however, was to assess him, which meant, like his bad attitude or not, she had to at least keep him in her sights. "But I bet you wouldn't mind having mine."

Medusa lifted her shoulder in a shrug, just small enough to send the bartender heading anywhere else but there to witness her flirting.

"Fine. I'll bite. Jake Sullivan." He held out his hand. "Hollywood's top entertainment lawyer. And you are?"

She engaged in another one of their silly human rituals by grasping onto his outstretched hand. "Medusa. World's next social media sensation."

He laughed, which made Medusa want to rip his head off. Literally.

"I get it. The hair, the long, pointy nails . . . The snake bag. It's a decent schtick in a city full of blonde-haired angels. I'm sure you'll be a hit with the scenesters. So where are you from?"

What did these meat bags say? Honesty was the best policy? Not that she was opposed to lying, but what harm would it do to tell the truth? He wouldn't believe her anyway, so why not have a little fun? Besides, things had moved quickly after her meeting with Eros. She'd barely had time to come up with a logo for her designer bag line let alone make up a backstory.

"The Underworld."

"Wow. You're fully invested in this brand persona, aren't you? Okay, well, it was nice talking to you, Medusa, but I've got a plane to catch." Jake tossed back the rest of his drink, the empty glass *thunking* on the wooden bar top a bit more aggressively than Medusa thought the conversation warranted. Humans were so sensitive.

Was this going to be the best vacation ever or what?

"I'm sure I'll see you around," she said, twirling one of her curls around her finger.

"Not unless you're in the entertainment business."

"Is that so?" she replied. "You must be a busy man, then."

"Sure am," he said, fishing out his wallet and opening it. "Good luck infiltrating L.A., *Medusa*."

"Infiltrating?" she asked, her chest tightening. How did he know?

"Yeah. Isn't that what monsters do?" He threw a fifty onto the bar.

She blew out a breath. He didn't know, he just despised her "mortal" existence. Her blood-red painted lips push up into a grin. If he only knew.

"Watch your step, Mr. Sullivan," she said, not missing the fact that he'd just tossed down enough money to pay for both of their drinks and still leave a pretty damned good tip. "I might eat you alive. If our paths cross again, that is."

Jake Sullivan shook his head before walking away.

"Can't wait until they do," murmured Medusa.

It was official. He was on her radar, but not simply as some uninteresting soul she needed to assess in order to report her findings back to Hades. Jake Sullivan was a challenge; one who conveniently owned the first heart, among other things, she was going to have the pleasure of breaking.

She finished the last of her whiskey before slipping off the bar stool, grabbing her black bag, turning on her ridiculously high heels, and sashaying out. Yep. It was going to be an absolute delight smashing this self-important prick's ego to pieces.

Medusa smiled politely as the bearded server set a steak down in front of her. "Here you are, miss. Can I get you anything else?"

"No, this is perfect. Thank you."

Perfect? More like torture. Trendy L.A. restaurant or not, she wanted to tear into her lunch in the worst way.

The server lifted his eyebrows, possibly still miffed at her request for her lunch to be left practically raw. Or it could have been her obvious struggle to keep the saliva pooling in her mouth from dribbling out.

"Very well. Enjoy."

She dismissed him with a nod and forced herself to unravel the napkin-clad eating utensils slowly. She bit her lip and refrained from grabbing the delectable cut of beef with her hands, opting to pick up the knife and fork instead.

The California sun beamed down through the glass, making a strong argument for the abundance of potted plants to go on living in captivity. The restaurant had a farm-to-table vibe, resembling a large greenhouse, and working like one, too.

Medusa broke out into a light sweat. It's not like she wasn't used to the heat but trying to eat her lunch with any amount of civility, so she wouldn't attract attention, was proving to be a bit difficult. She wanted all eyes on her, of course, just not for wolfing down a whole steak in one bite. What a pain in the ass having to chew. These human rituals —and manners—were so inconvenient. But, when in Rome.

After a few demure bites, Medusa took a sip of her chardonnay, catching the eye of a rather handsome man sitting at a table across from her. He was staring, and he wasn't being shy about it. His demeanor—one arm across his chest, tucked beneath the elbow of the other, a confident lean against the back of his chair, and a man-spread as wide as the Styx—broadcasted he thought he was a Very Important Person.

Medusa locked onto his gaze and turned up the intensity. He sat up straighter, switching his cell phone from one ear to the other in response, but didn't hang up. Although, he did stop talking long enough to send her a smile that said, *"I've noticed you and I like what I see."*

Medusa cocked her head at him, contemplating the message she should send in return as she took a sip of wine. The image of him taking her up against a wall in a darkened broom closet flashed in her mind, but just as quickly, she dismissed it. She had plenty of time for such debauchery. She'd had a trying morning, and right now all she wanted to do was enjoy her damn lunch.

She arched a brow, giving him a look that said, *"You? With me? Not a chance in Hades' Realm."* There were things to be done, like finding a place to reside, purchasing designer clothes to flaunt, and, most important, amassing a giant horde of followers.

"Excuse me."

Medusa flinched, surprised she hadn't heard anyone approach. When she saw it was a medium-statured twenty-something human female with fading green dye in her dirty blonde hair, Medusa relaxed. She looked about as non-threatening as they came.

"Yes?" answered Medusa coolly.

The young woman's mouth opened and closed a few times, but no words came out. This chick really had something to say. What stupid human rule had Medusa broken now? Perhaps she'd made a mistake in thinking Earth would be a vacation.

"I really love your bag," the girl finally blurted. "I've never seen that brand, though." She squinted, trying to make out the logo. "Is that Medusa's head? So freaking cool. Who's the designer?"

Medusa wanted to laugh out loud. So, the bag had been a good decision. She'd scrambled to put together a plan B the night before, in case the beauty guru thing turned out to be too much work. She thought either a line of designer accessories or a signature perfume would be something she could fall back on.

"I am. The brand is called Snake Head." Considering how well being truthful had gone earlier, she decided to make up a name. "I'm Melina Stone. But I go by Medusa." She thought about engaging in the useless, not to mention unsanitary, ritual of handshaking but thought better of it.

"Oh wow," said the girl, not seeming to mind skipping the pleasantry. "Your branding is tight. The hair, the make-up . . . And, seriously, I need one of your bags. I mean, when I get a job and have money, obviously. Do you have a store-front yet, or just a website?"

Ruin and damnation. Put that on the list. It seemed as though she had indeed been wrong; taking over the world would clearly *not* be a vacation. "Nothing yet. I just moved here from, um . . ." Where on Earth would be a good compar-ison to the Underworld? "The Midwest. I was waiting until I got here to set all that up."

The woman was still staring at the bag. "Oh yeah, that's smart. Create buzz first then build demand by making them wait. That snake-skin texture is amazing. Is it real? Can I touch it?

"It's embossed. I wouldn't dare kill a snake just to make a purse." Medusa took note of the woman's enthusiastic atten-tion to detail, and a plan began to form. "What's your name?"

"Dylan. I just moved here, too. Graduated from the Savannah College of Art and Design a few months ago and came out west to see if I could find an internship or some-thing. My parents think I'm crazy, you know, not having anything lined up, but I told them . . ."

Medusa nodded, pretending to be interested in the girl's life story. The only thing she was really interested in, however, was the idea that perhaps this fresh-faced kid could do all the work while Medusa reaped all the rewards.

A twinge of guilt tightened Medusa's jaw. This girl was way too naive. Did she have *any* clue that seriously bad shit—like being blamed for something you most certainly did not do and then being turned into a monster for it—could happen in the blink of an eye?

But this was *you scratch my back and I'll scratch yours* at its finest, an opportunity Medusa couldn't pass up. And it wasn't like she'd be taking complete advantage of the girl.

"You know, I'm looking for an assistant. How would you like to work for me?"

Dylan chewed on her bottom lip, her gaze flitting between Medusa and the bag.

"I'm kind of a big deal back home," continued Medusa, "so I can pay you, if that's what you're worried about. I just need someone I can rely on to help get my brand out there. I like your attention . . ." She was about to say *to me* but thought better of it. "To detail."

Dylan didn't look convinced.

Time to get slithery.

"I'm assuming you're working some shitty job, barely making rent for a tiny apartment in a not-so-nice part of L.A., am I right?"

Dylan paled, staring at Medusa with watery my-parents-were-so-right eyes.

Just one more little push and you'll be mine . . .

"Tell you what. When I find a place, you can sublet a room from me for a year. How about that?" Boy, was Medusa ever glad Hades had also approved unlimited withdrawals from Underworld Financial Credit Union during her vacation. Being appointed Assessor had its perks.

Although it was small and hesitant, Dylan finally smiled. "And I'd also be a partner?"

"Whoa there, slow down. More like an assistant who'll eventually work her way up to designer for a kick-ass, woman-owned brand she helped raise from the ground up before she has the experience and seed money to start her *own* line."

"Okay deal." Dylan pulled out a chair. "So, like, do I start right now or what?"

"Yes," said Medusa, tucking her Underworld Financial debit card into the bill holder the server had dropped off a few minutes ago. "And your first job is to find me a mansion in the hills with a crystal chandelier in every room.

CHAPTER SIX

The woman sitting next to Jake leaned in, hooking a hand around his shoulder for leverage as she stretched up to whisper in his ear. Sadie Parker, Hollywood's fastest rising star, smelled fantastic—felt even better—but he was done with women like her.

Actresses were one of the worst kind of L.A. monster.

"Do you really think this is going to work?" she whispered. "I signed a contract."

Her breath tickled his skin, his eyelids automatically closing as he swallowed. The close contact triggered memories of the night he'd met his ex-wife, an actress by the name of Natasia Nowak—Schmitt now, since she was already remarried—at a party in the Hollywood Hills.

He should have known what lurked beneath that angelic face of hers. That she was no different than any of the others who'd eventually left him for a bigger celebrity. Monsters, all of them. The only difference was he'd been stupid enough to marry Natasia.

And now here he was, tempted, and just by having a beautiful woman sitting next to him. Except, Sadie wasn't even coming on to him. She was simply attending her pre-trial, just like he'd requested she do. It was business, for fuck's sake.

Why were beautiful women always his downfall? He would take any other vice right now. Drugs, alcohol, gambling, Starbucks . . . anything.

Jake swept the thoughts from his mind and forced his eyes open so he could flash a lawyer's smile at his client. "Trust me. It'll work."

"I hope so." Sadie straightened. "I refuse to work with that man."

Jake knew she was referring to the A-list actor starring in the major motion picture she'd just been cast in. Sadie was due to be on set in less than a month, but a scheduling conflict wasn't the issue. The problem was she'd signed on to play the female lead *before* knowing who would be starring opposite her.

Big mistake. Had Jake been her lawyer then, he would have strongly advised against signing anything without reading the fine print. But the young starlet had hired him *after* she'd found out the actor who'd landed the role was one of Hollywood's hottest stars . . . Circa 1985.

The casting was definitely a head-scratcher. The actor was ancient, well beyond the appropriate age to generate any believable on-screen chemistry. And, of course, the script called for an excessive amount of making out.

Beside the lip-locking with someone old enough to be her grandfather, Sadie was more concerned about dodging some-thing else; the script had been re-written to include a sex scene, complete with full-frontal nudity.

In an action-adventure movie? Yeah, somebody pulled some strings to get the old bastard some action, all right.

Lucky for her, Jake "The Snake" Sullivan was the best of the best. If anyone could find a loophole and slither through, it would be him. Of course, he didn't believe his client should have to go through with something she was not one hundred percent comfortable with, but the bigger concern was his track record.

He'd fight dirty in order to win a case but, as far as he could tell, he wouldn't have to go that route. He had a few loopholes to choose from on this one. It was true that having to work with the guy's shriveled old-man wang hanging out was bad, but the actor was known to be notoriously difficult to work with, and also apparently very "hands-on" with his female co-stars.

And that was what Jake The Snake Sullivan referred to as a Number One Deal Breaker.

He would use the guy's handsy approach to his work first, and if that didn't do the trick, he'd uncover some other unsavory bit of truth—or gossip, didn't matter. Lord knew he had a lot of dirt, true or not, on people in this town, and if he didn't, he knew ways of getting it. He wasn't above using certain information to his advantage—that's what opportunists did.

Jake won cases by any means possible, and that's why his clients hired him. They trusted he'd get them off the hook, even if it involved being a snake in the grass, which he wasn't above.

The doors to the small courtroom swung open and a set of lawyers representing the film company strolled in, snickering at an inside joke. Tyler Monahan and his protege-in-training. In other words, Jake's greaseball arch nemesis and his equally slippery sidekick.

"Oh, look. A matching set. How cute. Mega Pix Studios has a uniform now?" taunted Jake under his breath, unable to stop himself.

But just look at them, with their slicked-back hair and Armani suits.

"Well, well, well. If it isn't Jake The Snake. Hey, buddy. Long time no see. I thought you might have retired after your big break up with . . ." Tyler turned to his sidekick. "What was that actress's name again? Natasha?"

The Sidekick smirked. "I believe it's pronounced Na-TAH-zia."

Jake clenched his jaw. He knew what they were doing, and he wasn't going to give them the satisfaction of getting thrown off his game before it even started.

It seemed they knew how to play dirty, too.

Jake cleared his throat, preparing to fire another round of insults, when the door behind the bench opened and the pre-trial judge ambled into the courtroom.

"Good morning, ladies and gentlemen. Let's get this show on the road, shall we? I've got another appointment at noon." The judge dropped a manilla folder onto the bench before wheeling out his chair.

A grin pushed up one of Jake's cheeks. What fucking luck. The honorable Judge Harold J. Davis. His father's long-time golf buddy. "Another appointment" was code for a noon tee time.

It was instances like this when Jake didn't mind bene-fiting from his father's social—and financial—status in Tinsel Town.

"Mr. Sullivan." Judge Davis nodded at him before addressing the other two lawyers in the room without so much as a glance. "Mr. Monahan, Mr. Jackson."

A good sign, but it didn't mean Jake wouldn't have to work his ass off to get his client's contract amended. Harry played by the book.

That was fine. Jake had his loophole.

"So, Ms. Parker is looking to get out of her contract, is she?" Judge Davis thumbed through the documents in front of him.

"Not necessarily," said Jake, ignoring the fact that Sadie had visibly stiffened beside him.

"What are you doing?" she whispered frantically.

"Trust me."

"Christ, Jake. I don't want my acting career to end before it even gets started."

"Just trust me."

Tyler piped up. "The contract is legal and binding."

"Thank you for that assessment, Mr. Monahan." Jake turned to address Judge Davis. "As I've stated, my client isn't looking to get out of her contract, but she is prepared to take the matter to court if a number of concessions aren't made."

"It's a done deal, Sullivan," muttered Tyler.

Judge Davis held up his hand, the creases in his forehead deepening. The one smack dab in the middle was Grand Canyon-deep by the time he fixed his gaze on Jake again. "Continue."

"It's true my client signed without knowing who would be cast as her co-star. However, the point of contention here is the script was re-written after she signed."

Tyler's sidekick elbowed him in the ribs for a conference. Their whispering was obviously meant to put him off his game.

"Which wouldn't be a problem, Your Honor," continued Jake. "If the re-writes were to enhance the plot and not add in unnecessary full-frontal nudity. This is an action-adventure movie, is it not?"

When no answer came, Judge Davis settled his shrewd gaze on Jake's opposition. "What is your answer, Mr. Monahan?"

"Well, yes, Your Honor, it's slated as one," replied Tyler, "but there are all kinds of factors the studio must take into consideration. Audience, demand . . . how streaming services will affect box office sales. It's not uncommon for scripts to be adjusted right up until production starts. Changes are sometimes even made *during* production. It's the nature of the beast."

All eyes were focused on Jake again.

Time to play the Deal Breaker card, Sullivan.

"Thank you for the rundown. However, my client, here, is a human being, not an entity, and I think we can all agree should be treated as such. Why should my client have to endure sexual harassment in the workplace? It's well known that her co-star, Mr. Alan Rockwell, is a serial offender."

"There is no evidence to substantiate that claim," blurted Tyler's sidekick.

"Well, I'm sure MPS wouldn't want to go through the process of finding that out, so let's prevent a very lengthy, very expensive, *very* damaging lawsuit, shall we?"

Judge Davis's gavel struck, a warning for Jake to slow his role—and to maintain a professional demeanor during this pissing match.

Jake watched as Tyler and his partner exchanged glances, and he almost grinned. They better be nervous, because he hadn't just played the Deal Breaker card, he'd laid trump.

And now it was time to go in for the kill.

"May I approach the bench, Your Honor?"

Judge Davis nodded. "You may but make it quick."

Jake took his time. Damn, he couldn't stop himself from pushing his luck even if his career depended on it, could he?

"All we're asking is for the studio to do the right thing, Your Honor, which is rethink their position regarding whether or not they'd like to risk a sexual harassment lawsuit." He leaned in, all conspiratorial-like, and said out of the corner of his mouth, "I mean, I'm no rocket scientist, but I'm guessing once it's filed, previously silent victims will have the courage to come forward to testify, as they should. My point is, we've all seen how that turns out. Lots of publicists working overtime to cover a bunch of asses, and, well, the studio would have so much more to consider besides audience and demand."

"Are you finished?" Judge Davis asked.

"I believe that is up to you," replied Jake.

Yep. Apparently, he would push every boundary there was to push.

Judge Davis sighed. "Please return to your seat, Mr. Sullivan."

Jake sauntered back to his chair, noting how his client bit her bottom lip, her perfectly groomed eyebrows crumpling under the weight of her anxiety. The subsequent smile he directed toward her was confident and meant to send the message that everything would be okay. Jake The Snake had just made her problem go away.

Jake felt Tyler's angry glare drill into him, which forced him to put his current train of thought on lockdown in order to focus on keeping a gloating smile off his face. He thrived on this shit, reveled in this level of *gotcha*, but he knew better than to celebrate victory before he'd been awarded the prize.

Judge Davis cleared his throat. "Since production has not yet started, I see no breach of contract. However, there are grounds for further negotiations regarding contractual obligations to take place. Mr. Sullivan, you will provide Mr. Monahan and his co-council, Mr. Jackson, with a list of more suitable replacements for the role in question. Mr. Monahan, Mr. Jackson, you will inform your client that if this concession is not met, the contract shall be null and void."

The gavel came down hard, and Jake had to force the smile off his face again.

After Judge Davis slipped through the door to his chambers, and Tyler and his sidekick gathered their paperwork and left the courtroom, Sadie turned toward Jake.

"Oh my God, Jake, you're amazing," she said, looping the strap of her designer purse over shoulder. "I can't thank you enough."

Jake nodded, too preoccupied with eyeing the bag's logo to respond verbally. Was that a head with snakes for hair? Where had he seen a bag like that before? When he realized his client had gone silent, he looked up and saw that her gaze had gone from thankful to hopeful.

"Maybe we should go for a drink to celebrate," she said, taking a fraction of a step closer.

Fuck. He'd been hoping that she wouldn't do this. A drink with a gorgeous woman would be nice right now. Not to mention, being high on the thrill of victory made it so much harder to say no, especially when his co-counsel, the one in his pants, was begging him to say yes. But he knew from experience that one drink would inevitably lead to two, and two drinks with a woman like Sadie Parker would lead him right to trouble's doorstep. He needed to just walk away before he was tempted to knock.

"It's what I get paid to do," he said, keeping his tone clipped.

"If you're sure," she said, arching a brow before slipping on a pair of Gucci sunglasses she'd pulled from her bag.

Jake knew that look, and it almost had him changing his mind. "I appreciate the offer, Ms. Parker, but I just don't think it's a good idea. I hope you understand."

"Suit yourself." She tipped a shoulder. "You have my number if you change your mind."

Jake blew out a breath as the actress headed out of the courtroom. He was quite proud of himself. The last thing he wanted to do was get trapped in another spider web. His ego couldn't afford to get tangled up in a relationship with another high-profile celebrity, and neither could his heart, quite frankly. What he needed was to keep things strictly business, because if there was a chance lightning could strike twice, with his luck, it would.

Sure, she'd been born and raised in the South, a nice all-American girl who *seemed* grounded, but that wasn't to say she couldn't be a monster in disguise. For all he knew, Hollywood just hadn't gotten its hooks deep enough into her yet to pull the worst to the surface.

She could be as sweet and innocent as she looked, but there was no way in Hell he was going to risk having what was left of his dignity torn to pieces to find out.

CHAPTER SEVEN

Medusa shook her head and sighed as she checked each of her social media accounts. Close to three and a half million followers in just over a month. Not as good as she'd hoped, but it was a start.

She suddenly got the feeling someone was watching her, and she stopped scrolling to look at the man who she thought had been sleeping in the bed next to her. Sure enough, he was staring up at her with a dreamy smile on his face.

"Morning, gorgeous."

It took all she had not to eviscerate him. To save her black satin sheets, she opted for pushing him onto the floor instead. "You can leave now."

Undeterred, his head popped up over the side of the bed almost as quickly as his ass had hit the floor. "Do you want to go get some breakfast?"

"No." Medusa pointed to a far corner of her room. "I think your pants ended up over there."

She peeked up from her phone to watch Daniel—or maybe it was Darren—slide a pair of jeans over his muscled thighs. She bit her lip, almost relenting when he tucked and then adjusted his ample manhood before zipping up.

No. Three times in one morning was more than enough. She had shit to do.

"Okay, well, can I see you again?" he asked, raking a hand through his tousled blond hair before reaching for another discarded article of clothing. "I had a really great time last night . . . and this morning."

Judging by how many pieces of furniture were knocked over—and the still red bite marks on his shoulder—he'd had a fucking fantastic time.

"Are you serious? You know nothing about me. It was just sex, Darren. Really good sex, but that's all it was. I thought we talked about this?"

"Derrek." He corrected before pulling on his t-shirt. He righted an overturned chair so he could put on his shoes. "We did, but I . . . I really, *really* like you, Medusa. And not because you're famous or anything." He fixed his blue-eyed gaze on her. "I don't know if I can explain this right, but I just can't get enough of you."

"Aww, that's sweet." She got out of bed, letting him get a good, long look at her naked body before slipping on a robe. This was all music to her ears, truly, but she'd grown tired of this human and all of his incessant babbling.

She'd only called him for sex and a fresh supply of compliments, but he'd apparently gone and caught feelings. She couldn't blame him, really, since she was a gods-damned delight, but she thought meat bags, especially the Los Angeles kind, were shallower than this.

She walked over and booped his nose. "But that's what they all say, Darren."

"Derrek," he whispered.

"Anyway." She turned away from him, no longer able to stomach the dejected look on his face. "I promise I'll call you later, okay?" The lie rolled off her tongue as easily as it would be to make him come running back. She stood inside the bathroom doorway and smiled innocently, batting her eyelashes at him as he nodded like an idiot.

And then she slammed the door shut.

Finally rid of that delicious but needy hunk of a meat bag, Medusa sipped the iced coffee he'd made her before he'd left. She sat at the kitchen island, scrolling through her Instagram feed full of models, beauty gurus, and former Vine stars who'd been forced to find another platform to get attention. Naturally, it wasn't long before her mind began to wander.

What was Jake Sullivan doing right now?

Probably being an asshole, which, if she was being honest, made wanting to know what he was up to at that very moment all the more tempting.

Before she could give it any more thought, Dylan breezed into the kitchen, all irritatingly cheerful like the morning person she was. "So gorgeous out today, isn't it?" she said, practically singing.

Medusa glanced out the huge windows framing her amazing view of the Hollywood Hills and grunted. "Is it, though?"

"I'm just about done editing this week's content for Youtube." Dylan snagged a mug out of the cupboard and set it under the spout of a fancy coffee machine before shoving something into the contraption and snapping the lip closed. "What else you got for me today?"

"Do you think being on SnapChat is enough to lure the youngsters over to the dark side, or should I be on TikTok, too?"

"I suppose it couldn't hurt," said Dylan, pressing buttons. "I mean, they do have more disposable income at their age than previous generations. I'll set up an account later this afternoon."

Medusa sighed over the gurgling machine and tossed her phone onto the Carrara marble countertop before picking up her tumbler and heading for the living room.

"It's all just so boring, though." Her deep-green silk robe fluttered as she threw herself onto the couch. "Having to create content sucks up all my time. World domination is taking longer than I thought. I should be living it up right now." Medusa added in a laugh, so it would seem like she was only joking.

"Taking longer? Girl, between all the platforms you're on, you've got over three million followers. You even have a fan club. The Snake Heads would slither off a bridge if you told them to."

Medusa flung her head back and shook out her hair, pretending to soak up the adoration as if she were basking in the skin-melting heat of Dante's Inferno. "I know, they just love me, don't they?" She sat up so she could properly pout. "But I want to *experience* that love, not read about it in the comments."

Dylan rolled her eyes. "Good Lord, woman. Diva much?" She swept her hand toward several vases filled with flowers. "Derrek hasn't provided you with enough attention?"

Medusa playfully hissed at her assistant. "Oh, he's just infatuated, which doesn't count. And I didn't come up here for just one admirer . . ."

"Up? I thought you said you were from Michigan?" Dylan took her steaming mug of coffee to the dining room table and sat down. Ready to work, she opened her laptop and logged-on to her email. Medusa had hit the jackpot by hiring Dylan and her good old-fashioned work ethic.

"You know what I meant. Anyway. I need to start meeting people. Rub elbows with celebrities, not Instagrammers," said Medusa, changing the subject. "I'm talking bona fide A-listers, mind you."

"Okay, but how do we do that?"

"You're resourceful, figure it out."

"Holy shit."

"What?"

"I might not have to figure anything out. You just got an email from Kitt Van Nightshade's publicist. You've been invited to the launch party for her new line of makeup called Shades of Death."

Kitt Van Nightshade was the lead singer of The War Mongers, a death metal band popular in the late nineties. Word on the street was she'd gone broke trying to get her label to pay up, probably so she could support her drug habit. Also, Jake was her lawyer.

Not that Medusa had Googled him or anything.

"That crafty old bitch. She's probably freaking out now that there's a new queen of darkness in town. Seems like a keep your friends close but your enemies closer move to me."

"Could be," agreed Dylan. "Or maybe she really wants to meet you. You know, being that famous is probably super lonely. Either way, this is your opportunity to get your foot in the door. Should I tell her publicist to put you on the list?

"Of course, I want my name on that list," said Medusa. "Now, shall we have someone deliver us lunch or should we go out? I'm starving."

Absolutely ravenous was more like it, and she couldn't wait to devour all the attention at Kitt Van-What's-Her-Name's party.

"We'll go out. I need to get my nails done," announced Medusa before Dylan even had time to answer. "Come with. You desperately need a makeover. I bet a nice set of acrylics would make you feel like a million."

Dylan held up her hands. "You want me to get fake nails

put on these sausage fingers? Autocorrect already owns my butt."

"Fine, just get some gel polish put on those sad little stumps, but you're coming with me. I don't want to go alone."

CHAPTER EIGHT

*J*ake sipped his whiskey, wondering how in God's name one person could make so much money selling eye shadow and lipstick. But that's exactly what Kitt was doing. She'd gone from heavy metal musician to makeup maven in just under a year and was now making more off mascara than hit singles.

He checked his watch, trying his best not to look bored. He was pretty sure he was failing. Not that he gave a shit. He wasn't planning on staying long.

As he waited for the countdown to freedom to tick by, he let his mind wander. Glancing around the room, which was blessedly empty at the moment, the memory of how they'd fought like hell with Kitt's record label several years ago came to mind.

They'd tried to get her a bigger percentage of what she had been raking in for them, which, at that point, even five percent more would have been quite a hefty sum. He thought the endeavor hadn't been very successful but judging by her lavishly furnished residence just outside downtown L.A., and its medieval torture chamber vibes, he supposed he hadn't done *that* badly. All these battle axes hanging on the wall had to have cost a pretty penny. Likewise, the full-scale iron maiden replica standing open on display in the corner couldn't have been cheap.

Of course, he'd found a loophole, that hadn't been the issue. The problem was, for him at least, was that it'd been so small he'd barely managed to squeeze anything through.

Despite still being a bit wet behind the ears, he had ended up getting Kitt some of her music rights back. Six, to be exact; the ones where he'd managed to convince the producer to list her as co-songwriter or the news about his illicit affair would be leaked to every celebrity gossip Website across the nation. That had gotten the rotten bastard to give her credit for at least a handful out of the nearly two decades and five albums worth of songs.

Thinking back, Jake should have gone for the jugular, so the band could have quit making music all together. Sadly, Kitt wouldn't let him, and his subsequent brush with having a conscience led to her and the guys going back into the recording studio.

He'd almost felt vindicated when Kitt had gotten so tired of fighting a losing battle with the execs, who'd ordered her to keep churning out crap, that she'd almost said screw it and dissolved the band. That would have been something because Kitt was hardcore. She'd been the poster child for sex, drugs, and rock and roll for decades.

Hard living was in Kitt's DNA, and she didn't do anything half-ass. But money is a hell of a thing to lose once you have it, and putting your heart and soul into shitty music just to hold on to it comes with a price.

Kitt felt she'd had no choice but to keep making music the label insisted would keep her "relevant." It damn near killed her, which was ironic because Jake thought it would have been the booze.

But, until her contract was up, auto-tuned crap instead of

real vocals and pop hooks instead of driving riffs were the lesser of two evils.

Jake couldn't say he blamed her. She was in her early sixties now. Pumped full of fillers in an attempt to compete with the younger pop stars, she was hardly recognizable as the influential rock vixen she'd once been.

The sad truth was Kitt Van Nightshade and The War Mongers were nearing the end of their shelf life as far as the record label was concerned, and they all knew it. The label was nearly done bleeding her and the band dry, and it would only be a matter of time before they were hawking *As Seen On TV* products just to make a buck. And that was why Jake had advised Kitt to diversify her revenue streams.

When Kitt told him her million-dollar idea was to create a branded line of makeup, it took everything in him not to spew his coffee everywhere. He'd been thinking a reality television show or something. Definitely not full-coverage foundation.

It looked like he'd underestimated the spending habits of today's youth and their love of contouring. Not to mention how many makeup artists needed to cover celebrity tats during filming these days.

He ran a hand through his hair before slipping it into a pocket. His fingers curled around his phone, and he contemplated pulling it out and pretending to be on a call. He'd still feel out of place, hiding in a house full of cosplayers dressed-up like every kind of dark fantasy character known to man, but at least that way he wouldn't *look* like he was. Looks were everything in L.A.

He hadn't felt like coming, to be honest, but Kitt was one of his most loyal clients, sticking with him even though he hadn't gotten her as much as he would have liked. Besides, it had been a while since he'd worked a crowd. Schmoozing kept his client list long. Being seen out and about was mandatory in his line of work.

His reputation as one of the most sought-after lawyers in both L.A. and NYC was no accident. It was calculated. Word of mouth contributed to some of his success, but family name did the heavy lifting. Not that he wasn't a brilliant lawyer, he was, but in a town like Hollywood, success was largely based on who you knew.

The irony was, even though he'd been eager enough to let nepotism help get his career off the ground, Jake had decided he couldn't coast on his family's name. Not forever, anyway. He no longer needed his father's money, or his penchant for pay-offs, but they did come in handy every once in a while.

When all was said and done, Jake was proud that he'd rolled up his sleeves and had actually started working for his reputation. The decision had yielded another benefit besides wealth. His workaholic tendencies kept the time he had to spend hearing his father yap about status and money and all the "work arounds" Jake already knew about to a minimum.

On the other side of that coin, however, was that his schedule, which he'd packed even more full after the divorce, didn't leave much time for Jake to hone his nice guy skills. A fact that made his old man beam with pride. Being a pompous prick was mandatory in the Sullivan family.

It bothered Jake sometimes because he wasn't like that. Not really. On the surface, yeah, but not deep down. And he'd be lying if he said it wasn't a kick to the gut there wasn't a single person in this goddamned city, apart from his twin sister, who knew that.

Well, he thought there had been one other person who'd known, who'd seen past the over-confidence and understood.

But she was a really good actress. And he had been sorely mistaken.

So, if being an asshole was how it had to be to make it in this town, then so be it. It wasn't that hard, honestly, especially if it kept him safe from falling for another fake.

Jake tipped his glass at a woman dressed as a Valkyrie

who'd peeked her head into the room. He noticed his glass had been drained of whiskey. The thought of venturing toward the bar for another crossed his mind, but that would make drink number three, so he dumped the ice in an overgrown potted plant and set his glass on the mantel, regretting his decision to venture out that evening.

He sighed, pulling his phone from his pocket while eyeing a . . . what was it, a throne? Jake sat, surprised the bejeweled chair was actually more comfortable than it looked.

He tapped the screen with a thumb. At some point, all celebrities ended up needing legal representation. It was a given Kitt's drunken soiree would be crawling with potential clients. Since none of them were going anywhere for the next couple of hours, Jake decided to check his email before rubbing elbows.

He scrolled through dozens of unread notifications until Kitt's raspy voice pulled him offline and back into the dim corner of her creepy-ass mansion.

"Snakester!"

He didn't particularly care for her version of his nickname, but he went with it.

"Ms. Van Nightshade." Jake stood, almost knocking over a massive standing candelabra as he slipped his phone into the back pocket of his jeans.

Not surprising, since the damn things were everywhere. The shadows flickering across the walls gave the room a certain macabre ambiance—rock star or makeup mogul, Kitt had a flair for the dramatic—but damn if they didn't present a huge fire hazard around this many intoxicated humans.

"How many times have I told you, Jake? *You* get to call me Kitty," she said before planting an air kiss on each of his cheeks, failing at her attempt to keep red wine from sloshing over the rim of her over-sized goblet and onto the rug.

Honestly? He was surprised she could move at all, considering how tight her leather pants were. Or that she hadn't tripped over the sheer, floor-length jacket slash cape thingy she was wearing. She was relatively fit for her age, so she was sort of pulling it off, but Jesus, the shit these people wore got weirder and weirder every year.

Whatever ridiculous getup she was wearing wouldn't matter once he quietly slipped out the medieval-castle-inspired doors now that she'd noticed he'd shown up.

"Staying out of trouble, Kitty?" He scrubbed his jaw, reminding himself not to gawk at her for too long. Her boobs were enormous, and definitely in no need of help from the push-up bra she was wearing. Her face was stretched into a permanent wrinkle-free—and painful-looking—grimace. It took effort, but he forced a smile onto his face wide enough to pass as legit.

"Barely. Good thing I've got you, right?" Her cackle, gravelly from years of unfiltered Marlboros, was too theatrical to be sincere. "You know, if I didn't like the ladies so much, I'd be all over you." She gave him a once over, as though contemplating switching teams for the night, and then abruptly grabbed his arm.

"Oh! Come with me, Snakester. I just remembered, there's someone I want you to meet."

God damn son of a bitch. Not staring at the caricature his client had become was a piece of cake right now compared to not busting his teeth out of his skull from clenching his jaw so hard. So much for leaving.

Obliging, he followed behind Kitt as they climbed a staircase before she continued to weave them through a seemingly endless crowd. Damn, her place was bigger than it looked. A labyrinth of doors and rooms and long hallways. Add in the eerie sounds of a cello soundtrack being piped into every one of those rooms and hallways, and it made him feel like he was walking toward his death in a horror movie.

When she finally stopped at a small group of people mingling near a set of doors that led out to a balcony, he groaned. They weren't off to the side or even out *on* the balcony, like courteous adults, but standing right in the middle of the open doors, blocking access to fresh air and the spectacular view of the downtown skyline like a bunch of jerks.

Be that as it may, Jake couldn't help but notice the woman with the killer hourglass shape. As if her backside wasn't already alluring enough, an explosion of curls spiraled down her back, accentuating her curves.

Unfortunately, the pair of hopefuls displaying their waxed chests like peacocks succeeded in ruining the lovely scene.

They were doing the dance; drones trying to impress a queen bee. He wanted to tell them it wasn't worth it. He knew because he'd been there, done that. Once. And he'd vowed never do that dance again.

Kitt handed her goblet to the hopeful wearing guy-liner, so she could hug the woman from behind. "There you are, darling. Are you having a good time?"

When the woman turned around, more than Jake's jaw clenched. It was the woman from the airport bar. The one who called herself Medusa.

Another round of colorful curses exploded inside his head. Of course, the person Kitt wanted to introduce him to would be *her*, the snake chick.

Normally he liked a bit of confidence in a woman, but she'd managed to turn him off within the first three words that had come out of her gorgeous mouth.

Why couldn't Kitt have introduced him to a strung-out rock star in need of a new music deal? Why did it have to be someone he really did not care for? What made the whole thing worse was this Medusa woman had told him he'd be seeing her again, and she'd been right.

Jake offered a curt nod. "We've met. Medusa, isn't it?" He knew full well that was the ridiculous name she insisted on

going by, but the asshole in him refused to give her the satisfaction.

Medusa stared at him with that intense gold-and-green flecked gaze he remembered. It had taken him aback when they'd met. He remembered all to well how the air had suddenly seemed scarce, and a little too thin to pull in a proper breath. Unfortunately, her eyes hadn't lost any of their power to suck all the oxygen from the room.

Thank God he was a lawyer, practiced in the art of quick recoveries.

"Mr. Sullivan." Medusa leaned in for the standard Hollywood greeting, an air kiss to the cheek.

She smelled divine. Like honey and vanilla and exotic flowers. Like trouble. Like wrapping men around her finger to get whatever she wanted no matter who she destroyed.

Like the kind of woman he had trouble staying away from.

Fuck. "It's nice to see you again," replied Jake.

Oh, but was it?

Preoccupied with the strange air pulsing between him and Medusa, Kitt didn't bother to introduce either of the men, which was fine by Jake. The alpha of the two was clearly furious at the interruption, and it would be better if Jake just kept his mouth shut. He might be tempted to point out how the dude didn't have that much game in the first place.

Accepting his defeat, Alpha Boy bowed his head before saying, "It was a pleasure talking with you, Medusa. I hope we shall meet again soon."

Jake almost laughed out loud when he saw the man was wearing fake vampire fangs, as in actual veneers and not just molded plastic. He thought that trend had died out a while ago. He pressed his mouth shut, but it didn't stop Alpha Boy from shooting him a dirty look before stomping down the hallway toward the staircase.

What a tool.

Not sure what to do now that his leader was gone, Guy-liner handed over Kitt's goblet and headed after Alpha Boy without a word.

Kitt lifted the cup to her lips, murmuring, "Interesting," before taking a sip of wine. The moment had been far from interesting, or subtle, but Jake didn't know if she was referring to Alpha Boy's abrupt and sulky departure or the animosity between him and Medusa.

Either way, Kitt wasn't budging. She stared at them, waiting for someone to make a move.

It was now or never.

"I'm afraid I need to get going as well. Kitt, it was nice seeing you—"

"Really?" cut in Medusa. "What are you, eighty? It's only ten o'clock and you're already going home? Stay and talk to me."

"Who said I was going home?" he shot back. "Maybe I'm meeting someone."

"Maybe she can wait."

Irritating *and* presumptuous.

Jake's head began to spin. It was most likely the whiskey, but the way her lips curved seductively didn't help. Something primal in him sparked to life, burning its way through him as he looked her up and down, contemplating what to do next. His mouth made the decision for him when he returned her cocky smile with one of his own.

Perhaps he could stay a little longer.

Kitt's eyebrows shot up as she drained the contents of her cup. She would have to have been an imbecile not to notice the mood go from seething dislike to intense sexual attraction in exactly four words.

"Well, then. My work here is done. Enjoy yourselves, kiddies. I need more wine."

Jake's gaze switched from Kitt's flowing cape thingy billowing behind her as she walked away to Medusa, and damn if his lungs didn't start acting up again.

Sex. That's it, Jake. If you're actually thinking of giving her the time of day . . . Just sex.

He cleared his throat, hoping it sounded like he was more annoyed than affected by her in any way. That's how defense mechanisms worked. "All right. You've convinced me to stay. Now what?"

"First, we get you another drink," she said, brushing past him and toward the upstairs bar.

Of course he followed her. He was on autopilot. And the moment she handed him a glass of whiskey and said, "Second, I seduce you," he knew his resolve for nothing more than a one-night was in danger of crashing and burning.

CHAPTER NINE

*D*amn the gods to Hades' Realm, seducing this guy was going to be a lot more fun than Medusa had originally anticipated.

She *thought* she might just want to jump straight to sex, but now, seeing the look on his face—so full of confidence, like *he* was the one in control—perhaps it might be more fun to drag it out.

Really make him suffer.

A warm breeze blew, lifting the ends of her hair, and she shook them out to add to the effect. An extra dose of allure to really get him good and worked up.

When her skin broke out in goose bumps, she told herself it was because she still wasn't used to temperatures that fell below hell-fire hot. But a nagging suspicion she'd just received a warning from Hades to not mix business with pleasure prompted her muscles to tense, cutting the shiver racing up her spine short.

Jake rested his forearms on the railing surrounding the balcony, dangling his drink recklessly over the edge.

"So, are you going to tell me your real name before we do this or not?"

"Does it matter?" she said, annoyed he saw right through her ruse and straight to the end game.

He'd cut straight to the chase, or rather, the catch. His directness about what was inevitably going to happen, either out here on the balcony, in one of the rooms of this house, or even back at his place, tipped the balance of control ever so slightly. And not in her favor.

"No, I guess it doesn't." A sly smile curled his lips before he raised his glass of whiskey for a sip. "At least tell me where you're from, then."

Why was he trying to force the small talk? Maybe he was nervous, or perhaps it was to assuage the guilt of going through with the one-night stand he was about to have.

Either way, his rambling made her want to cackle with delight. He was fighting harder than a Titan to gain control over his libido. How cute.

And futile.

She pushed a laugh out through her perfect new nose. "Why, so you can dig up the dirt on me? Let's just say I come from somewhere and leave it at that."

Medusa moved to stand next to him, holding her phone up at just the right angle to take a selfie with L.A.'s top entertainment lawyer.

And for later, when she was alone with her dirty mind.

Jake blocked her shot by moving his head and shoulders away from her phone and out of frame. "I don't do selfies. Sorry."

"Ooh, motion denied," laughed Medusa. It was forced, since he was really starting to get on her nerves now. "It's just a picture. I would have let you approve it before I posted."

"Famous last words," he said, still turned away from her.

Medusa tossed her phone into her handbag. "You can turn back around . . . I put it away."

Jake faced her again. Damn. Those eyes. They sure made it difficult to conduct any type of business.

A streak of desire shot through her, reminding her why she was even there in the first place. This man was one tasty snack.

She swallowed the saliva pooling in her mouth as she pictured all the ways she would possess him. All the compromising positions she'd put him in.

Oh yeah, she was going to mix all the pleasure she wanted with her business, thank you very much. The only thing she'd asked for was a vacation, yet somehow, she'd ended up a pawn in Hades' tedious and never-ending fight with Zeus. Hades would just have to deal with however she decided to get the job done. She would assess Jake's soul in due time . . . Right after she had her way with him.

Medusa fixed her gaze on him, nearly laughing out loud at the way every wheel spinning inside his head showed up on his face. It frustrated him to no end that she would not give up the goods because that's how he gained the upper hand. That's how he wriggled his way to victory.

She could tell because that was exactly what she did. The difference was, she would win this game they were playing, even if it took all two hundred and some odd days she had left of her vacation.

But what if that strained look was because the poor man was grappling with something far more harrowing? Self-doubt was a hell of a thing, and Medusa knew all too much how real *that* struggle was.

Maybe dragging him into a game he wasn't equipped to play would be more than she had bargained for. Perhaps she just needed to make her assessment and let destiny run its course.

Speaking of fate, when the middle sister, Lachesis, deemed your time was up, there wasn't really much anyone could do about it. Jake's days were numbered, and Medusa needed to have her fun with him while she still could.

With the way he kept trying to wrestle the upper hand from her, she wasn't sure they'd even get to the fun part.

"What about you?" she blurted, suddenly and inexplicably wanting to fill the silence.

"Born and raised here," he replied.

The sadness in his voice tugged at her heart.

"Why don't you sound happy about that?" she asked, genuinely curious.

He dropped his head, sighing before lifting it again. "Because I'm not."

The light pounding in her chest turned into a more aggressive hammering. "Why is that, if you don't mind me asking?"

Hades' wrath, now *she* sounded like the sad one, as in a sad sap who actually cared where he'd grown up.

This night was turning out to be just full of surprises, wasn't it?

Jake remained silent as he looked out over the City of Glitz and Glam. She'd hit a sore spot, obviously, but instead of pressing on it, she surprised herself, yet again, by joining him in appreciating the enticing lights for what they were— beautiful but dangerous, so easily ensnaring all who walked into their sparkling web.

As she did, long forgotten feelings floated to the surface. Memories of how utterly lost and alone she'd felt in those first few decades after she'd been turned.

Sometimes she *still* felt that way.

"Sometimes I hate where I come from, too," she murmured, the words just slipping out.

Jake turned his head, tilted it, his green eyes flashing just as dazzlingly as Los Angeles at night. "Yeah?"

Medusa nodded before looking at him. Those eyes, that mouth. His lean, muscular body and, damn it to Hades, his silky voice. They did things to her, making her desire to possess every part of him grow stronger.

But, right now, she almost felt human again, and the longing to connect on a deeper level, learn more about him—to tell him more about her—was currently more powerful than her lust.

"Yeah," she said. "I haven't always had it easy. Haven't always been this . . . Worshipped."

She had nearly said *loved*, but her adoring fans didn't love her. Mortal or immortal, no one did. Not by a long shot.

Her cheeks warmed when he scoffed, but it didn't upset her. Quite the opposite.

"I didn't mean it like that," she said. "I just meant . . ." She couldn't exactly tell him what she'd meant, but for some strange reason she wanted to at least try.

"You probably won't understand," she continued, "but I've always been horribly ugly, until recently, and I had to practically sell my soul to look the way I do now. So what's wrong with wanting to be beautiful?"

Jake shook his head and shrugged. "Nothing. You fit right in. We're all beautiful around here . . . on the outside."

Medusa's brow crumpled. What was he implying?

"I hear you about the selling your soul part, though," he continued, before she had time to fully react. Total lawyer move. "Except I'm not even sure I had one to begin with. I was a spoiled little rich kid who followed in his father's deviant footsteps. I'm a goddamn cliche."

A whirlwind of thoughts funneled around Medusa's brain. The least of which was that he hadn't said or done anything close to deviant. In fact, she was starting to wonder if she would even be able to call his assessment work.

"Over-confident, maybe, but cliche?" she said. "Please. You're unlike anyone else I've ever met, Jake Sullivan."

"Is that so?" he asked, one eyebrow sliding up.

What to say now? The conversation had definitely veered

off into Making Connections territory when it should have stayed squarely in Making Out by Now.

It seemed she had forgotten rule number one of vacay: Do Not Get Attached. And here she was, starting to find him quite likable . . . *relatable* . . . and maybe even a little charming.

Shit. She needed to reroute this train back to Vacation Station, and quick.

"Okay, scratch that," she said. "You're a total self-absorbed prick, just like the rest of them."

She sent him a teasing smile, slitting her eyes and pouting her lips for added potency. But his eyebrow dropped, and his face hardened, his walls flying back up the same instant he turned to look out over the skyline again.

Her grin, the one she thought had been sexy, faltered.

"But so is everyone else here," she offered, the ball of worry that she had upset him dropping into the pit of her stomach. "And I can relate, you know? I'm trying to be someone different, just like everyone else here. It's kind of exhausting, really. I thought coming to L.A. would be so much . . . easier." She stepped closer to him, close enough to place a hand over his wrist. "We may *seem* shallow, you and I, but we're both more complex than people give us credit for."

A tiny smile tipped the side of his mouth. It was almost imperceptible, but it still had the power to make her head spin, and she leaned on the railing to steady herself.

Some seductress she was. And what the hell? Who was she, Doctor Phil? Wouldn't that just be the something if those were her last words, all empathetic and shit, before she lost her balance and went careening over the railing?

Medusa tried again, sending him another sultry, come hither look. She was in charge here, and it was high time she get back to the top order of business: Pleasure.

What did she care about his upbringing? What did it matter if he was a fragile being underneath all that bravado?

"But enough with the small talk," she purred. "You want me, I want you, so let's cut the . . ."

The words caught in her throat when he straightened. He was tall, six two, at least, and his gaze was intense and hooded. "I couldn't agree more."

He licked his lips as he took a step toward her, more than ready to stop talking, and Medusa let her bag slide off her arm and fall to the ground.

Their mouths met in a collision of disdain and desire so powerful it was hard to tell which was fueling them more. The faint sound of breaking glass barely registered, same with the sharp crunch beneath her feet as Jake walked her backward, toward a shadowed recess of the balcony. It wasn't until her back hit the siding, and his hands were gripping both hips, that she realized he must have dropped his glass of whiskey to free them up.

Her lust came back, full force, and she snaked a leg around one of his to draw him closer. His body was hard, and the part that was currently the hardest felt delicious pressed against her.

She sucked the whiskey off his bottom lip, trying not to rip open his shirt and gulp him down in one bite. His hands slid up her thighs, the hem of her dress going along for the ride.

When some asshole opened the door, stuck their head out, and said, "Oh. Sorry," she had to stop herself from flying into a rage.

"Shit." Jake exhaled as he unhanded her, stepping back. "Not here."

Frustrated, she hooked her fingers into the front pockets of his jeans and tugged his hips forward. "Why not? Hollywood loves a good show, right?"

"Too many cell phones." He ran his fingers through his hair. "We can go to my place if you want."

Without waiting for an answer, he walked over to retrieve her bag. When he handed it to her, she arched a brow at him.

"Your place, then," she said, hooking her bag into the crook of her arm and turning toward the door.

A sudden urge to be real with him—well, as real as she could get under the circumstances—made her stop just before they reached the threshold. She turned to face him.

"Melina," she said.

He tilted his head. "What?"

"My name, it's Melina Stone."

His face lit up with understanding. "Really?"

She blinked at him, abashed for the first time since she'd arrived on Earth.

"What do you mean *really*?" It was a made-up name, and she kind of felt bad, but it wasn't as if she could tell the truth.

Also, lying by omission, as it turned out, was an incredibly uncomfortable, especially considering his opinion was supposed to mean nothing to her.

Jake shook his head, and that small, barely-there smile came back. "I just didn't expect you to actually tell me is all. It's pretty."

Her heart flew into her throat. Sweet Persephone. It seemed like she was about to go flailing over the proverbial railing anyway. How far she would fall, however, had yet to be determined.

CHAPTER TEN

*J*ake couldn't stop thinking about Melina, and the things they'd done all night long. She'd left before he'd woken up, which was standard as far as one-night stands went, but he wouldn't have minded taking her to breakfast.

It was just as well. He already had plans, brunch with his sister and niece.

He pulled into a parking spot—no valet at their favorite hole-in-the-wall—and threw his Range Rover in park. He hurried across the pavement and into Vega's Starlight Diner.

When he finally got to their usual booth by a side window, Jake held a fist up to his twin. "What up, sis?"

"Oh, the usual." Kara bumped knuckles with him before sliding into the worn red pleather booth. "Death, taxes, stopping Judith and Mort from turning my child into a spoiled little brat."

Jake squatted, opening his arms wide for his seven-year-old niece, Hailey, whom he called Comet because she was the brightest thing in his universe. Also, Kara had named her Hailey, and Jake thought it would be a fun play on words.

"She would never act like a spoiled little brat. Would you, Comet?"

Hailey stepped back from their hug. "I'm not little."

"Oh, that's right," said Jake, moving out of her way so she could climb into his side of the booth. "She prefers acting like a *big* spoiled brat."

Despite his packed work schedule, Jake always made it a point to keep his longstanding every-other-Sunday-brunch date with his sister and niece. He looked forward to it. It was the only time he felt like he could breathe. The rare few hours he could be himself and not cringe when he looked in the mirror afterwards.

He looked down at his niece, who had wasted no time ripping open the cellophane-wrapped trio of cheap crayons to color on the paper placemat in front of her and shifted into Uncle Jake Mode. Time to allow his sensitive side a few leg-stretches.

"You excited for Uncle Jake's big Halloween party next weekend?" Kara asked her daughter.

"Mm hm," murmured Hailey, setting down the red crayon and picking up the green one.

Hailey's father, some slick-talking salesman from Glendale, conveniently disappeared when he'd found out Kara was pregnant. Turned out he already had a wife.

Oh, and three other kids.

Jake gave his sister a half-smile from across the table. She'd learned some pretty hard lessons about trying to change people. They both had. When you grew up having everything you wanted, you thought you could bend people to your will with a snap of a finger. When they didn't do as commanded, or couldn't be bought, and you realized you weren't so special after all, well, it humbled you. Made you get your priorities straight.

Or, if you were like Jake, made you an even bigger asshole.

Of course, thinking about Hailey's deadbeat dad always made Jake remember the moment he'd first laid eyes on her. He could still see Kara laying in the hospital bed, chewing on her lip as the nurse placed Hailey in his arms. Kara had been mentally preparing for the smart-ass remark her big-shot lawyer brother would say about his niece's cleft palate.

It always made his heart ache whenever he remembered the way his sister had cried as she nodded in agreement when he'd said, "She's absolutely perfect, Kara."

From that moment on he'd stepped up, standing in as a father figure to Hailey when her piece of shit dad was nowhere to be found, which had been every milestone and all seven birthdays so far.

Of course, their parents made sure Hailey went to the best private school in the area. There was no way in Hell Judith Sullivan would stand for having her granddaughter enrolled in the public education system. It was bad enough her daughter had chosen *nursing* as a profession, let alone being a single mother.

Judy's philosophy regarding love and marriage, on life in general? Wealth could cover up all the unsavory bits. A huge bank account could fill any void. And money could hide the fact that your daughter chose to live as a commoner.

While Kara never let on how much their parents' thinly veiled disappointment hurt, she did let them provide Hailey with the things she couldn't afford on a nurse's salary.

She was down with their parents footing the bill for the private education thing, but it was Jake she relied on to help with the stuff that mattered. Like making sure Hailey didn't grow up to be an entitled rich kid. Or, as Kara had so eloquently put it, *"A raging butthole like you, Jake."*

He was all in for that challenge, fully committed to being a source of stability in Hailey's life, but he was also Judith and Mort Sullivan's son. He didn't worship the almighty dollar like his parents did—well, not quite as much, anyway

—but he could definitely appreciate the power that came along with having it. His only saving grace, if he did say so himself, was that he knew how to use it for good and not evil.

Mostly. For the things that really counted.

Like helping his sister pay for the multiple cosmetic surgeries and dental procedures required after the initial correction, so that Hailey had the best chance at not having to deal with a lifetime of other people's bullshit. And like sponsoring a charity ball every October to help kids whose parents couldn't afford the multiple surgeries and procedures in order to do the same.

He ruffled Hailey's hair. "What are you dressing up as this year, Comet?"

"Medusa," she answered without hesitation. "And not the fake one, the real one on Youtube. Can I have your phone, mommy, so I can show him?"

Jake almost choked on his sip of water. He knew exactly who Hailey was talking about. He should, since he'd just had a one-night stand with the woman.

"Sure, babe," said Kara, digging around in her purse. "There's a new beauty guru," she stopped rummaging to throw air quotes around the words beauty and guru, "who goes by the name of Medusa. She's everywhere. Hailey loves her. She's actually kind of a badass."

"Ooh, mommy, you said ass."

"Don't repeat that word, Comet. It's for grown-ups." Jake rubbed his forehead, a distressing thought popping into his head. "Christ, Karalynn, you're not letting her wear make-up, are you? To cover up . . . you know."

"Of course not, *Jacob*. She's only seven." Kara looked at her daughter. "Plus, Hailey knows her scars are nothing to be ashamed of, don't you, babe?"

"Yep." Hailey nodded her head absently, which didn't seem very convincing to Jake. But he trusted his sister, even if she did run fast and loose with swear words around her seven-year-old. He trusted she knew what she was doing when it came to the Raising A Well-Adjusted Child Considering the Circumstances Department.

"I know her, you know," said Jake, picking up the blue crayon and marking an "X" on the tic-tac-toe grid printed on Hailey's placemat.

"You know who? Hailey?" replied Kara, resting her elbows on the table with a confused look on her face.

"No, Medusa."

Hailey's head snapped up from the phone screen, and he bit the inside of his bottom lip to stop himself from saying another grown-up word—the four-lettered kind.

That started with an F.

"You do?" Hailey bounced in her seat when she turned the phone towards him, a picture of Melina in all her snaked-out glory lighting up the screen. "Is she coming to the Halloween party? Please, oh please, oh *pleeeaaase . . .*"

"Uh . . ." Jake stalled, trying to think of something to say. He had said he knew his niece's latest obsession out loud why?

Hell if he had any clue, the words had just slipped out.

"Well, Uncle Jake. Is she?"

"I don't know." It was the only thing he could say without lying. "She hasn't RSVP'd yet."

Yeah, that's because he hadn't sent her an invitation. And, fuck, now he'd have to because while he may have been doing a halfway decent job over the last year and a half of not getting involved with any more of L.A.'s monsters, there was one female he had zero willpower against. She was looking up at him right now, putting him on the spot with her big, brown eyes.

Thankfully, the conversation was derailed when the server came by to drop off their food.

"Oh look, pancakes," said Jake, glad to be out of the hot

seat. That was until he noticed the server's gaze lingering a bit too long on Hailey's scars. "Why don't you take a picture? It lasts longer."

He was being one thousand percent childish, and he knew it, but damn if he didn't get sick of people blatantly staring at Hailey. He could deal with a quick glance, he'd kept his mouth shut plenty of times for that, but when they stared, with their mouths hanging open like morons? Didn't they realize how ignorant that was? How detrimental to a little girl's self-confidence it could be?

The waitress's face turned beet red. "I . . . I'm sorry. I didn't mean to—"

"Don't worry about it," said Kara. "Can we get some ketchup, please?"

"Uh, sure. Be right back," replied the waitress, spinning on her heels and hightailing it as far away from their table as possible.

Hundred bucks she'd send someone else to drop off the ketchup.

"Wow. Take a chill pill, bro." Kara arched a brow as she slid Hailey's plate over to her.

Kara was older by four minutes. Sometimes, mostly when Jake did something rash and stupid, it felt like years, possibly even decades.

"Well, she was staring, and it was rude."

"Hailey knows the drill." Kara nodded at her daughter. "Don't you, babe. The bigger the flair . . ."

Hailey wiggled in her seat, see-sawing her shoulders as she said, "The longer they stare." She picked up the syrup decanter and began to pour. "They're just jealous of my flair, Uncle Jake. That's all."

"Exactly," said Kara. "And Hailey won't ever learn to be comfortable with her *flair* if her Uncle Jake keeps doling out sick burns on her behalf every time someone says or does something rude." One of her fingers flew up. "That's enough syrup."

The staring still pissed him off, but his sister had a point.

"Well, Uncle Jake is sorry, then."

"It's okay," Hailey reached up and patted his arm, her hand sticky with syrup. "You can make it up to me by taking me to the zoo or something."

Jake shook his head, beaming with pride. No, he wouldn't let her become a raging butthole, but he would make sure she knew how to find the loopholes, so she could work the angle to her advantage whenever she needed.

"You drive a hard bargain, Comet, but motion granted," he said, pausing from the annihilation of his hash browns to point at his little lawyer-in-training's plate with a fork, his sleeve covered in syrup and his heart full of unconditional love. "Now eat your pancakes before they get cold."

edusa adjusted the headpiece made of plastic snakes. They used to be the real deal. What a shame. The girls would have gotten a kick out of attending a fancy party like this.

A smile curled her lips just thinking about what fun they'd have striking out at all these strangers, turning their asses to stone, but then her chest tightened when another thought hit her. She was dressing up as herself instead of *being* herself. Somehow, that was sadder than her snakes missing out on the opportunity to raise hell.

A valet opened the car door, scattering her thoughts, which was good, because she didn't want to be thinking right now, let alone feeling.

The well-groomed young gentleman held out his hand, and Medusa took it, letting him help her out so she wouldn't trip over her floor-length gown; a hunter-green, form-fitting number that hugged her curves like a second skin.

Like snakeskin, to be exact, and she planned on shedding it in the backseat of someone else's—preferably Jake's—limo by the end of the night.

She'd snort-laughed when Dylan had tossed a pile of

envelopes on the counter that morning. Who sent snail mail anymore? Even a monster from the Underworld knew that was archaic as hell.

Turned out, she'd gotten an invitation to a fundraiser from some plastic surgeon. She'd been poring over the details, trying to figure out why Hollywood's premiere fixer-upper was begging for money, when she'd spotted one name in particular, in tiny letters, listed as a sponsor.

Jacob Sullivan, Sullivan & Sullivan Entertainment Law.

When she saw Jake's name, she'd practically choked on her mimosa demanding that Dylan RSVP immediately.

Even though it was basically just a boring Halloween gala, celebrating the wonders that plastic surgery can do for horribly ugly people, she would go. And even though attendees were encouraged to wear a costume, something which she found equally trite, hers had been a no-brainer.

Champagne fountain. Fancy hors d'oeuvres. The hot meat bag who she was on a mission to seek and destroy. All in one place? There was no excuse *not* to go, really.

Medusa sashayed across the red carpet and into the venue with a mission. Okay, two missions. The first, to be seen *and* heard, a requirement for all the attention she was about to soak up. The second, locate her chosen target. If he was here, she would find him.

But first, a drink.

She breezed past the champagne fountain and over to the bar, where a zombie scanned her up and down as she approached, lingering on her ample cleavage.

"What can I get you, miss?"

Medusa patiently waited for him to recognize her, which was something because patience was not her strong suit. Thank Hades, it didn't take long.

"Hey, aren't you . . ."

"That hot new influencer who *everybody* is dying to get to know?" She licked her lips, slowly, savoring the dazed look on Zombie Man's face as the blood vacated his big head and made its way down south in a hot hurry for a smaller one.

She almost laughed at how easy it was to arouse mortals. Women were a bit tougher to know for sure, since their hard-ons were much, much smaller, but lady boners definitely counted.

"I'll have the strongest stuff you've got behind that bar, brain eater," said Medusa, winking. He was decent looking as far as meat bags went, so why not?

She should have a back-up, any way. In case Jake didn't show.

"Brains aren't the only thing I like to eat," he said, just loud enough for her to hear as he poured a glass of Elijah Craig bourbon.

Before she could fashion a response, she spotted a pair of broad shoulders and a tight backside that looked suspiciously like they belonged to Jake Sullivan.

"Pour another, will you?"

"I'm not allowed to drink on the job," said the zombie, his gaze darting around the room before continuing, "but I can see if I can get someone to cover for me so we could—"

Medusa snapped her head toward him with such force it hurt a little. She needed to remember to take it easy. For all intents and purposes, she was one of them now, and needed to be delicate with this banging bod so she wouldn't break it . . . or shake it loose or whatever.

Trying not to wince at the literal pain in her neck, she stared at the figurative pain in her ass, stone-faced, all interest gone.

"It's not for you."

Cheeks turning red under the spotty green face paint, the bartender poured her a second drink. She nodded politely as she plucked both glasses off the bar top and headed toward her preferred target.

Medusa admired the way Jake's broad shoulders tapered

to a trim waist, even in a suit. The smirk on her face widened into a mischievous grin as she silently thanked the designer whomever he was wearing that evening for knowing what they were doing with a needle and thread.

As she weaved her way through the crowd, taking inventory of her wittiest quips, her stilettos suddenly felt too high when a woman sidled up to Jake and kissed him on the cheek before threading her arm through his.

Medusa's confident stride faltered, but only slightly, and although she nearly threw both drinks across the room in a fit of rage, she refrained, managing to curb the impulse by gripping the glasses tighter.

Ignoring the strange twisting going on in her midsection, she resumed her march toward the epic battle in which she would reclaim the conquest that was rightfully hers.

"Fancy meeting you here," said Medusa, plastering on a smile she hoped came off as more sweet than vicious as she waited for Jake and the woman to turn around.

That was the trick with meat bags, especially around these parts; batting false eyelashes and feigning nonexistent innocence while pretending to care.

When they finally turned around, Jake looked like a deer caught in headlights. Scratch that, a ghost in headlights?

His face and hands were painted white. She had no idea why, nor did she care, honestly, because the surprised look on his face had been enough to give her that delicious shot of adrenaline she loved whenever his feathers got ruffled.

Surprises of all surprises, she was starting to crave the rush.

The woman on his arm, though, she had the gall to look pleased as punch. She also looked lovely in the Grecian-inspired gown she was wearing.

Before Medusa had any more time to ponder their strange and poorly executed costumes, and before Jake could even respond, Medusa shoved a glass into his hand, nearly spilling the expensive bourbon down the front of his perfectly tailored suit.

"I know how fond you are of good whiskey," she said, "so I brought you a bourbon. It's Elijah Craig."

Medusa batted her eyelashes at him, and as soon as he had a firm grasp around the glass, she went in for the kill. She held out her hand to the woman who had unwittingly just become her opponent.

"Hello. I'm Medusa." She tried not to wince as the woman moved in for the Hollywood handshake and air-kissed both of her cheeks.

"Medusa! Oh, wow, it's so nice to meet you in person."

Disarmed by the woman's seemingly genuine response but not deterred, Medusa refocused. This woman was good, but Medusa was better.

First rule of Hades' Realm? Always come prepared for a fight to the death. Always. How dare this woman try and disarm her by being so . . . non-combative. Well, since Medusa didn't have claws anymore, she'd just have to cut a bitch down to size with words.

"I would have brought you a drink as well, but I don't think they're serving piña coladas tonight."

"Oh, no worries. I don't drink alcohol."

The woman smiled with such genuine sweetness that Medusa opened her mouth to impart another thinly veiled yet viciously back-handed compliment.

But Jake beat her to the punch and spoke first. "Medusa, this is—"

"Uncle Jake! Mommy!"

Medusa resisted the urge to hiss when a tiny human dressed as some sort of hideous monster came barreling toward them. She managed to keep a snarl under wraps but couldn't help but take a step back when the screeching mini-meat bag skidded to a halt in front of her.

Medusa blinked down at the spindly little thing staring up

at her with wide eyes. Snakes. The girl had snakes for hair. Plastic ones, but still, she could see the girl was dressed up as a certain infamous gorgon.

Medusa's eyes narrowed, and her lip lifted in preparation to unleash a growl, but when she noticed how visibly the child was shaking, her chest tightened for the second time that evening. Or was it third? Either way, another long-forgotten feeling shot to the surface, conveniently stopping at her heart to wring every ounce of malice from it.

What a strange development. Medusa may not have encountered a child, or have even seen one in a very long time for that matter, but it didn't mean she wanted to frighten the poor thing.

Then, in the midst of her maelstrom of conflicting emotions, something else hit her. What if the matchmaker's illusion had slipped? Had she indeed accidentally shaken it loose over by the bar, and now it was hanging off her real face like a rubber Halloween mask?

Medusa's hand flew to her cheek. Praise Hades below she felt smooth skin instead of rough scales. She touched a hand to the back of her head next, exhaling when she discovered hair instead of snakes.

Speaking of snakes, now the white face paint made sense. Jake was made up to look like he'd been turned to stone.

Oh, how clever. Even if it was a painful reminder—and a touch hurtful—she could appreciate the level of care taken in regard to authenticity.

She would have painted on a few cracks in that stone, though. Speaking from experience and all.

"Oh, my dear little mortal," said Medusa. "You're dressed up as *me*. I'm so honored. You look absolutely amazing."

"Thanks!" said the girl, loudly. "I can't believe you came to my Uncle Jake's party. I'm going to tell all my friends I got to meet you in person. Can we take a selfie?"

So much vim and vigor—and volume—for such a small

creature. Medusa smiled at the little girl, realizing she had been shaking with excitement instead of . . .

Wait a minute. *Uncle* Jake?

"Of course," said Medusa, standing again. Her gaze landed on Jake first, then flicked over to the woman before going back to him again.

Same thick, dark hair. Same green eyes, though Jakes were decidedly more alluring, and similar facial features.

"Medusa, this is my sister, Kara, and my niece, Hailey," said Jake, a little on the dry side and a lot on the way-to-over-react side.

CHAPTER TWELVE

Jake relished the surprised look on Melina's face when he introduced Kara and Hailey. Seriously, did the woman think she had any kind of effect on him whatsoever? They'd had sex. That's it.

Now if only he could just stop replaying it over and over in his mind . . .

He needed to stop. No, *she* needed to stop. Stop looking at his niece so adoringly. So tenderly. It was making his heart thud in his chest without permission. And he didn't like it. Not one bit.

Connecting with this woman on a deeper level was *not* part of the arrangement he'd made with himself. He would *not* let her sink her claws into him.

But dammit, she'd knelt down so she could get eye-level with Comet, and it was shit like that he couldn't resist. He'd been expecting—almost hoping—she'd say, *"Well, aren't you quite the little monster,"* or something equally as backhanded.

But she hadn't. She'd actually given his niece, an impressionable little girl, a genuine compliment. It had caught him off guard, causing his heart to melt quicker than an ice cube in Hell. He hadn't thought the woman had it in her.

Well, shit, maybe she *had* managed to dig her claws in.

"You're delightful, Hailey. Can I have a hug?" asked Melina with a grin.

Jake tried not to wince as her claws sank a little deeper.

Compliments, hugs . . . Dazzling, brilliant smiles. These were the tactics monsters used to reel in their prey. Every last bit of it was fake. He knew *that* from experience.

Then why was he so powerless against it right now?

"Will you take a picture of us, mommy?" Hailey wiggled out of Melina's arms to tug on the designer gown he'd bought for his sister.

Kara had wanted in on the themed costume action—Comet would go as Medusa, he'd be turned to stone, and Kara would go as a Greek goddess. He'd used it as an excuse to treat her to a luxury she couldn't afford on her own, and had refused to indulge in on principle.

"Sure, babe," said Kara. "If it's okay with Miss Medusa."

Melina knelt down again, nodding and beckoning Hailey to her. "Of course."

Jake gnawed on the inside of his cheek, wishing he could bust up the whole scene with a few choice grown-up words as he watched Kara take pics of his niece and Melina.

Christ, they were both mugging for the camera like two college girls on spring break. There was no way he could be an asshole now, not when Comet was so excited. Besides, he needed to concentrate on not letting a smile overtake his face.

The gnawing turned into clenching, and the muscles over his jaw bunched as he ground his teeth. Being a dick might be his only recourse to stop the bullshit fluttering going on with his heart. Even if the damn thing was having a hard time seeing Melina for the succubus she was, with all this genuineness going on, his brain knew the truth.

Yet, his current conundrum remained. If she kept showing this side of herself much longer, complete with crippling levels of authenticity, the stirring in his chest would wind up in his pants.

Again.

Goddamn it, Jake. End this shit now. Find the loophole.

"Uncle Jake?" asked Hailey, walking over to him and cupping a hand around her mouth to whisper something into his ear.

"Yes, Comet?" Jake raised his eyebrow as he leaned down. She had that look. The one he was never able to refuse.

"Can Medusa come with us to the zoo on Saturday?"

Jake's gaze cut to Melina. She was biting that luscious lip of hers, anxious to hear his answer.

God save my soul. "Sure," he whispered back. "If she's not already busy."

"Okay," whisper-yelled Hailey. "Can you ask her right now?"

Jake swallowed hard and straightened, shoving his hands into his pockets as he ran his tongue along his teeth. How in the hell had Comet managed to put him in the hot seat again? So thoroughly on the spot he just might end up stammering the next words that came out of his mouth if he wasn't careful.

He had to hand it to the little shit. She kept slamming shut any loopholes he was finding—which, oddly enough, weren't nearly as many as he'd hoped—with a resounding bang. The grasshopper was quickly becoming the master, indeed.

He cleared his throat. "I'm sure you're probably busy, but would you like to go to the zoo with Hailey and me this Saturday?"

"I'm not busy at all and I'd love to," Melina replied without hesitation. A shit-eating grin spread across her face, and he hated that his heart—among other things—twitched at that display of genuineness, too.

"Yay!" squealed Hailey.

Jake went to say something else when feedback from the audio equipment screeched, making the guests groan. He decided it was a blessing in disguise since he wasn't sure, exactly, what else would have come out of his traitorous mouth.

"Whoa. Sorry about that, folks," apologized the emcee, who was dressed as a skeleton. "Let's try that again. Good evening, ladies and gentlemen. Are all you ghouls and goblins having fun tonight?" Light laughter and a round of applause rippled through the crowd of vampires and brides of Frankenstein as they stopped their chatting to turn toward the stage. "We'll let you get back to it in a just a few minutes, but right now, let's hear a few words from the host of this annual Halloween shindig, shall we? Please welcome Dr. Shane Williams to the stage to talk about this year's Superstar Smiles mission."

Jake shook his head, pushing a chuckle through his nose as his friend, dressed as Doc from Back to the Future, bounded onto the stage with erratic and bewildered movements, totally playing the part.

As far as business colleagues went, the man wasn't a saint, the price tags on his cosmetic procedures were outrageous, but he was a good man with a big heart. When Jake had approached him to see if he'd be interested in starting the Superstar Smiles Foundation with him, he'd been delighted to learn that Dr. Shane, as his clientele called him, was as passionate about making sure kids had beautiful smiles as he was making a set of double D's happen.

"We're up next, Comet." Jake held out his hand and Hailey grabbed it, quickly taking the lead and pulling him toward the stage as if she was an old pro a public speaking.

Jake nodded at people in the crowd as they made their way to the platform. This was the portion of the evening that always made him nervous. He felt awkward, even though he was known for his commanding presence in the courtroom, which he'd shown plenty of over his lucrative career.

Still, he wasn't keen on having to make this particular speech every year. It required him to show humility, and he didn't like trotting that guy out very much. It was too risky.

He also never knew what to say, especially when it came to taking credit for such important work. He wished he could do more than just give money. Sometimes he even wished he was the surgeon instead of the lawyer. That way, at least he'd be giving instead of taking. But he'd made his choice.

Or should he say the choice had been made for him?

Good old Morty hadn't given him another option, not really. He'd needed someone to take over the law firm so he could vacation in St. Tropez half the year.

But that was fine. Jake had been hungry for the fame and fortune back then and had accepted the baton willingly. It sure as hell had been a lot easier than taking the brave route and breaking away from their parents' expectations like Kara had.

He'd made his bed long ago and it was best to just lie in it, continuing along the path of least resistance he'd chosen. But he'd do it without resentment or complaint on this night, it was the least he could do. He'd grin and bear it as long as it helped raise funds for Superstar Smiles.

"Good evening," said Jake, adjusting the microphone. "Thank you all for coming to the seventh annual Superstar Smiles Halloween Gala."

A video screen descended from its casing, whining thinly from behind him. He'd wanted to do something different during his five minutes on stage this year, something that did the talking for him. Tugging on people's heartstrings tended to loosen their wallets. However, since he usually rubbed people the wrong way when he opened his mouth, he figured a montage of Hailey's baby pictures might do a better job of pulling in the donations.

He swept Hailey up into his arms. "It's because of this bright little star's birth seven years ago the Superstar Smiles Foundation was born."

CHAPTER THIRTEEN

What an unexpected development. Jake's niece was utterly delightful, and meeting her had reminded Medusa just how much she liked children. Too much time in the Underworld had made her forget.

As if it would make her any less bitter about her ugliness, Athena had deemed Medusa the official protector of women and children. It had been an ironic twist to say the least, considering she was no longer a woman and had no children, but she'd taken the duty seriously. Well, for a little while . . . until the irony had become too dark and she'd said screw it.

She'd gone to Hades, getting hired on as an intern first, then biding her time and paying her dues while stepping on all the other monster toes clamoring up the corporate ladder. Competing for the top spot in Hades' Realm had caused her "appointment" by Athena to fall by the wayside.

She hadn't been mad about it, either. In fact, she'd decided being *the* most powerful monster in the Underworld had much better perks.

Also, becoming Head Monster had been the biggest *eff you* to Athena she could think of at the time.

Speaking of work, she had a job to do. It was the reason she'd accepted the invitation to the gala in the first place. Part of the reason, anyway. She was hoping for more sexy time with Jake.

Reminiscing about the old days wasn't going to get either of those two things accomplished.

Honestly, this whole assessment thing was turning out to be way more complicated than she'd anticipated. Never mind the fact that she was dressed to the nines at a charity event he'd founded to help underprivileged children and their families deal with the expense of being born with a birth defect, which didn't exactly scream bad guy, but then there was the one hundred percent certainty that it made him ten times more attractive.

Who was she kidding? She already knew where he belonged, so why was she dragging her feet sending her final assessment to Hades?

Medusa realized she'd been chewing on her lip and stopped. She took a sip of her drink, assuming a semi-disinterested stance so she could continue to think uninterrupted. He was probably skimming off the top of his charity. If not, he was benefiting off people's pain and suffering *somehow*. She needed to figure out what that somehow was . . . In case . . .

Was she really thinking of sending a man who clearly belonged in Elysium to Hades' Realm?

She sighed, a twinge of guilt prompting her to lift the glass to her lips again. As vicious as she looked in real life, she didn't have the heart to be needlessly cruel. She knew what it felt like to be on the receiving end of an egregious injustice, and she wasn't *that* monster.

Or was she?

"So, Kara." Medusa took the last sip of her bourbon before putting the glasses, both now empty, on the tray of a server passing by. "Tell me how a guy known as "Jake The

Snake" in multiple cities manages to have the time to be so philanthropic?"

She'd give it more time, to gather the proof she needed to make sure her final decision, whatever it was, would be the right one.

Kara's smile widened as she continued to watch the video, but as soon as she turned to look Medusa in the eyes, it morphed into something else entirely. Something Medusa knew all too well.

Defensiveness.

"You seem surprised," said Kara, lifting an eyebrow.

Medusa ignored the challenge. Although she didn't make it a habit to walk away from the heady thrill of a fight, collecting more evidence took precedence over ripping an opponent to shreds.

The goal had changed. It was no longer just to have fun while it lasted. It was to get Jake to trust her completely, so he would reveal his bad side. She had to have iron-clad reasoning to take him with her when she went back to the Underworld. Wasting time going head-to-head with his sister would only delay Medusa's new plan.

So, she *did* plan on being that monster.

Kara had gone back to watching the video, and Medusa did her best to smooth the frown she could feel creasing her face as she did the same. The thought of Jake spilling the tea on himself, making it an open and shut case for selfishly sending him to Hell, suddenly felt underhanded.

She glanced at Kara, quite possibly the only other adult on Earth that Jake trusted implicitly, and a thought formed in her head. The woman shared his DNA, an advantage that could perhaps be a way to work smarter and not harder.

Siblings were the staunchest of allies—or enemies—when it came to the art of war, figuratively and literally. History had proven that time and time again. Not having the support of a blood relative of influence could be quite the troublesome obstacle to overcome.

In other words, piss Kara off and Medusa would have to work ten times harder to gain Jake's trust. Win her over, on the other hand, and it could be as simple as, *"You know, Jake, I like Medusa. She seems like a really good person."*

Plus, Medusa wouldn't have to destroy Jake, not completely. If Kara provided the evidence, or at least a few leads Medusa could investigate further, then the job would be done, the final decision made. It would be settled, and she could go back to enjoying the original reason for being here.

"I'm sorry. That came out wrong," began Medusa. "Let me start over . . . I just meant that I find it strange people would refer to him as a snake when he seems like such a good guy. I mean, I'm all for snakes, of course, but it is a bit curious."

"Well, he does kind of deserve it," said Kara, some of her defensiveness lifting. "He's done some pretty shady lawyer shit, but yeah, underneath it all, he's a good guy."

Medusa smiled at the cuss word. Kara seemed so refined. Medusa hadn't expected the woman would have the mouth of a trucker. Then again, looks could be deceiving, and who knew that better than an ugly-ass gorgon?

"Really? Like what?" said Medusa in her best you-can-trust-me-tell-me-everything voice.

Kara bit her bottom lip, contemplating how much to divulge. Medusa softened her expression to help coax the words out. It wasn't hard to see the woman was desperate for a friend, someone to confide in.

Even so, Medusa still had to play her cards right.

"I'm sorry, that was rude of me," she said, shaking her head regretfully. "I didn't mean to pry. It's just that he seems like such a nice guy, with such a big heart." Medusa glanced toward the stage where Jake still held Hailey in his arms. "I can't imagine anyone thinking he wasn't."

Medusa's chest tightened as soon as the words left her mouth, or maybe her stomach dropped. Whatever happened, it definitely wasn't normal, and it most certainly wasn't pleasant.

"He's pretty much destroyed his ex's new husband's acting career," blurted Kara. "No one wants to work with the guy now. Jake's got so much dirt on everyone in this town . . . He's got them all by the nut sack. They're scared shitless."

Okay, it was definitely Medusa's chest causing trouble. Her lungs more specifically, and the air they couldn't seem to pull in. His black-mailing ways were definitely grounds for a trip south, but what had really caught her off-guard was . . .

Jake had an ex-wife?

Why did she find that shocking? Why *wouldn't* Jake have been married? It was a rite of passage for mortal men like him. Rich, powerful, and good-looking. The quintessential wolf in sheep's clothing.

But was he, really?

Obviously, the split hadn't been amicable. Medusa didn't need to be a genius to figure that out. Whoever she was, she'd hurt him, and by the sound of it, not just hurt but *destroyed* him.

Wasn't that exactly what Medusa intended to do?

She swallowed down the irony.

"Oh, wow," she said. "So, he filed for the divorce I take it?" She already knew the answer, but she wanted to hear Kara confirm it out loud for some reason.

"One hundred percent. She was sleeping with one of her co-stars." Kara unleashed a derisive laugh. "All of them is more like it."

"May I ask which actress?" Medusa folded her arms so her fingers wouldn't curl into claws.

"Natasia Nowak." Kara's lip lifted in distaste. "God-damned harpy. She deserves an Oscar for the way she had

Jake fooled. She didn't even *try* to keep the sex tape from leak—"

Medusa inhaled sharply, not wanting to hear anymore. She'd already heard too much. If Kara uttered another word on the subject, Medusa might be tempted to go find this Natasia Nowak person. She needed to change the subject, and quick.

"Well, he seems like a pretty good uncle."

"The best." Kara's dark expression lightened. "I don't know what I'd do without him."

Medusa tried not to cringe, disguising the attempt with a thoughtful tilt of the head. She'd almost forgotten that, courtesy of fate, Kara would be thrust into a life without her brother only several months from now, and for the first time in a long time, Medusa felt a pang of sympathy.

Actually, it hadn't been that long. She'd been feeling them for weeks now.

"He's been a huge help raising Hailey," continued Kara. "It's been good for him, I think. Keeps him on his toes . . . and off his high horse, thank God."

He should go to Olympus popped into Medusa's head. Assessing his soul was simply a formality at this point. All she needed to do was send word of her assessment to Hades.

Not yet.

More wanted more time with him. He'd piqued her interest and, as it turned out, genuinely excited her. He made her feel good, and wasn't that exactly why she'd needed to get away in the first place?

Medusa distracted herself by taking in her opulent surroundings. The round tables set with the finest silverware and fanciest place settings. The wainscoting and wallpaper, hallmarks of taste and elegance. Her gaze slid around the richly appointed room, from one thing to the other, but the question she was trying to avoid nagged her regardless.

What if she lied? It wouldn't be that big of a deal, would

it? Not if she could have Jake for herself when she was back in the Underworld. She had come here to find some poor soul to do her bidding, hadn't she?

Conscience aside, the bigger issue on the table was going against Hades. He expected the results to be in his favor. He'd look like a fool if Medusa went against expectation and determined Jake belonged in Hell. That particular judgment call would undoubtedly spark his temper, and the King of the Underworld would not be happy if he were forced to concede to his brother. Not after sending a major middle finger in writing. And then there was the matter of being betrayed by someone who he'd thought was on his side.

Medusa shoved the thoughts on the matter to the back of her mind. She had time. Hades hadn't given her a deadline, although she wouldn't put it past him to get impatient and demand an answer sooner.

But she wouldn't think of that very real possibility right now. What she would do was continue to dig up the dirt on Jake. If she did decide to go that route, she needed at least one bullet-proof reason Jake belonged downtown.

She also wanted insurance she'd keep her head. Oracles knew, it wouldn't be fun losing *that* again.

"So, no one crosses Jake Sullivan, huh?" Medusa asked the question casually, careful to not let on how interested she was in how Jake went about settling his vendettas.

Kara snorted. "Not if they want to make it in Hollywood."

"I can't say that I blame him, honestly," snorted Medusa, "I would have probably done the same thing."

Kara turned, holding Medusa's gaze and regarding her shrewdly. They'd come to the point where niceties fell away so scrutiny could take over. Friend or foe, ally or enemy. Jake's twin, and staunchest supporter, was trying to decide.

Medusa hoped she settled on friend.

A smile finally curled the corners of Kara's mouth. "You know, I can't either. I wish I had some of his ruthlessness when it comes to getting revenge. Some people just deserve it. Take Hailey's father, for instance."

Medusa nodded her head. "That bastard should be given no mercy," she murmured.

She had been thinking of Poseidon, but the same applied to the degenerate who'd decided not to be a part of such a sweet and innocent child's life.

Medusa wasn't so naive to think Kara didn't realize she was interested in spending a whole lot more time with her brother. She had expected Kara to do a little assessment of her own, and was relieved it'd gone well.

"Would you like to have lunch sometime, Kara?" asked Medusa. Both because it just made good business sense and also because she wouldn't mind it.

"Sure." Kara smiled, a tentative alliance shining in her eyes. "I'd like that."

"Me too," said Medusa, her heart dancing in her chest so hard she thought it might waltz right out and do a few twirls before plopping onto the floor. She'd just done something she hadn't expected to do while vacationing on this trash heap of a planet.

They weren't besties yet or anything, but the door to having a friend had been opened.

CHAPTER FOURTEEN

Melina's Mediterranean-style abode, with its white stucco and red clay tile roof, was a monstrosity compared to Jake's sleek 2,500 contemporary square footer. Not too shabby for a Youtuber.

His pulse raced as he and Hailey walked up the front steps. What the hell? It was just a trip to the zoo with his niece. Oh, yeah, and a woman who was supposed to have been a one and done. A hit and quit.

What were the chances he could get a double dip?

Jesus Christ, Jake. No.

"Are you excited?" he asked Hailey as he rang the doorbell.

She was still nodding vigorously when the vine-colored front door swung open. He had to stop his mouth from dropping open by clamping it shut. Melina had rushed up behind the young woman who'd answered her door, almost unrecognizable in a pair of canvas slip-ons, skinny jeans, and a simple black tee.

The key word being *almost*, since the t-shirt was undoubtedly designer and probably still ridiculously expensive. The green sunglasses resting atop her head were also surely the latest trend in eyewear. The frames donned a subtle snake-skin pattern, with the same logo he'd seen on his client's purse screen-printed on the reflective lenses.

Jake had to literally bite his tongue so he wouldn't say something sarcastic. Or worse. Something nice.

"Hey, guys." Melina grinned from ear-to-ear, as if she was actually happy to see them. "This is my assistant, Dylan."

The genuine smile on Melina's face snatched the wind right out of Asshole Jake's sails. It also deflated his resolve to act like a smug bastard. She'd opted for no makeup and a low-maintenance ponytail. It was a significantly pared-down version of her Medusa persona, which he was grateful for since the last thing he wanted was people with cameras following them around.

Whether she had decided to go out in full make-up or a burlap sack, Jake knew it would look good on her. Those lips of hers would still be alluring with or without lipstick.

Jake's stomach muscles trembled, and he realized he was sucking in his gut for all he was worth. He wasn't sure why, since he worked out regularly and didn't exactly need to—

Would the court please turn their attention to Exhibit A? Here you will find evidence strongly suggesting that no matter how Ms. Melina Stone presents herself, the result will most assuredly always be a fluttering inside Mr. Jacob Sullivan's chest. This, ladies and gentlemen of the jury, proves a clear and present danger . . .

It took all Jake had not to physically shake off his thoughts, even though he wanted to fling the damn things right into the proverbial garbage can in the farthest reaches of his mind where they belonged.

The effort made him press his lips together even harder. When Melina quirked an eyebrow at him, he forced a smile onto his face, sliding his hands into his pockets, where he could at least hide his clenched fists with relative ease.

"It's nice to meet you," chirped Dylan.

Jake had been perfectly content with a quick nod, but she'd stuck out her hand and, wouldn't you know it, his inner nice guy shook it.

"Same."

And apparently his inner nice guy was awkward as hell.

Jake's fist went back into his pocket as soon as the handshake was over, but when Melina opened her arms to Hailey and said, "Bring it in, sister," the tightly balled hands in his pockets loosened. Then his clenched jaw followed suit. Well, shit, then one thing led to another and he melted like butter, figuring the least he could do was cut his inner nice guy some slack.

Melina had taken the low-key thing seriously, and no matter what kind of power struggle was going on inside his head, he appreciated it. He'd been prepared to cancel this little soiree based on the argument she would go all out with the Medusa thing and attract a bunch of unwanted attention. She'd saved him from having to break Comet's heart.

Yeah, sure. He was glad *Comet* wouldn't be disappointed. That was it.

"You ready?" he mumbled, immediately regretting how dumb Nice Jake sounded. Of course she was ready, she was standing there. Ready.

"I love your sunglasses!" squealed Hailey, effectively delaying his attempt to get this show on the road so he could get his misery over and done with.

"They just came in." Melina pulled the glasses off the top of her head. "Here, try them on." She handed them to Hailey, who wasted zero time shoving them onto her face.

This will all be over soon. All he had to do was grin and bear the strange lure this woman had over him for the next several hours, and then he'd never have to see her again.

"Okay you two fashionistas, we should get going. It was

nice meeting you Dylan," said Jake before turning on his heels and heading out the door and down the front steps. He heard Dylan say, "Have fun!" and Melina and Hailey giggle as they followed behind him.

Somehow, he just knew they were holding hands.

Jake opened the door of his Range Rover so Hailey could climb into the backseat. He buckled her in, taking his time checking that the already secure strap wasn't going anywhere.

No, he did not need a few more seconds to mentally prepare to be in such close proximity to Melina. Hailey's safety was the reason, that was it.

Hailey stared at him through the snake glasses, head slightly tilted, and her lips curled into a tiny, knowing smile. The damning evidence of his discomfort was written all over his face, and his motion to strike it from the record had been denied.

Seriously. How was he consistently getting his ass handed to him by the tiniest lawyer in town?

Jake rolled his eyes playfully at his niece and mouthed the word "no" before shutting the car door. When he slid into the driver's seat, he snuck a glance at Melina as she searched for something in her bag, presumably another pair of sunglasses.

Despite his carefully orchestrated nonchalance, he inhaled deeply, pulling the scent of warm vanilla in through his nose.

God, you smell good.

He wanted to think what he'd just done was involuntary, the coincidence of needing to breathe, but who was he kidding? It had been one hundred percent on purpose.

Christ. It was going to be one hell of a long day.

Melina slipped on a pair of oversized sunglasses before flipping down the visor to inspect her appearance in the attached mirror.

You look great.

Jake let out a small huff at his inner nice guy's apparent lack of self-control but smiled politely when Melina looked over at him.

He couldn't tell if her eyes had gone wide or not, but he could see her cheeks were tinted the slightest shade of pink, and his palms started to sweat.

She broke eye contact to snap the mirror shut then fold up the visor. "Thank you for inviting me along. I've been dying to go to the zoo, you know. I hear they have an awesome reptile exhibit."

"Sure, no problem." Nice Jake piped up before Asshole Jake could stop him.

Jake snatched his own sunglasses from the console, nearly poking his eye out with one of the stems as he jammed them on.

Sure, no problem? Sure, *no problem?* He was supposed to be figuring out a way to end this—whatever *this* was—before it went any further.

Jumping into the sack hadn't helped, and the worst part about the whole thing, the reason he was mentally kicking himself in the ass right now? He had known better.

No problem my ass. You've got a huge problem on your hands, Jake. You sniffed her like a damn dog.

To build off of Asshole Jake's argument, he was complimenting her; in his head, sure, but it wouldn't be long before Nice Jake was doing it out loud.

He knew how that song and dance went. Him doing these things meant she was dangerously close to going from someone he didn't give two shits about to someone he could end up liking. A lot.

Why couldn't she have despised kids? Why couldn't she have been as vapid and shallow as he'd previously determined? Jesus, Mary, *and* Joseph. He needed to find a technicality to get him off the hook, like yesterday.

Because right now, right this very moment, he was quite possibly a single afternoon away from having the case he'd painstakingly built against her blown right to hell.

he girl's hand was tiny, and Medusa had to keep reminding herself not to squeeze too hard, so she didn't accidentally crush it, but the longer she held it, the more she got the hang of it.

What she was really having a hard time getting used to was the sun. Not the heat, necessarily, but the brightness.

She adjusted her sunglasses, thinking she might have to bring a pair of Snake Heads back with her as a souvenir for Hades. She could see him wearing them to staff meetings, just to be funny. Hopefully they wouldn't melt into a plastic mess on his face.

She bit back a laugh at the thought, and Jake asked, "What?" as he walked beside her, hands stuffed into the pockets of his chinos.

"Nothing. Just . . . Having a good time."

One of his cheeks shot up, and she grinned in response, wide enough to be classified as a smile.

Holy regenerating hydra heads, what was she doing? Monsters didn't *smile*. Not at things that weren't evil and torturous, anyway. The mere thought of him being able to coax this level of . . . Well, whatever it was he was getting out of her made her head spin. And to think, he'd achieved it with only half a smile.

Maybe it *wasn't* the sun that was making her dizzy.

She tested her theory. "Thanks again for inviting me."

His other cheek slid up, spreading his mouth into a smile so brilliant and warm, her head snapped forward when she felt lightheaded again.

No, no, no, no, no.

Medusa veered so suddenly Hailey stumbled. "Look at those lovely striped cats," she said, first steadying and then rushing the girl over to the tiger exhibit.

Once Medusa regained her composure, they continued to wander through the zoo, side-by-side, looking at the animals trapped behind barriers that barely sufficed for their natural habitat for what seemed like an eternity.

By the time they stopped to get ice cream, she was sweating again. Another feeling had settled over her. It was heavy, but didn't carry the depressing weight of sadness, exactly. It was something else, an emotion she couldn't quite name.

Whatever it was, heavy was definitely not the right word. In fact, she felt light enough to float in the clouds like a goddess. And that shit was concerning, because she despised goddesses.

A very specific goddess, to be more precise.

Back when she was mortal, she'd dedicated herself to Athena, swearing an oath of chastity to the goddess she admired above all. At the time, she'd been positive that's what she'd wanted—to live a life of worship, service, and virtue.

She had been content in her decision, or at least she thought she'd been. Sitting here now, with this child, perhaps she hadn't given the matter enough consideration. She had been young, after all, and hadn't realized what she would be giving up. Clearly, she had also put too much faith in a goddess who had zero ability to see past her own ego.

But as this tiny mortal girl swung her feet without a care in the world while she went to town on her ice cream cone, Medusa could pretend none of what happened in her past had transpired. Instead of being cursed to be a monster, ugly and alone for all eternity, she could imagine what life would have been like if she had fallen in love.

Medusa shoved the last of her cone into her mouth. Damn it to Hades. Who knew attending this menagerie would dredge up these sorts of memories?

She did, and it appeared that after a millennium or two, she was still adept at making rash decisions. Because now here she was, thinking useless thoughts and entertaining the idea of reaching for a ridiculous dream so she could realize an even more ridiculous reality.

What good would finding love or knowing real contentment do her now? No matter how she looked on the outside, she would always be an unlovable monster.

"Ready for the reptile exhibit?" She pulled a paper napkin out of a nearby dispenser and Hailey nodded thoughtfully as she handed over the rest of her ice cream to Jake. "We saved the best for last, didn't we?"

Medusa dipped the corner of the napkin into Hailey's cup of water and began to wipe the ring of chocolate from around the girl's mouth. What would she have named her if she'd have been her child? Calisto, *most beautiful*?

She heard a crunch and looked up at Jake, who was finishing what was left of Hailey's cone with a strange look on his face. His brow was furrowed like he was in pain, and the half-smile from earlier was nowhere to be found.

Medusa pulled out another napkin. As she walked toward him, another thought flashed through her mind. What if her fate had been different? What if Jake had been born long ago and she had fallen in love with *him*.

She handed Jake the napkin, determined not to entertain such thoughts. That hadn't been the case then, and it wouldn't be the case now. Fate would make sure of that.

She had a job to do. That was it. And he was a plaything.

"You're about as skilled at eating a melting ice cream cone as your niece."

He took the napkin from her, and she made a circular motion around her chin, helping him locate the spot where the delightful frozen cream and sugar had dripped.

"Thanks," he said, avoiding her eyes as he wiped his mouth.

Medusa couldn't help but stare at him while he did it. He might be just a mortal, but his eyes were such a beautiful shade of green . . . his mouth so tempting.

She pursed her lips to contain the nervous laugh threatening to break free. Everything about him—every move he made—was more interesting than it should be.

"Come on, Hailey." Medusa took the girl's hand. "To the snake pit we go."

"Yay! To the snake pit we go," repeated Hailey, jumping up and down.

When she stopped to look at Medusa with a serious expression on her face, Medusa thought the pre-ice cream churros they'd had might have been a mistake. The poor girl looked like she was going to be sick.

She surprised Medusa by saying, "You can call me Comet. Uncle Jake is the only one who calls me that, but you can, too. If you want."

Medusa glanced at Jake. Judging by how tightly his lips were pressed together, he obviously had thoughts on Medusa being invited in on something that had previously been shared just between uncle and niece.

But Hailey's comment had genuinely delighted her, and Medusa couldn't help but smile. "I'd be honored."

She almost furrowed her brow at Jake's incredulous huff,

but she knew what she had done so there was no use pretending. She'd crossed a line, even though she hadn't meant to, not necessarily.

Or maybe she had.

Medusa sent Jake a weak smile. The lines between business and pleasure were getting blurrier, which was definitely not in the game plan.

If you would have asked her a few days ago how she felt about having successfully put the man standing in front of her looking absolutely beside himself in check mate, she would have reveled in the fact that she was winning the game they were playing—that *she* was playing.

Now, with all these strange emotions making an appearance, horribly uncomfortable feelings of tenderness and longing, she wasn't so sure the prize was worth winning.

"Okay then, Comet. Let's go see some snakes," said Medusa, careful to keep her tone light, casual. Non-threatening. She succeeded at not sounding smug but failed miserably at not swallowing hard enough to crush a beer can with her esophagus.

Medusa pulled herself together, yet again, as the three of them made their way to the reptile exhibit. It was cooler inside the building, which, twist of all twists, she actually didn't mind. But that was probably because she had started sweating bullets again.

She shivered as they walked toward the enormous glass enclosures, lit and warmed to the correct temperatures to simulate the proper environment for the inhabitants inside.

"Wow," whispered Hailey, letting go of Medusa's hand to press her nose against the glass holding the amphibians.

She smiled at the wonder and amazement Hailey held for the colorful tree frogs dotting the lush foliage. It appeared the girl possessed the same smile-inducing power as her uncle.

"Wow is right," said Jake, placing a hand on the back of

Hailey's head as they stood trying to pick out the camou-flaged amphibians. "Look at that one, Comet. You can barely see him."

"Where?"

Jake crouched down, pointing at the rainforest within. "Right there . . ."

"Oh, yeah!"

Medusa could tell that Comet didn't see anything but shadows within the leaves, and she thought she might faint from the adorableness.

"Let's go check out the snakes," said Medusa, nodding her head toward the entrance of a smaller room.

When they entered, an Eastern Green Mamba, so bright under the light it seemed neon, lifted its slender tapered head from the branch where it rested. Like called to like, and Medusa sent it a silent greeting. The snake's tongue flickered, and it lowered its head slightly, bowing to Medusa.

She nodded back, just enough to offer her respect. The mamba was quite a specimen, as dangerous as it was beauti-ful. One bite could take a mortal man down in as little as thirty minutes. Of course, Medusa could take one down in three seconds, but who was counting?

Oh, right. She was counting. Because she always counted. Also, she *used* to be able to take a man down.

Hailey interrupted Medusa's random thoughts. "There's a boy from my class over there. Can I go say hello?" asked Hailey politely, but before either of them could say no, she was skipping away merrily.

Her cheeks had looked like little apples, and Medusa knew what that meant. The poor thing was crushing hard.

Wasn't she kind of in the same boat right now?

No. Nope. No way. Uh-uh.

Medusa turned on her heels and headed for one of the long benches to sit down. She needed a moment. Jake followed, but instead of saying anything he focused a watchful eye on Comet. When he was sure she wasn't leaving the premises, he took a seat next to Medusa.

"So. How's the beauty guru business going?"

"It's going well, actually. Thank you for asking. How's the lawyer business?" Seriously. Who was she right now?

Jake chuckled. "It pays the bills."

"I noticed it was a family business. Sullivan & Sullivan. Won't you need a son to take over for you?"

Jake flat out laughed. "Not if I can help it. If Comet wants to get into law, and if she wants it, the firm is hers. I'd never push her into it, though."

"Like you were, I assume," replied Medusa, knowing all too well about not having been given a choice.

She could feel the resentment rolling off him, as heavy and brooding as a storm cloud.

"Yeah, like I was."

"What if she wants to be the next beauty influencer? What will you do then?"

"Don't even say that." He shook his head, as though appalled by the thought. "All those influencers are—"

She fixed her gaze on him. "Vapid? Vicious?"

Yeah. They were, but she had been asking because she wondered what he thought of her, specifically.

"Vain," replied Jake.

In the silence that followed, Medusa heard sniffling.

She ripped her gaze from Jake, zeroing it in on the boy Hailey was talking to as she shot to her feet. The boy stared back, defiant, as if he had set out to cause trouble and had achieved that goal in record time.

She marched over toward the two children.

"What did you do to her?" snarled Medusa, narrowing her eyes and wishing she still had the power to turn mortals to stone.

"He . . . he . . . said he d-didn't t-talk to u-ugly girls," stammered Hailey, hiccupping the whole way.

Medusa glared at the boy. "Is that so? Well, I don't see any ugly girls here." She folded her arms. "Where are your parents?"

Head Monster or not, she was technically still the protector of woman and children, and if one of them was acting like a rude little asshole then all bets were off.

The boy darted into another room of the reptile house without a word—or an apology—and Medusa was set on following him when Hailey stopped her.

"It's okay. William is just jealous of my flair," she said in a small voice that made Medusa's heart actually *hurt*.

There was nothing she wanted to do more than go grab that ignorant little shit by the collar and give him a taste of the real gorgon within, but Hailey was more important.

Way more important.

She knelt down and began to wipe away Hailey's tears. "Oh, Comet. What he thinks doesn't matter, not one bit. Don't waste your time or energy on him, he doesn't deserve it. You can be the most beautiful person in the world on the outside and it won't matter if you've got an ugly heart. And you, my darling, have the prettiest heart. You're beautiful inside *and* out. Do you understand me?"

Hailey nodded, falling into Medusa's arms. She held the girl loosely, so as not to constrict her little lungs, stroking her hair as she waited for the crying to stop. An overwhelming sense of protectiveness washed over her, and she kissed the top of Hailey's head. She would miss this child when vacation was over, but as long as she was on this Earth, she would do everything in her power to make sure she was happy.

"Why don't we head home, huh?" Jake said softly. He'd knelt down to rub Hailey's back. The other rested on Medusa's shoulder.

She nodded, letting Jake scoop Comet up so he could

carry her back to the car. She followed behind, letting out a hiss of frustration when Jake was out of earshot.

Medusa was still fuming, but it seemed Hailey had recovered somewhat once they got to the parking lot. By the time they merged onto the expressway, Medusa's blood pressure had come down and Hailey was almost back to her usual verbose self. About halfway through the ride home, the random chitter chatter from the backseat had gone silent. Sure enough, when Medusa turned to check on her, Hailey was asleep.

Jake parked his car in front of what she assumed was Kara's apartment building. His half-smile made an appearance again when he saw that his niece was conked out.

When he shifted in his seat to face Medusa, his expression was serious, just like Hailey's had been back at the zoo.

He cleared his throat. "Thank you."

He took her hand, and sweet Persephone, she thought the weak mortal heart beating inside her chest was going to burst. Also, what was going on with her mouth? It had suddenly gone dry as a bone. She glanced down, and another shock wave tore through her when his thumb brushed across her skin.

"For what?" His thumb stroked the back of her hand a second time and she tried not to crush beer cans with her esophagus again, but it was no use.

"For being so good with Hailey."

"Why wouldn't I be? She's a sweet kid."

"You know what I mean, Melina. What you said. Hearing it from you . . . I was wrong, not all influencers are vain."

Medusa sighed. How did he do that? Make her float at the top of the world with a single look? Call her out in that way of his without provoking the full extent of her gorgon-ness, but instead, making her think.

Or was it *feel*?

If he only knew who she really was. How she actually looked. That she was a real, honest-to-gods monster.

"Yes, I know what you meant," she said. "You're welcome."

When his tongue slipped out over his bottom lip, teeth grazing over it seductively, she thought he was going to lean in and kiss her.

Just like she wanted him to.

But he asked her a question instead. "Hey. You hungry?"

"Starving," she replied, even though she knew she was about to jump into an even deeper hole, and the knowledge that it wasn't food she was starving for grabbed hold of her like a boa constrictor and squeezed.

It was attention. More specifically, Jake's attention. All of it. His time, too. She wanted nothing else, and it was quite possibly one hundred and ten percent official that she would spend the rest of her vacation trying to get it.

"Would you like to go to dinner with me?"

Son of a child-eating Titan. Was Jake playing the game she'd just abandoned, or was he being real? Did he want to spend as much time with her as she did him, or was he just angling for more sex?

Honestly, she wasn't sure she cared. It was too late. Even if he was playing games of his own right now, she was all in. Because, after a really, *really* long time, Medusa wanted to give more than she wanted to take.

And it felt really, *really* good.

CHAPTER SIXTEEN

Jake's leg bounced underneath the table as the server poured water into their glasses. The place was casual, and he'd asked to be seated outside versus in a quiet corner. Not that he couldn't get into somewhere trendy on such short notice, or that he had a problem with indoor dining, but he feared that might be too much.

The day had gone so well, and Hailey had such a good time. He'd been pleasantly surprised Melina had turned out to be so . . . adaptable.

He'd had his doubts. Even though she'd toned down her persona, it didn't mean she couldn't have turned out to be awful.

He had pegged her as less patient and more high maintenance, but she'd gone with the flow, handling every sudden change of plans the day had thrown her way as if she were an old pro at parenthood.

Plus, the way she had handled the incident with the boy, wiping away Hailey's tears and replacing them with words of comfort and strength, she'd blown all his theories about her being a monster to bits.

He'd felt the need to show his appreciation, for both

comforting Hailey and surprising him, so he'd thrown caution to the wind and asked her to dinner, to say thank you.

That was it. A nice evening to end a wonderful day. They were one hundred and ten percent not going to wind up in bed again.

Jake took his time sliding his hand up Melina's thigh.

The moonlight illuminated the curve of her hip, and he took in the lovely sight, appreciating its beauty, but he didn't exactly need to see where he was going.

He'd tried sticking to just dinner, but the conversation had been lively, the whiskey barrel-aged, and when she'd looked at him with those bedroom eyes, what little resolve he'd had evaporated like water in a desert.

They'd hastily finished their food so they could go back to his place.

And now here he was, again, his fingers skimming over the edge of her lace underwear—everything else had already been discarded—before gliding over the delicate folds beneath. His touch was light, the fabric thin, and there was definitely no desert for miles around.

Fuck. This was only supposed to be dinner.

The thought made his head spin. He could blame it on the whiskey, sure, but he'd stopped at one, and he'd nursed the second so it didn't count.

There was no pinning his inability to think straight on the alcohol, but he was intoxicated, all right. Drunk on *her*. Everything about her tempted him. Her throaty laugh . . . that confidence, bordering on arrogance . . . that sultry smile.

An arsenal of weapons. And what weapons they were. They threw him off balance—had since day one—before he could even duck.

Duck? He should have run.

In his defense, ladies and gentlemen of the jury, he'd tried.

The heat radiating from her body made his own skin flush. Needing to feel her, he pushed aside the lace. He took his time searching for that deliciously sensitive part of her, and when he found it, he circled it lightly with his finger.

The breathy sound of her sigh made an equally sensitive part of him twitch.

He had promised himself he wouldn't get involved, that it would be in his best interest to leave well enough alone. He knew asking her to dinner would be a mistake, would create a bigger mess—put the promise he'd made to himself to never get tangled up again at risk—but he'd done it anyway.

She's not like the others. . .

She writhed under his touch, panting softly when he applied more pressure, more speed. He pressed himself into her hip out of sheer animal instinct, desperately trying to relieve his own throbbing.

Why couldn't he have stuck with the plan and listened to the asshole within? That was the question. Change of plea? By reason of insanity? Petition for more sex?

Guilty. Guilty. So fucking guilty.

He moved his hips in time with hers as she rode his hand. He kissed her neck before venturing down to take a nipple into his mouth. Her lips parted, and her brows dipped in pure carnal bliss.

He sucked it, and when it hardened, he licked it.

He could—would—do this all night, devour every inch of her. She was a glorious creature, and the way she arched her hips in ecstasy made him want to bury himself deep between them.

But not yet.

He moved his hand to cup her other breast. She whimpered in protest at the sudden departure, but forgave him when he kissed her hungrily, tasting the whiskey they'd had earlier, that had gone down like water.

He couldn't stop a moan of his own from escaping.

To make up for the switch in focus, he slipped a finger inside her as he explored her mouth. She sucked the air in through her teeth when he pulled it out to tease her again, right on that spot he knew would drive her to the brink.

"You like that?" He whispered the question on her lips, and she answered by finding him inside his boxer briefs and squeezing, stroking, until he had to gently remove himself from her grip or he'd be done for.

"You're going to love this, then," he said, dragging the only undergarment she was left wearing down before throwing it off into some far corner of his room.

He didn't think he could get any harder, but when she kneaded her breasts, pinching both nipples in anticipation as she opened up for him, he proved himself wrong.

He was in so much trouble.

And right now, quite frankly, so was she.

He lapped at her until she twisted the sheets in her fists. Before long, he licked harder, flicking his tongue before gently sucking.

She threaded her fingers through his hair, grasping and pulling. His cue to wrap his arms around her legs and open them wider.

He didn't have to be told twice.

He worked a finger inside her again, and when his tongue found the right rhythm, it was all over. She threw her head back and unleashed, shaking and shuddering as her orgasm rocked her body.

She pulled him up, groping at his briefs, indicating in no uncertain terms he needed to remove them immediately.

"Take those off . . . now," she said, her voice low and raspy.

He wasn't about to argue with that, and so he obliged,

then reached for the condom he'd set on the nightstand—there hadn't been any illusions about what they'd come here to do—and tore it open.

He could barely get it on fast enough, and when he caught a glimpse of those rock-hard nipples perched on top of perfect breasts bathed in silvery moonlight, he had to grab the base of his cock and close his eyes.

She laughed, and when he opened them, he found a wicked grin on her face. He watched as she worked herself over, taking a moment to let the exquisite ache build. When he couldn't stand it any longer, he went down on his elbows, sliding into her velvety smooth warmth so deep she gasped.

He pulled back his hips, and despite the greedy way she tried to pull him forward again, he held steady, moving at a leisurely pace until she gave in and went with his slow roll.

"Fuck, this feels good," he murmured into her ear.

Not just this, *but you . . . us.*

He trapped her wrists, moving them up and out so he could capture her mouth. He wanted her, all of her, and when her tongue brushed his, inviting him to take her, it drove him to the edge.

Her nipples grazed his chest, her skin hot on his, and before long the sound of their bodies crashing into one another had him aching for release. Her gasping moans, rising higher, getting louder, drove him to move faster, thrust harder, plunge deeper.

She pulled her arms free and dug her nails into his back before dragging them across his shoulders and then reaching up to pull his face toward hers.

And then she kissed him like she meant it—like it wasn't just sex—murmuring "yes" over and over again as she came.

It would have been nice if it was his name, but he'd take it. The sound of her ecstasy alone was enough to send him careening over the edge, and he pushed himself in to the hilt and let go. She held him tight against her, grinding herself into his hips as a moan tore out of him.

He looked into her hazel eyes, feeling the tiny earthquakes of her pleasure gripping and releasing around him, and he couldn't move.

Couldn't or didn't want to?

She must have sensed his internal struggle. This was supposed to be casual, yet Jake was pretty sure he'd just made love to her.

It seemed as though Melina was having the very same thought, and they stared at each other, wide-eyed and startled. Until Jake bit his lip to keep from saying something stupid and Melina blinked before looking away.

He shifted, dropping down onto the bed next to her, pulling the sheet over them both.

Perhaps asking her to dinner had been a way to gather the proof he needed to walk away. That she was only pretending to be different, putting on a good show in front of Hailey, but would show her true colors once they were alone.

Maybe it had been a last-ditch effort to find a loophole so he could dive through that mother fucker and slam the door shut behind him.

All it had done was prove he was in over his head. That he wanted more than just dinner, and possibly a lot more than just sex.

"Go to Greece with me," said Jake, the words falling out before he could stop them.

She turned onto her side so she could face him. "Excuse me?"

He followed suit, going up on one elbow and then reaching out and tucking an errant curl behind her ear. "Sorry. Would you like to go to Greece with me? That's where the Superstar Smiles mission is this year, in a few weeks, just after the holidays. I'd love to take you with me."

Panic clouded her face.

Shit. Way to freak her out, dumb ass.

"It's okay if you don't want to go," he said. "Or if your schedule is too crazy. It's kind of short notice, so I totally understand."

She chewed on the inside of her cheek as she thought about it. Her indecision made his heart hammer, so he rolled onto his back and tucked his hands behind his head. He had to prepare himself for rejection somehow.

It was probably better if she said no, anyway.

"Okay." She assumed the same position as him before tapping his ankle with her foot underneath the sheet. "But only if you're not sick of me by then."

Sick of her? Jesus. If she only knew. It would probably be *her* that would get sick of *him.*

"Even if I am . . ." He rolled toward her again. "And I'm not saying that I will be . . ." He reached out and pulled her to him. "But Superstar Smiles could use some attention, and who better to get it noticed than the biggest social media star in L.A.?"

Her hands, which had been caressing his chest, stilled. "Oh." Another one of her blinks, followed by a smile. "Of course."

Shit. Why had he added that last part?

Melina rolled over, and he moved in for the spoon. She caressed his arm when he wrapped it around her, but he barely noticed because he was trying to figure out why he was such an asshole.

CHAPTER SEVENTEEN

The sun was blessedly weak, the light coming in through the expansive windows gray and dim. Medusa had gotten up early and, after having made coffee, was now languishing on the sofa, intent on relishing the rare dreary day in Southern California.

It hadn't been long before her thoughts wandered to Jake. She thought of him morning, noon, and night at this point. She secretly wished Helios would peek out from behind the clouds for an hour or two, so Jake might get the bright idea to call and ask if she wanted to go hang out at the Santa Monica Pier. She'd say yes in a heartbeat, but the sun god hadn't obliged, and it hadn't been long before she'd moved on to inspecting the chipping polish on her nails.

Medusa sighed, letting her hand fall into her lap. It was no use. She couldn't stop thinking about Jake long enough to properly convalesce.

He'd asked her to go to Greece approximately thirty-six hours ago, and even though she'd said yes, now that she thought about it, she had mixed feelings about going back to the place where tragedy had ended her mortal life.

It had been a calculated move on Jake's part, only asking

her to go so he could get more attention for Superstar Smiles, but she had to give the man credit. His marketing prowess was impressive.

Medusa got up from the couch and walked over to Dylan's work nook. It had originally been a dry bar, and it still was, but her live-in assistant had taken it over. The printer sat out in the open, along with a cutesy placard with a bumble bee on it informing no one in particular to *Bee Kind,* a potted plant, and one of those meshed wire file organizers.

She plucked a pen out of the pencil holder, took out a notepad from one of the drawers, and then set to work on making a to-do list at the dining room table.

- *Get nails done*
- *Back out of Greece?*
- *Make final decision and send*

Going on the mission with Jake was just part of the game, she knew that. Posting and sharing the work he was doing on social media would put the Superstar Smiles Foundation in the spotlight, and since he didn't have any kind of digital footprint, the next best thing was to collab with someone who did.

It was a solid marketing plan, since his end goal was to attract more donors. It was exactly the kind of thing she would have done if she were in that position and an opportunity, sporting stilettos and millions of followers, had presented itself so willingly.

So, what the hell was gnawing at her?

It's not like he'd wronged her in any way, and she could still get him to do whatever she wanted with a playful pucker of the lips here and a lingering caress of a fingertip there.

Yet, despite still having him under her thumb, she felt like she was losing control. Not so much over him, exactly, but over her own feelings.

More accurately, her actions.

She underlined *Make final decision and send*, but instead of moving on to the next order of business, which was to text Jake she'd changed her mind about Greece, the pen hovered over the marks she'd just made.

Did she even want to back out? It would be the logical thing to do, to ensure she maintained the upper hand, but it wasn't like she was opposed to helping Superstar Smiles gain some attention. Besides, a trip to Greece with Jake might be fun.

It was settled. She would hold off on making her decision, at least until after Greece.

- *Get nails done*
- *Pack for trip to Greece*
- ~~*Make final decision and send*~~

Medusa pushed the thoughts about Jake and Greece and losing control away to focus on a more pressing matter. Her nails. They had to be done before Jake's parents' annual holiday party.

He'd asked her yesterday over breakfast, and she wasn't mad about it. She was actually a little excited to meet the two people who'd created such a god in the sack, and she wanted to look her best.

Dylan stumbled into the kitchen in her pajamas, rubbing the sleep from her bleary eyes.

Medusa smiled. Dylan always seemed to know when it was her cue to walk onto the set of *The Medusa Show*.

"Good morning," said Medusa.

Dylan moaned, glancing out the massive living room windows as she opened a cupboard and grabbed a mug. "Is it?"

Medusa stifled a cackle. It seemed she was rubbing off on the girl.

"Want to go to the nail salon with me?" asked Medusa. "My treat."

Dylan flipped open her laptop while waiting for her coffee to brew. "Can't. I've got lots more editing to do."

Medusa tilted her head, noting the dark circles under Dylan's eyes. "Is everything okay? You look terrible."

The setting of Dylan's jaw was slight, but Medusa still caught it, and the notion that maybe she had something to do with that tension dropped into the pit of her stomach.

"Dylan? What's wrong?"

"Nothing," said Dylan before going in for a sip of her steaming coffee. "Fuck!"

The hot liquid sloshed over the brim when she jerked it away from her mouth, burning her hand and causing her fingers to abort mission and let go.

The mug shattered on impact with the Travertine.

Medusa pressed her lips together to hide her amusement. Dylan hardly said the F-word, and it made Medusa watch the scene unfold with equal parts confusion and pride.

But there was something else lurking in that mix, too.

Dylan hurried over to the paper towels and plucked the roll off the holder.

"We'll need to have another photoshoot soon. I'm waiting to hear back from the photographer about when we can get on her schedule," she said, wiping up the mess she'd made during her spat with a scalding-hot cup of coffee.

Her scowl deepened with every unsuccessful pass, and her scoffing got more aggressive with each paper towel she added onto the soggy pile.

"Okay," said Medusa, heart picking up pace. Dylan was upset, clearly, but Medusa wasn't sure what to do about it. "Can you make sure it's scheduled before I leave for Greece next week?"

"Of course, Medusa," muttered Dylan. "Right away, Medusa."

The swirling in Medusa's gut intensified. Ignoring the elephant in the room had been the wrong choice, but addressing it hadn't exactly been an appealing option.

It required listening. It took empathy, and Medusa had already been doing too much of both those things lately.

"Excuse me?" she snapped, the monster within triggered. This human adulting business was for the harpies.

Dylan shook her head. "It's nothing. Just forget it." She unleashed several exasperated huffs as she transported the soaked and dripping paper towels to the trash.

Medusa pushed the pen and notepad aside. "No. Tell me what's wrong."

"Okay, fine." Dylan slammed the tall cupboard that hid the trash can. "I didn't realize I'd be doing everything. I'm working *twenty-four seven*, Melina. I thought I'd at least have the weekends to work on *my* stuff. But you're never here anymore, and there's so much to do, and now you're going to Greece . . ."

She'd avoided eye contact as she paced around the kitchen, but now, she pierced Medusa with a glare from the other side of the center island.

"You may think I'm just some stupid kid, eager and willing to do your bidding because you're an influencer, but I'm not. I've got goals, too, you know." She narrowed her eyes, driving the point she'd just made deeper into Medusa's heart. "I have dreams. I have *a life*, and I'll be damned if I give them up just to work for someone who doesn't appreciate that. I'm going to go take a shower."

The buzzing inside Medusa's head, which had started right around the time Dylan had begun speaking her truth, grew louder. She couldn't have known how close to home she'd hit, and as Dylan headed toward the hallway, the hum turned deafening.

Before she could stop herself—or the anger she knew was misplaced—she yelled, "Don't you dare walk away from me!"

Dylan whirled around, unafraid. "Or what? You'll fire me?" She laughed, short and cynical. "I was up all night, for the fourth night in a row, single-handedly manning your business, managing *your* brand while you were off living it up. You're not going to fire me because *you need me.*"

"What needs to change, then?" ground out Medusa. "More money?"

Dylan's arms flew up in exasperation. "How about some fucking help?"

"I told you upfront this wasn't a partnership," Medusa said calmly, even though the bubble of panic in her gut had grown so big it was wobbling and on the verge of bursting. "I mean, honestly, what did you expect? Me to help you manage your time?"

"Of course not!" shot back Dylan. "I just thought that maybe the weekends would at least be mine, you know?"

She emoted with her whole body, and the display caused Medusa's chest to tighten and her teeth to grind, the theatrics only throwing more fuel on the pile of guilt burning in her gut.

"You *knew* coming into this you'd be my *assistant.*"

Dylan lifted her chin. "Yeah, I knew. But I guess I just didn't know what an ugly bitch you'd turn out to be."

The trio of Graces, mocking and jeering, flashed behind Medusa's eyes, instantly sparking her long-held belief that she was unworthy—of kindness, of sympathy, of the *chance* to be considered anything other than horrible—and it lit her fear up like kindling.

Heat crept up Medusa's neck until it settled in her cheeks, the air thinning every time her lungs tried to pull it in. Dylan was right—she was doing everything, and she was burning the candle at both ends to do it. If she left, Medusa would be screwed, and not in the good way.

But that wasn't what made Medusa so angry. She needed Dylan to stay, one hundred percent, but there was a much more frightening reason—Medusa *wanted* her to stay. She liked Dylan, so much she might even consider her a friend.

Maybe all this—the sponsorships, the money, the attention—hadn't been what Medusa had been after all along. Perhaps she'd just wanted to know if it was even possible that she, a terrifying gorgon of myth and legend, was capable of having friends.

Monsters don't need shit, remember?

It was too late to tell herself that lie. The truth, both Dylan's and Medusa's, had been dragged out of the dark and hoisted into the light.

Pride and fear joined forces, firing the next round of words from Medusa's mouth with lightning speed and frightening force. In fact, if she'd still had the power to turn Dylan into stone, it would have already been done.

"Get out," hissed Medusa. Her powers might be suspended but she could still wound with words. "You're a shitty assistant and an even shittier designer. Bravo on the confidence, Dylan, but here's a tip: I don't need you. Now go get your shit and GET OUT."

Sometime during her rant, Medusa had snatched the Bee Kind placard off of the office nook counter, and now she hurled it at Dylan.

It collided with her forehead, but any satisfaction Medusa felt at having landed a direct hit drained out of her. Dylan had gone as white as a sheet and was standing there so still it was as if she were . . . stone.

Fuck. Had Medusa's tantrum somehow caused her power to switch on for a split second?

The buzzing returned, now with a dull ache in tow. A faint crackling, like the one that always accompanied the transformation of warm flesh hardening to cold stone, filled her head. But she didn't *feel* the pulsing zaps of electricity like she normally did when her power surged, so that was a good sign.

Medusa rushed over to Dylan, barely hearing herself call the girl's name over the sound of her heart, which was pounding in her ears like a timpani drum.

"Dylan?" Medusa took her by the shoulders and gave her a gentle shake. "Dylan are you okay?"

Dylan didn't answer, only stood there staring at nothing with vacant eyes.

Medusa released her, a wave of nausea rolling through her so powerful she thought she might need to run to the kitchen sink and vomit. If she'd actually managed to turned Dylan to stone, she might not be able to forgive herself.

Might not? More like never.

It also meant that her ugliness had trumped even a goddess's power, and while that would be thrilling under a different circumstance, it was not something to celebrate in this one.

It was proof the Graces were right. She'd become so ugly, truly hideous inside and out, that no magic in the universe could disguise it—or suppress it.

Medusa wrapped her arms around Dylan and began to weep. "I'm sorry," she sobbed, unabashed now the floodgates had been opened. "I do need you, and not as an assistant . . . As a friend. I don't even know what I'm doing anymore."

Her sorrow bloomed into a painful pressure inside her chest when she was still met with nothing but silence. Her throat swelled until it ached, and the tears kept coming, stinging and hot.

Heartbroken, Medusa squeezed tighter. "Say something. Please," she whispered, as if it would somehow reverse what she'd done.

She supposed she should start figuring out how to explain how a statue that looked suspiciously like a young woman who'd just graduated from design school before heading off to California never to be heard from again had ended up in her kitchen. But she couldn't help but stand there and blubber like an idiot.

Turning a friend to stone was definitely not going to be a highlight of her vacation.

"I can't . . . breathe," croaked Dylan.

Medusa let out a yelp of relief before taking a step back. "Charon's coins, you're okay!"

"Who's Karen?" Dylan rubbed at the giant goose egg rapidly forming in the middle of her forehead. "And that *hurt*."

Medusa grimaced. The center of the goose egg had morphed into an angry reddish purple. "I'm sure it did." She gestured toward the dining room space. "Sit. I'll go get you some ice."

Dylan eyed her suspiciously. "Are you sure you're not going to get a kitchen knife to finish the job?" She pulled out a chair and sat. "I think you might have anger issues."

Medusa fished a dish towel from the drawer and filled it with ice from the dispenser before twisting it into an ice pack.

"You might be right. Here."

She handed it to Dylan, happy to see the color had returned to her face.

"From here on out the evenings and weekends are yours," said Medusa. "And we'll get everything done and scheduled before I go, so you can work on your own stuff while I'm gone."

"Melina, I might have said some things that . . ."

"No," Medusa shook her head, guiding the ice pack, which Dylan had still been holding in her lap, to the swelling. "It's the truth. Harsh, but the truth, and I can't hold that against you." Medusa let go of Dylan's hand so she could swipe her phone from its spot next to the pen and notepad.

"Let me call and have lunch delivered, and then you can show me how to upload videos to Youtube. I should really learn how to do that anyway. We'll divide and conquer. Now, what are you hungry for?"

"I'm kind of in the mood for sashimi," said Dylan.

Medusa wanted to gag, but she smiled instead. She still didn't care for seaweed, and she'd rather consume raw flesh than raw fish, but it was the least she could do for her friend, who still looked a bit dazed and confused.

"Of course," replied Medusa.

As far as Dylan knew, it was only her feelings and her forehead that had been hurt. In reality, Medusa knew the woman nearly had her spirit crushed . . . And that was in addition to quite possibly almost being turned to stone by a hideous monster.

Medusa winced at the ridiculous amount of holiday decor hanging from Jake's parents' massive front porch. As far as dwellings went, the size of their home didn't impress her all that much. It was the blatant show of extreme wealth that raised her brow.

The Underworld may be dark and smell like a sweaty jock strap in some places—okay, pretty much all of it reeked, especially when Queen P wasn't there to fumigate it with a heavy dose of fresh air—but the miles-long veins of gold and silver that ran through her boss's domain, deeper than any mortal could find unless they earned themselves a one-way ticket to Tartarus, made Hades one of the richest gods in existence.

Even with its ominous and foreboding vibes, Hades' Realm was still one of the most opulent places to live. He might be dark and brooding, but he appreciated the finer things immortal life had to offer, and his palace gleamed with as much luxury and wealth as his brother's place up on Olympus.

It was just a shade or two darker.

Even the minions that did Hades' bidding, including

Medusa, were filthy rich. She had to admit, Mort and Judith Sullivan's mortal abode succeeded in giving her place at the Underworld Condominiums a run for its money, but it was still no comparison to Hades' obsidian palace.

She'd definitely give it an honorable mention in the Money to Burn Department, though, especially with the thousands of twinkling lights strung above a life-sized nativity scene, complete with three kings on camels making their way toward the manger and a real drummer boy—no doubt some hard-up musician trying to make ends meet until his band hit it big—hired to stand on the front lawn and drum his ass off for guests as they arrived at the Sullivan's annual "small" holiday gathering.

"Thanks for agreeing to come to this thing," said Jake as they climbed the front steps together.

"I'm surprised you even asked me, to tell the truth."

It wasn't so much the fact that their relationship was moving at lightning speed that surprised her, she was down with that, but the man seemed to be having less trouble opening himself up and being vulnerable around her than she thought he would have had at this stage of the game.

Asking her to accompany him to his parents' holiday shindig, where she would undoubtedly meet them, was kind of a big step forward, for both of them.

"I had to . . ." He cleared his throat. "Comet let the cat out of the bag I was spending a lot of time with someone. The fact that she kept referring to that someone as Medusa piqued Judith Sullivan's interest and—"

"She wanted to see just how unfit I was for her son with her own eyes, in the company of her closest friends."

"It's the Sullivan way. My mother is . . . Well, sometimes you have to throw her a juicy piece of meat to release her jaws from the bone she's sniffed out."

"So I'm the juicy piece of meat? How sweet."

"Trust me, it's best to just introduce her to the woman I've been spending my days with."

"Shall I entertain her and her guests with stories about how you've been spending your nights?"

A nervous laugh bubbled from Jake's throat, and she had to suppress a thrilled shiver from rippling through her at the mere thought he was uncomfortable. She knew *he* knew she'd do it.

Thank Hades her boldness was one of the things he'd said he liked about her.

"Hey, Reeves." He nodded at the butler who had opened the door before Jake could let them into his parents' home on his own.

"Good evening Mr. Sullivan."

"How many times do I have to tell you, man? Call me Jake."

"Of course, Mr. Jake. It's nice to see you again."

Jake ushered Medusa through the door and into the grand foyer, where an enormous evergreen decorated with twinkling lights, oversized mercury-glass bulbs, and gold ribbon that spiraled up to the glittering star at the top greeted them. On either side of the festive display was a set of elegant staircases, the banisters wrapped in the same gold ribbon as the tree.

They'd barely had time to hand over their coats when Kara came rushing toward them.

"What took you so long? I've been on my own for forty-five goddamn minutes with these barbarians."

Jake kissed his sister on the cheek before affecting a haughty accent. "Whatever do you mean, Karalynn? Every one of these people are close, personal friends. By the way, are you still shaming our family name working as a nurse?"

"Oh, Jacob," replied Kara in the same mocking tone. "You've always been my favorite child."

When an impeccably dressed older woman dripping with

diamonds and entitlement abandoned her conversation and headed straight toward them, Medusa knew exactly who she was.

"Jacob." The woman practically pushed Kara out of the way to grab Jake by the shoulders and plant a real kiss on each of his cheeks. "I'm so happy you decided to come, my darling boy. It's good to see you."

Jacob wasn't a boy, he was a man, and Medusa could already tell his mother was a monster, and an abusive and controlling one at that.

Medusa checked the woman's eyes for any signs of immortality as casually as she could. Who knew, this woman might be a harpy in disguise.

Also? Both Jake and Kara had nailed their impressions of her.

"And who do we have here?"

"Mother, this is Melina Stone. Melina, this is my mother, Judith Sullivan."

"And what do you do, Ms. Stone?"

Wow. That escalated quickly. Not even a, *"It's so nice to meet you."*

"I'm a designer," replied Medusa.

Jake placed a hand on the small of her back. "Melina owns the very successful Snake Head brand."

His hand slid up, rubbing a small circle when it reached the spot between her shoulders. He'd probably felt her shaking. He just hadn't known it was from rage and not fear.

How sweet. He was trying to comfort her.

"Yes, it's the hottest line of bags and accessories in the world right now." She tried her hand at levity. "Selling like . . . hot snakes."

Jake stifled a laugh. Judith, on the other hand, did not see the humor.

"Designer? I thought I heard somewhere she was one of those . . . Oh, what do they call them, Karalynn?"

"Influencers."

"On some sort of thing called . . . What do they call that thing?"

"Youtube," answered Medusa, trying to remain calm. She was standing right in front of this woman, and she was talking about her as if she were invisible.

Damn, Judith Sullivan's horse was high, almost as lofty as the one the graces had perched themselves on.

Well, guess what? They weren't on Olympus and Medusa didn't have to take this shit. Time to help this woman down from her privileged pedestal.

"Yes, I'm also a content creator. Seventy percent of my target audience is on the Youtube platform. Ninety-five percent of that audience is fashion conscious. I provide them with entertaining, day-in-the-life videos of what it's like to be me and they buy my merchandise. It's called capitalism."

"She's a beauty, Jacob. Even with all that makeup. And rather witty, I see," whispered Judith out of the side of her mouth. The comments weren't meant to be private; they were meant for Medusa to hear.

Oh, she'd heard all right, and the audacity sparked her temper.

"I also have brains to go with that beauty."

"Well, then you just might make it into the club, darling," said Judith, not to be outdone. "The last one lacked any strategy at all."

Jake's nostrils flared, and the muscle over his jaw bunched, and when Medusa saw it, a funny thing happened. His discomfort made her want to claw his mother's eyes out.

Who did this woman think she was? What right did she have to talk to anyone that way, let alone her own child?

Medusa held her anger in check, seeing as she was one to talk. She'd delighted in the discomfort she herself had caused him not even fifteen minutes ago.

She'd recently almost turned her friend to stone. There was that, too.

Judith clicked her tongue. "Karalynn, darling. Stop frowning like that. It makes your lines worse. You should really let Dr. Shane take care of that. It's all that stress from taking care of . . ." She clicked her tongue disapprovingly. "I can't believe you're still breaking your poor mother's heart by working as a nurse."

Not that Medusa hadn't believed them, but they'd been right. Kara's chosen vocation was the perceived black spot on the family name and not arrogance. This woman was a Grade-A piece of work.

Medusa opened her mouth to impart the nobleness of taking care of people when they were sick when Jake jumped to his sister's defense.

"She likes helping people, Mother."

"Oh, Jacob. How sweet of you to defend your sister's questionable choices in life. You always were my favorite." Judith sighed. "Well, if you'll excuse me. I have guests to entertain. It was nice to meet you, Melanie," said Judith, nodding at Medusa.

Was it? Medusa couldn't tell.

"You, too, Judy," she said under her breath.

Once Judith Sullivan was out of earshot, both Jake and Kara sighed, as if they'd narrowly squeaked by a Kraken unscathed.

Medusa joined the silent conversation by offering them a look of sympathy. She knew the meaning of abuse and dysfunction, but wow, this woman took the cake.

"That actually went pretty well." Kara patted Jake on the shoulder. Then she turned toward Medusa, raising her eyebrows. "Now all you have to do is live through meeting Mort."

"Speaking of Mort," said Jake, his tone indicating he was irritated with his sister for pointing out the obvious. "I bet he's teaching Hailey the basics of the Ponzi scheme as we speak."

Kara mouthed the words, "Good Luck," before leaving the scene in order to locate her daughter's exact whereabouts.

Medusa tried to hide the fact that she was a bit shaky again. Only this time it *was* because she was nervous. She suddenly wanted to make a good impression. Not with Jake's father—she didn't care what he thought of her, Judy, either—but with Jake.

For some crazy, totally effed-up reason, Medusa felt the need to make Jake proud of her.

CHAPTER NINETEEN

drenaline exploded inside Jake's chest, the aftermath ringing in his ears as a surge of panic shot through his body, finally settling in all four of his limbs and making them prickle.

"Fuck."

Medusa stepped closer, gliding a hand over his chest and onto his shoulder. "Now? I'd love to. Shall we go upstairs?"

If the bane of his existence wasn't headed straight for them, maybe.

Jake widened his eyes and nodded at the tall blonde sauntering over. "I meant fuck as in *fuck, that's my ex-wife headed this way.*"

Melina stiffened, a tiny huff escaping before she pursed her lips. It wasn't hard to see she was annoyed; maybe even downright pissed. Rightfully so, since this had been the first time she'd heard of his marital status.

Well, not the first, technically speaking, since Kara had admitted to spilling the tea about Natasia at the Halloween gala back in October.

Instead of getting angry, he'd been relieved Kara had done

that bit of dirty work for him. He hadn't broached the subject afterward, either.

What else could he have added? He avoided his ex like the plague. In fact, he'd made it a point to stay as far away from the whole Hollywood scene as he could.

He certainly hadn't thought he'd run into Natasia here, of all places, but once again, he'd underestimated how much pleasure his mother derived from other people's pain, which apparently included her own son.

"Oh great," said Medusa. "She's beautiful, too."

"Yeah, but she's dead inside" he replied, trying his best to smooth things over. Judging by the distressed look on Melina's face, he was failing.

"Goddamn it, Judy," he muttered. "Why would you do this to me?"

"Jaaaacob," lilted the bane of his existence as she walked up to them. "How are you?"

The mere sound of her Eastern European accent made his jaw tighten, and he had to actually grind his teeth in order to stop himself from firing off a round of insults.

The divorce had been over with relatively quickly, but it had been messy, and he was still bitter about what she'd done. How much she'd embarrassed him. She hadn't just embarrassed him, she'd humiliated him.

There was no telling what was going to come out of his mouth.

"Hello, Natasia."

So far, so good.

He pasted on a smile, inhaling a fortifying breath as discreetly as possible. He hadn't seen her since the divorce a year and a half ago.

It was obvious she'd had more work done, and he tried not to grimace at her ridiculously pronounced pout. She was beginning to look like a Bratz Doll. The shitty thing was the woman was barely even thirty.

Natasia took her time scanning him up and down. If he knew her, she was trying to determine how close she was to being back on his good side.

"You look good."

Jake's nostrils flared, and his lips automatically pressed into a thin line. Of course, typical Natasia. Zero fucks given about his heart, only the usual focus on his appearance.

But hadn't he just done the same thing? Judge her, as if what she'd done with her body was any of his business.

God, he needed to get out of L.A. Maybe he should move to the Midwest, to a cabin in the woods somewhere. He wasn't exactly outdoorsy, but he could learn. Beards were in, right?

"What are you doing here, Nat?"

He'd intended for it to be an innocent question, but Asshole Jake had taken over at the last second. She hated when he called her that.

"Last I heard you moved back to Poland." *Don't do it, man. Don't be a dick.* "Or maybe that was just wishful thinking. I take it you and Judy are on speaking terms again?"

Natasia narrowed her eyes at him, his Americanized nickname for her doing its job.

"Your mother and I were never enemies, Jacob," she said, flipping a lock of perfectly tousled Malibu Beach-waved hair over one shoulder. "It was you and I who parted on bad terms, remember?"

Hold on to your ass because here we go, people. Ready, aim, and . . .

"Oh, I remember," spat Jake. "Do you remember *why* we left on bad terms, Nat?"

She inhaled sharply, bracing herself for impact, which made the insult he was about to sling even more satisfying.

"I believe several of your co-stars can remind you if you've forgotten."

Her mouth dropped open.

To see the shock on her face that he would go there filled Jake with a feeling almost as gratifying as ripping apart one of Tyler Monahan's weak-ass arguments in the courtroom.

This woman had absolutely destroyed him. Took him for all he was worth. Not his money or his status—she had plenty of her own—but things that were far more painful to lose. His time. His trust. His heart. And he'd be damned if he was going to pretend all was forgiven.

He was out for blood.

He noticed Medusa's gaze flick to his set jaw out of the corner of his eye. When she placed a hand on his back, returning the comforting circles he'd given to her earlier, he relaxed a little.

"Jacob. *Kochanie.* I regret—"

Jake glared at Natasia, despising her and the way she could put him into such a negative headspace so easily. Leave him seething with rage in less then, what had it been, five whole minutes since they'd said hello?

And how dare she still refer to him as *honey*.

"Let's be real, here, Nat," he sneered. "The only thing you're sorry for is getting caught."

Jake sighed, closing his eyes for a second to adjust his attitude. Although the tears brimming in Natasia's eyes were most likely part of the act—which made him even more furious—he still didn't want to lose his composure.

He didn't want Melina to witness the utter carnage if he let his ruthless side out.

"Actually, I'm over it," he said. "In fact, let's start over, shall we? You look great, Natasia. I'm glad you and my mother still keep in touch."

"Thank you, Jacob," said Natasia before fixing a pointed gaze on Melina.

What he wanted to do was walk away, but he'd backed himself into a corner by being nice, so he introduced Melina instead.

"This is my girlfriend, Melina Stone. She's an up-and-coming designer. Her new line of bags is making a big splash in the fashion industry."

Jake glanced at Melina to gauge her reaction. They were definitely sleeping together, and there might be potential for more, but there hadn't exactly been a discussion about their relationship status. The only talking they'd done so far was dirty.

He gave Melina a thin smile. Or was it a wince? Either way, she stood there as motionless as a statue, her expression hard as stone.

Yeah, he might have just fucked that up.

"Oh, yes," said Natasia, her eyes suddenly drier. "You are that Youtube star called . . . um . . . ah . . ." Natasia moved a hand in a circular motion, the universal symbol for insulting one's ex-husband's choice of rebound.

"Medusa," replied Melina. "And you're that . . . um . . . ah . . ." She furrowed her brows as she cocked her head, the universal symbol for *fuck you, bitch*. She looked at Jake, pursing her lips and shaking her head for added effect. "Actress, did you say?"

Jake tried not to grin like a fool as he wrapped an arm around Melina's waist. She'd surprised him yet again.

He rather enjoyed the fact that Melina had hopped onboard the Ego Express. Not only that, but she was in the seat next to him as he traveled to Revengetown.

What more could he ask for in a rebound than that?

CHAPTER TWENTY

The bombshell standing in front of her looked harmless enough, innocent even, but Medusa knew better. Looks could be deceiving.

Take her, for instance. She didn't look like a monster, so why would Natasia? She wasn't a *real* beast, straight from the Underworld like Medusa, but that didn't mean the woman wasn't capable of just as much destruction here on Earth.

Medusa bit the inside of her cheek as she sized the woman up. Obviously, she didn't have the capacity for fidelity, but that wasn't what bothered Medusa. It was who the woman had been unfaithful to that ruffled Medusa's scales.

Natasia had hurt *Jake*.

The thought of it incensed Medusa, and although it shouldn't, she couldn't stop herself from being outraged on Jake's behalf. In fact, if she still had her claws right now, they'd so be out.

Medusa couldn't deny that she'd grown somewhat fond of Jake, or at least his company. She'd spent enough time with him to know that even giant assholes could have hearts. They just erected walls. Outer shells, tough exteriors, whatever terms you wanted to use to described them, they all had the same purpose. How else was one supposed to protect their vulnerable soft center?

Maybe annoyance with Natasia wasn't what Medusa was feeling, then. Perhaps it was sympathy, for Jake. His mother *and* his ex-wife treated him carelessly, and Medusa couldn't quite figure out why. He was easy on the eyes, of course, but he also had a sense of humor. It was cynical most of the time, but that was par for the childhood trauma course.

Jake Sullivan had a lot to give. Any fool could see he just didn't know the best way to give it. The women who'd been most important in his life, save for Kara and Hailey, had taken—were *still* taking—advantage of that.

She heard Jake inhale sharply, pulling her out of her head just in time to notice the rather attractive man walking up behind Natasia. Medusa wanted to wipe her sweaty palms on her dress in the worst way, slow the rapid-fire beating of her heart, stop that swirling feeling in her gut. She pasted on a smile instead.

When Jake mumbled, "Jesus Christ, you've got to be kidding me," under his breath, she knew the man must be one of the previously mentioned co-stars, undoubtedly the one that had put the final nail in his marriage's coffin.

Jake nodded politely. "Chad."

"Jake." Chad flashed his perfectly white—and very obvious—dental veneers.

Yep. This was the guy Natasia had left Jake for, and Medusa would bet her life if she still had one that she'd deliberately poured salt on the wound by bringing him with her tonight.

Medusa suddenly felt the need to prove who was the bigger monster.

"Oh my goodness, you're Chad Smitt," she said, letting her gorgon out to play. "I loved you in your new movie . . . oh, the name escapes me . . . what was it called?"

"Swiping Right III," supplied Chad, falling right into her wicked trap.

"That's right. It's a shame it wasn't in theaters very long." Medusa waved a hand at him—and his acting—dismissively. "I thought it would have been a blockbuster."

A corner of Chad's mouth twitched. He'd received the message loud and clear: *I know what you did, and exactly what role you played in it. Mess with me—or the man standing next to me—at your own risk, buddy.*

And my, wasn't Natasia looking a bit caught off guard? Like bringing her new B-list actor husband to her ex-mother-in-law's holiday party just so she could rub it in her ex's face had been a mistake?

"I'm glad you liked it," said Chad before giving Natasia a look so pointed it was almost sharp.

"Well, it was nice to see you, Jacob," purred Natasia. "I should go find Judith and say hello." She glanced after Chad, who was already halfway to the other side of the room. "Pleasure to meet you, Melina."

"Medusa," corrected Jake, flashing her a tight smile.

Natasia tilted her head. "Pardon me?"

"She goes by Medusa," he repeated before leaning in ever so slightly and whispering, "But the more important thing is . . . I dodged a huge bullet divorcing you, Nat. I'd have never met this beautiful and talented creature on my arm if I hadn't." He glanced at Melina before sending his ex a sinister sneer. "Hope you and Schmitt have a long and happy life together—Oh, until you find someone else to destroy."

Medusa's mouth dropped open, but she quickly recovered with a prim smile. Damn. He'd gone savage on the send-off.

Under normal circumstances, it would have been exactly the kind of ammunition she could use to back-up her decision to send him to the Underworld. But Nat was one of the worse examples of unscrupulous human beings she'd encountered thus far. Well, unless she were to count Judy, but they were neck-and-neck.

So, the question was: Could this really be counted against him?

Her thoughts began to race, and she pressed on a temple in an attempt to slow them down, even for two seconds. It wouldn't be right sending Jake to Hades' Realm, especially knowing his ruthlessness was coming from a place of hurt. He wasn't a questionable soul. On the contrary. He was proving himself to be very much otherwise.

Underneath all the machismo he was a decent human being, just doing his best with the fate he'd been given.

Jake didn't deserve to be punished. In fact, the thought made her want to wrap her arms around him in the here and now instead of her legs every night in the Underworld.

"What's wrong?" asked Jake, cutting into her thoughts. "Do you have a headache? I can get you some aspirin if you need it."

Medusa realized she had gone from pressing on her temple to massaging it. "Oh, no." She shook her hand loose. "I'll be fine. I could use a drink, though."

"You and me both," he replied, offering his elbow to her. "Let's go find one."

She looped her arm through his, relieved to be over the ex-wife ordeal. "Lead the way, kind sir."

As Jake ushered them farther into the lion's den, Medusa smiled demurely at all the guests who'd stopped their conversation to raise eyebrows and whisper about who the woman on Judith Sullivan's son's arm could be.

She seemed to be impressing them, just by being there, and it was a wholly new experience. One that almost had her giggling with sheer delight at the way they nodded approvingly as they inquired about which house of Hollywood royalty she hailed from in hushed tones.

Jake swiped a glass of champagne off a serving tray as

they continued to make their way through his parents' home, if it could even be called a home, and handed it to her. He squeezed her other hand, which he was now holding, and she hoped he wouldn't notice how clammy it was.

Did he really think she was beautiful *and* talented.? She would agree, of course, but that wasn't what had her insides tumbling faster than a swarm of drunk butterflies.

Had he only said that to get back at Natasia? To hurt her for hurting him, or had there been some truth to it?

Well, whether it was the truth or a lie, it was concerning. It was fine if Medusa had somehow developed feelings of fondness. She could handle it; she was mentally prepared to walk away after her vacation was over. Jake, on the other hand, was a mortal, with fragile human feelings to consider.

As if on cue, Jake squeezed her hand again, this time brushing his thumb across the back of it tenderly, confirming her predicament might have reached Oh, Shit Status.

She gulped down half of her champagne. She needed to find out where his head was at. Seeing as she was more skilled in the art of stone turning than truth seeking, that might prove difficult.

"So, I'm your girlfriend now?" she asked when they stopped in front of a set of large wooden doors, two obscenely large sconces on either side.

"I'm sorry." Jake scrubbed a hand over his jaw. "I know it was inappropriate, but I just couldn't let her—or him—think I still felt something for her."

"Do you?"

"God, no."

"So, you're telling me you feel nothing when you see her?" probed Medusa.

Jake raised his eyebrows, but when he saw she was asking a serious question, they dropped, and his face took on a less quizzical expression. "Not a thing. Well, unless you count all-consuming anger."

"You just wanted to make her suffer . . ." she continued, "because she hurt you so badly?"

Jake sighed, his eyes not meeting hers. "I suppose I did. But . . ." He dragged his gaze to Medusa's and opened his mouth to explain.

She already knew what he was going to say; he had been ruthless toward his ex-wife, but he would never be that way to her.

"Hmm. I like how you operate," she said, stepping closer, in order to divert the truth train down a different track. "Maybe I *should* be your girlfriend." She slid her hands up his chest to rest on his shoulders. "It doesn't sound like it would be the worst thing in the world."

"Yeah?" He circled his hands around her waist, drawing her closer still. "You think we should label it?"

"Why not?" She toyed with the hair on the nape of his neck, just the way she knew he liked. "I mean, we're already sleeping together."

"That sounds circumstantial to me, but you make a good case."

"Are you saying you need hard evidence." She pressed herself into him, grinning when she felt the growing bulge in his pants. "I'd say we've found it."

Even though things had just gone from Oh, Shit Status to a What Have I Done? Red Alert, Medusa couldn't help but give him a wicked smile.

CHAPTER TWENTY-ONE

Medusa waited until after Jake kissed her to tell him that his plastic surgeon buddy was waving at them from down the hall.

"I didn't know Dr. Shane was a close personal friend of your mother's."

Jake clasped his hands in front of himself to hide Exhibit A before nodding at Shane. "Are you kidding me? He's my mother's secret weapon to looking ten years younger."

"Does she know it's not working?" asked Medusa, but before Jake could answer, Shane was already standing in front of them tugging at the ugliest garment she'd ever laid eyes on.

Shane adjusted one of the blinking ornaments attached to his sweater. "Hey guys. Merry Christmas, Happy Hanukkah, season's greetings, etcetera, etcetera."

If Jake liked Shane, then Medusa decided she liked him, too. With his blond hair, tanned skin, and easy-going manner, there wasn't much not to like.

"Is Kara here yet?" asked Shane.

"Probably hiding in here." Jake tipped his head toward the doors.

"I hope Hailey is with her," replied Shane. "I haven't seen her since the fundraiser. I need my fix."

Shane's face flashed even brighter than the lights on his sweater at the mentioned of Kara and Hailey, and a fleeting thought slipped through Medusa's mind.

Does he . . . ?

"Come on," said Jake. "We could use some downtime as well. Melina just met my mother."

"Oh boy," said Shane. "How'd that go?"

"As well as can be expected."

"That bad, huh? My condolences."

Medusa laughed. "Thank you, Shane, but I held my own. Don't you think, Jake? Both times?"

"Both times?" asked Shane. "Did Judith reject the first attempt?"

"My mother invited Natasia," said Jake flatly.

Shane winced. "Oh, shit. Double whammy."

Jake nodded, opening one of the doors. "And Melina did great. Better than I did, that's for sure. She even kept me from causing too much of a scene."

"That's right, Sullivan," said Medusa as she entered what appeared to be a library. "Do you even know how much I love causing scenes?"

When they were all inside and Jake had closed the door, Kara and Hailey looked up from their game of Connect Four.

"Hi Shane," said Kara, dropping a blue chip into one of the slots in the plastic game board. Hailey mimicked her mother, staring at the holes with a look of deep concentration before dropping a red chip and saying hello.

"What's up, ladies?" Shane walked over to an enormous solid cherry wood desk they were using as a table—Hailey, of course, was sitting in the gigantic leather office chair—and put his fist out for a bump.

When Shane greeted Kara for a second time, Medusa detected a breathlessness, confirming her suspicion. Shane had a thing for Kara but was hiding it. She, on the other hand, seemed completely clueless.

Two questions popped into Medusa's head. One, who was going to take the place of Jake in Kara and Hailey's lives when he was gone? Two, why was Eros slacking on this love match?

Medusa made a mental note to check into it. Not that she wanted to tell the matchmaker how to do his job, but it was obvious these two needed to be together.

Another question wormed its way into her brain. What if she scheduled a meeting with the Fates, to see if she could get a revision on Jake's life? At the very least, maybe they'd agree to an extension.

Yeah, sure. Just add a meeting with the notoriously difficult sisters to her to-do list. No problem.

She almost flinched when Jake touched her shoulder as he leaned in and whispered, "I know, he's just so cute and funny, isn't he?"

Medusa tried to hide the fact that she'd been absently staring at Shane for several minutes. Well, not so much at him as the general area where he was standing.

"What?" She rolled her eyes to further cover up her space out. She'd been thinking of others again—how to *save* one of them, in particular—and it was getting her into all kinds of trouble. "Are you kidding me? I only have eyes for assholes."

"Okay, good. Just checking."

His gaze dropped to his shoes, and he swallowed hard before finding her eyes again. Whatever he was about to say, she got the feeling he didn't say it often.

"Speaking of assholes, I shouldn't have used you like that earlier. I saw the opportunity to put Natasia in her place and I took it. It was a total dick move, and I'm sorry."

Medusa's heart pounded in her chest. He'd caught her off guard and finished his apology. There was nothing to do now but go with it.

"I get it. I'd have done the same thing." Maybe acting like it was no big deal would stop him from showing any further emo—

"No, I shouldn't have used you like that."

Should she deflect with humor or aggression? That was the question.

"Why stop now?" she asked, pursing her lips.

Defensiveness flashed across Jake's face, the muscle in his jaw working as he ground his teeth. "What's that supposed to mean?"

Oops. Too much aggression. Time to temper it with a bit of irrefutable truth.

"I may be hot, Jake, but I'm not stupid," she said. "I know that's the main reason you asked me to go to Greece."

"I . . . That's not . . ." stammered Jake.

"It's okay," said Medusa, stepping closer so she could toy with his hair again. "It's a smart move, and I don't mind giving your foundation some love. It's for a good cause, one that would be perfect for boosting my image even more. Honestly? I'm actually looking forward to it."

His eyebrows furrowed. "You are?"

"I am."

Now his brow was arched. "It's not exactly a vacation, you know."

She traced a finger over his lips. Partly because they were so soft-looking and partly in an attempt to stop him from saying anything else. "I know, but I'm still looking forward to it."

"And why is that?" he continued before trapping her fingertip between his teeth.

"Because I'm going as your girlfriend," she whispered.

And just like that, she was telling the truth, the whole truth, and nothing but the truth.

He smiled, releasing her finger before moving in for her lips.

CHAPTER TWENTY-TWO

Jake hadn't meant for the kiss to linger. He'd actually gone in for a quick peck, but like every other thing when it came to Melina, here he was. Lingering.

"Get a room," said Shane.

Jake opened his eyes, unable to hold back a smile when he saw that Melina was gazing back at him with a grin of her own. He could feel Shane, Kara, and Hailey staring at him, too, so he broke away, only slightly embarrassed at his inability to control himself. He'd have to work on that.

Oh, and also the fact that he was supposed to be looking for a loophole out of this fling that was quickly becoming a thing. There was also that.

Melina bit her bottom lip, feigning innocence on her part regarding their very public display of affection, and Jake had to talk his co-counsel into settling down at the sultry look in her eyes. Screw the loophole right now. He needed to concentrate on finding an opportunity to leave, so they could be alone.

Jake went through a list of excuses in his mind. Not feeling well. Early morning—it was Saturday, so that wouldn't work. Although, it might, since Jake basically worked 24/7 . . .

She thinks she's your girlfriend now. That's not good, man.

Leave it to Asshole Jake to ruin the moment.

Medusa released her bottom lip so she could run her tongue along the top one before whispering, "You. Me. Later."

She grinned, her scarlet lips curling ever so slightly at the corners before she made a sound that was a cross between a moan and a sigh, as though she could hardly wait.

Jake ran a hand through his hair as he watched the way her hips swayed when she walked over to Hailey and Kara. "I call dibs on playing the winner."

It's moving too fast, man.

Yeah, but when you know, you know.

You were wrong before, hot shot.

Jake scanned the room. There had to be some liquor somewhere. He needed to drown out the voices in his head right the fuck now.

He spied the liquor cabinet on the other side of the room, the sparkling crystal decanter of brandy, or scotch, or whatever it was that didn't matter because he needed to take the edge off in a hurry, sitting behind glass calling to him.

"Anyone else need a drink?"

"Sure, I'll take one." Shane took a seat in one of the leather wing-back chairs in front of a massive fireplace. "Thanks, man."

Jake poured a small amount of the amber liquid into a snifter, swirling then sniffing before taking a sip. Cognac.

"Ladies?" he called out as he poured a second glass.

When Melina and Kara each murmured a, "No thanks," he replaced the stopper before swiping the glasses from the cabinet.

"Here you are, my friend."

Shane took an eager sip, as if he needed a hard edge soft-ened, too. "Damn this is good."

"Did you expect anything less from Mort Sullivan?"

"I think it must run in the family." Shane lifted a brow. "I see you've gotten cozy with the hottest influencer in town. Is it serious?"

"No."

"Oh, is that why you asked her to go to Greece with us?"

"It's called marketing strategy, bonehead."

"Is that what you're calling it? It looked like a lot more a few minutes ago."

"That's called lust."

"If you say so. I just hope she knows she's on Jake The Snake's agenda."

"Look, if she can get some eyes on Superstar Smiles, and we don't have to put as much of our own cash into the mission, then where's the harm?"

"The harm, my friend, is you're a sucker for women like that. You married one and look what happened. I mean, don't get me wrong, Melina seems like the exception." His gaze landed on the two women across the room. "Beautiful, with brains *and* a conscience. *That's* the kind of woman you marry, you know."

Jake glanced over at Melina, who had Hailey on her lap, letting her help strategize against his sister. "And good with kids. Yeah. I know." He took a sip of cognac. "Fuck."

Medusa pointed to the slot where she wanted Hailey to drop her chip. "Jake and Shane didn't ask you to help with the mission this year?"

"Oh, they did . . . well, Shane did, and I'd love to, but I just can't take that kind of time off work. Besides, who would look after Hailey?"

"Couldn't your parents do that?"

Kara looked up from the game, her cocked eyebrow saying it all. Medusa read the *You did just meet my mother, correct?* expression loud and clear.

"Of course, they would, but Hailey would miss her mommy too much, wouldn't you, babe? Shane always brings Brit, anyway."

"Brit?"

"Brittney something or another. She works for him. Volunteers every year. I think they're a thing."

Before Medusa could interrogate Kara about Brittney any further, the study doors swung open, one of them practically banging into the wall, and a fit-for-his-age, silver-haired fox strode into the room.

"How did I know I'd find you two in here? Jacob, Kara-lynn, you know how much your mother hates it when you ignore her guests," said the man Medusa knew in a single instant was Mort Sullivan. "Come on Hailey, you as well."

"We're playing a game right now, papa," said Hailey, unbothered. As if she was used to her grandfather's demands. "We'll come out when we're done."

Mort pursed his lips, even smirking a little with apprecia-tion for his granddaughter's dismissive tone. As if he'd taught her well.

"Well, hurry up, then," he snapped.

All his posturing reminded Medusa of Cerberus, Hades' vicious three-headed watchdog. Perpetually crabby and forever barking out orders.

The trick to Cerbie was charming him instead of chal-lenging him. Running your mouth got you nowhere with Hades' gatekeeper. She still had the bite marks to prove it.

"I don't think we've met," began Medusa, gently removing Hailey from her lap so she could stand. She handed over the rest of her chips before continuing, "I'm Melina Stone, Jake's girlfriend."

One of the man's eyebrows arched, his gaze flicking to his son before landing on Medusa for further assessment.

"It's a pleasure to meet you," she said, lifting her chin, the corners of her lips curling into the barest hint of a smile.

He regarded her for a few more seconds before his brow evened out, his rigid demeanor relaxing with it. "Mort Sullivan. A pleasure to meet you. I didn't realize my son had such exquisite taste."

That was more like it. Definitely a tamer version of the man who had burst into the room a few minutes ago, snarling orders at his grown children.

Medusa laughed, smooth as silk and fake as hell. "Like father like son." She gestured toward her surroundings. "You have a beautiful home." She kept her movements fluid and serpentine as she glided closer. "And your wife, Judith, is an absolute gem."

She was fully aware Jake was staring at her in awe, shaking his head and chuckling at how quickly she had won over such an elitist bastard like Mort Sullivan. She'd struck with lightning precision and deadly force, just like a viper.

If he only knew the half of it.

Medusa winked at Jake as she engaged his father in conversation about, what else, how he'd made his millions. Jake raised his glass at her and smiled, letting her know just how incorrigible he thought she was.

It had been a piece of cake, really. Good old Morty may be ferocious, protective, and indignant, but he was easily subdued if you knew how to approach the damn beast.

In fact, she'd broken them all down quite easily. All she'd had to do was insert herself into their lives, charm them with lies, and she'd been accepted without much effort on her part.

She'd won them over, including Jake, it seemed. Six months and he was calling her his girlfriend.

On that note, she was rather enjoying the results of the

time and effort she'd put into Jake so far. It hardly seemed like work, to be perfectly honest. Experiencing him go from arrogant asshole to tender lover who apologized for enlisting her to help him put his ex-wife in her place, well, it thrilled her. More than that, even. It made her happy.

Along with that happiness, however, came something far more unsettling than really starting to enjoy—crave—his company. None of them had a clue who she truly was, even his best friend, who seemed to be a great judge of character.

None of them had picked up on the monster that lurked within.

She was in the perfect position to slither the rest of the way into Jake's heart, burrow deep into its cute little ventricles and start ripping them apart. She had played the game perfectly, made all the right moves, and she had Jake Sullivan right where she wanted him.

Then why did being the snake she was, feel so wrong?

CHAPTER TWENTY-THREE

As the private jet sailed through the sky, Medusa smiled at the way Jake's eyes moved beneath his lids.

His head rested against the seat, and his chest rose and fell with his deep, even breathing, and she found the mortal necessity to sleep endearing now that she was seeing it through new eyes.

This thing—this connection—they had going on between them was even better as his girlfriend.

The hum of the jet's engine was trying its best to talk her into doing the same; close her eyes and let sleep take over her mind for a while. It was tempting, to let go and fall asleep beside him, but, knowing her luck, she'd probably start dreaming of a life she could never have, with a man who could never be hers.

Well, he could be. His fate wasn't up to her, but where he ended up was. If she wanted him, all she had to do was lie. Something she should have no problem doing. And yet . . .

When she looked down at their joined hands, her throat tightened. That would have been easy to do six months ago, but now that she was his lover, starting to feel things and actually *enjoying* feeling those things, she couldn't damn him to Hades' Realm like that.

She sighed. To say things had gotten complicated was an understatement, and this trip was probably *not* going to help matters.

She slid up the windowpane and looked down at the earth below. A tiny popping sensation bubbled in the pit of her stomach. They would be landing soon, and she would be setting foot on the soil of her homeland for the first time in thousands of years. Hundreds of thousands.

It was strange and exciting and terrifying all at once. Not quite how she envisioned this little vacay of hers would go, but so far, she wouldn't change a thing.

Well, except having Jake's ultimate happiness in her hands.

Jake stirred beside her, shifting in his seat a bit before slowly opening his eyes. "How long have I been sleeping?"

"Couple of hours," said Medusa at the same time Shane shouted, "Three days," from the seat behind them. Brit, who of course was sitting next to him, snorted when she laughed.

Turns out her last name was Thomas, and Ms. Thomas had laughed at practically every word Shane had uttered thus far. Even when he'd very seriously asked the flight attendant for a cocktail to take with his Xanax to calm his nerves.

He thought he was afraid of flying, but Medusa knew, like all mortals, he was really afraid of not being in control of his fate. Of not being able to do a damn thing should they fall out of the sky.

It had been a while, but some small part of her could still relate to that fear, even more so since she'd been hanging around humans for the past several months.

"So not very long, then?" chuckled Jake, squeezing Medusa's hand. "Sorry. Planes always knock me out. Was I snoring?"

"Yes," answered Shane. "Hey, I know a guy who is top-notch at correcting deviated septums, you know."

Everyone laughed except Jake, who turned toward Medusa with a mortified expression on his face. She quirked her lips and shook her head.

"Quiet as a temple mouse," she said, fighting off the urge to take him into her arms and hug him anaconda-style. She brushed a lock of dark hair off his forehead instead. "And cute as a button."

Cute as a button? Jesus fighting a Kraken. What kind of sappy shit was she allowing out of her mouth lately? Maybe keeping such close company with mortals hadn't been a good idea.

"You say that now," he leaned over and kissed her, "but give me time. I'm sure I'll change your mind on that one."

She kind of hoped he did, and that this was all just some dream she was having, that she was just passed out on her sofa with Lucifer playing on the television. That she would wake up and discover she didn't have to leave Jake's life in the hands of the Fates when her vacation was over.

A sharp pain when her teeth sliced through the inside of her mouth pulled her from her thoughts. She tasted blood, and realized the mere thought that Jake's life would be over much sooner than she wanted it to be literally hurt.

The seatbelt signs lit up, followed by a soft click from the loudspeaker.

"Good afternoon, ladies and gentlemen. We are beginning our descent into Athens International. Please fasten your seatbelts for the duration. Local time in Athens, Greece, is 2:36 p.m. The temperature is currently sixty-three degrees. We should touch down in approximately twenty minutes."

The plane landed, and after waiting for what seemed like a lifetime at baggage claim, they hailed a taxi and made their way to the resort.

Jake hadn't chosen the largest hotel in Athens, but it was

still luxurious. It wasn't in the center of the city, where the clinic was, but a few miles away, nestled along the coast of the Saronic Gulf. She actually preferred to be off the beaten path, so she didn't mind.

Once inside, Medusa waited off to the side with Brit and Shane as Jake checked them in. She took in her surroundings, the decor that was sparse but modern, spa-like.

The large glass doors slid open and a man with no luggage walked through. Their eyes met, and her heart stopped, a burst of adrenaline prickling through her so strong she nearly cried out.

Hermes smiled and headed straight for her.

Medusa widened her eyes at him, since there was no way she could shake her head with Brit and Shane sitting next to her. Sure, Brit was preoccupied with staring at Shane, who was scrolling through his phone, but Medusa couldn't take any chances.

She got up from her chair. "Be right back. I need to run to the restroom. Brit, will you watch my suitcase?"

Brit nodded without looking over, and Medusa hurried off toward the restrooms, trying not to look frazzled. Gods-damned Hermes. Whatever he had to tell her better be important.

Her heels clicked as she hurried toward the lavatories. Thankfully, they were located around the corner and a short distance down a hall. More importantly, out of sight.

Hermes came around the corner with a huge smile on his face, as if he was actually a long-lost friend of hers.

"*What* are you doing here?" she whispered, folding her arms so she wouldn't take a swipe at him.

"Well, I knew you were here, and I hadn't been to Athens for a while, so I thought it might be fun to zip down and hit a few museums and whatnot while I waited to see if you needed any help."

Did he say he'd wanted to see if she needed any help? Now that was just ludicrous.

It was also sweet, and even though she wanted to remain furious, she couldn't.

"Thank you, but I've got everything under control." She waved him away. "Now go have fun at your museums and whatnot, okay?"

CHAPTER TWENTY-FOUR

It seemed to take forever, but when Jake finally finished at the front desk, he joined the group and began to disperse key cards.

Shane barely looked up from his phone when Jake handed him his, and Brit's shoulders fell, ever so slightly, when he handed hers over.

Melina smiled when he winked and stuffed theirs into the pocket of his button-down.

They headed toward the elevators as a group, and when the doors opened, and they saw there was just enough room for two people and not four, Jake nodded at Shane.

"Why don't you guys take this one."

"Sure," agreed Shane, pocketing his phone. He glanced at Brit, who was already wheeling her luggage into the elevator. "See you guys at dinner, right?"

"Yep," confirmed Jake. "Around Seven-ish?"

Shane stuck a thumb up right before the doors closed.

"I think she's in love with him," said Melina.

"Nah," countered Jake.

Melina tilted her head. "She's been trying to talk to him for the last fourteen hours and he's had his nose glued to his phone screen. When have you ever known Shane to miss out on the opportunity to be the center of conversation?"

"Interesting," replied Jake. The elevator dinged and the polished metal doors slid open. "I don't see it, though. He's got some long hours ahead of him. I think he's just getting into the right headspace is all. This mission means a lot to him."

"Well, be that as it may, I think he's in love with your sister," said Melina as they stepped inside.

Jake laughed. "Who are you? Cupid?" The woman was hot, but she was off her rocker. Shane would have told him if he was interested in Kara, he was sure of it.

"Go ahead, laugh. But I'm right. You'll see."

Medusa linked her arm in his and sent him a smile. It was genuine and sweet, dazzling and sexy all at the same time.

He squeezed her arm tighter to his side when she rested her head on his shoulder. She was in a playful mood. Now was as good a time as any to tell her what he'd done.

"I have a confession to make."

She lifted her head, looking up at him warily, as if what he was about to divulge was that *he* was Cupid.

Or that he might feel more for her than she did him.

Even if that was the case, there was no way it would work long-term. What mattered right now was being here, together, enjoying each other's company while it lasted.

"I might have told the receptionist that we were newly-weds so we could get a bottle of complimentary champagne."

One of her eyebrows shot up, causing his heart to climb into his throat.

"Oh, so I'm your *wife* now?" she said, releasing his arm so she could fold both of hers.

Well, shit, now his palms were sweating. He'd just thought it might be a way to let loose, you know, since they'd be working nonstop all week. He'd wanted the first night to be fun, at least.

Or had he wanted to make it special?

It didn't matter because he had a feeling it was about to be over sooner rather than later if he didn't convince her it wasn't that serious.

"Hey, what can I say? I'm a sucker for free stuff." He shrugged. Great. His pits were damp now, too. "Plus, we got upgraded to a room with a jacuzzi tub. I didn't think you'd mind."

She thought about it for a few seconds before her lips curled into a smile. It wasn't long after that when she pushed him up against the wall. Good thing they'd let Shane and Brit take the first elevator, and this one had been empty.

"I'm not sure we'll need the jacuzzi," she murmured. "I'm already wet enough."

Jake inhaled sharply when she cupped him through his pants. If this elevator ride got any hotter, he'd disintegrate.

They'd managed to make it down the long hallway and into their room without shedding any clothes. He fully expected to finish what they'd started, but as soon as they entered their room, Melina made a beeline for the bottle of bubbly chilling on ice. Damn, this place worked fast.

"Ooooh, it's Cristal, too. Good call, Mr. Sullivan."

Jake walked over to the glass doors that led out onto the small balcony and opened them. A crisp sea breeze billowed the sheer curtains, and he inhaled deeply, hoping the fresh air and spectacular view of the water would chill him out.

Too bad the most gorgeous woman he knew was making that extremely difficult.

She was breathtaking, even now, popping the cork of their complimentary champagne in her leggings and trendy crop top. He wanted her whether she wore cotton or silk. And the thing of it was, no matter what he tried to tell himself, what lie he came up with, he wanted to be around her, not just in her.

And it scared the ever-loving shit out of him.

She handed him a flute and then clinked it to his. "Here's to us, Mr. Sullivan."

Here's to us, Mrs. Sullivan.

He wanted to say it out loud, try on the words even if they would never be anything more than something said to get free champagne.

Melina tucked herself into an overstuffed chair, and after setting her flute on the small table next to her, she checked her social media.

He nodded toward the balcony. "Want to catch some of this Mediterranean sunset with me?"

She stopped scrolling to think about it for a second. She placed her phone on the table next to her still fizzing champagne. She unfolded her legs out from under her and stood.

"Sure," she said, breezing toward him. "Then maybe we can test out that jacuzzi tub before dinner?"

"I like the sound of that," he said, opening the door.

They stepped out onto the balcony, moving the chairs closer together before sitting. They sat in companionable silence, watching the sun hanging over the horizon.

When he looked over, her face was bathed in a warm glow, and her lovely eyes were lit up and shining with emotion.

He wanted to reach out and take her hand, pull her into his lap and hold her. He wasn't sure the exact moment things had shifted, but he could picture them together, like this, for a long, long time. He just didn't know if she could.

"You okay?" he said, hoping the moment was real enough that she'd say all the things he couldn't.

"Yeah," she sighed, fanning her face before dabbing at her eyes. "I'd just forgotten how beautiful sunsets were."

A moment later she was out of her chair, removing her top in one fluid motion as she stepped in front of him. "What do you say we go try out that jacuzzi?"

She gazed down at him in that arrestingly sexy way of

hers, and he knew he was done for. Knowing how much stamina the woman had, probably until dinner.

But it's not just sex anymore, is it?

No, he didn't think it was. Not when urgent grasping need had been replaced with slow and gentle caresses. Reverent, languishing kisses got him just as hard as the hasty greedy ones.

But that was him. He had no idea what Melina thought. For all he knew, she was living in the moment, and this was temporary for her. It was too soon to feel the way he did, and the sooner he stopped entertaining the idea that it wasn't, the safer his heart would be.

Maybe asking her to come hadn't been a good idea.

Jake pushed himself out of the chair and followed her back inside. He should have listened to Asshole Jake. Because when this house of cards came tumbling down, it would be him standing there with a mess scattered at his feet. Again.

There was only one problem. Despite knowing the footing he had with Melina was shaky at best, he couldn't *not* be with her. He was defenseless against the force that drew him to her. It was stronger than anything he'd ever felt before.

So strong, he could no longer deny that it existed. He hadn't invited her to come to Greece because of Superstar Smiles like he'd been desperately trying to convince himself. He'd asked her because, somehow, despite desperately trying to prevent it from happening, he no longer liked the idea of being apart.

Shane and Brit were already seated when the hostess showed Jake and Melina to the table. They were sitting across from each other, so Jake and Melina were forced to do the same, which was fine. It wouldn't be so obvious when he stared at her all night.

He pulled out a chair for Melina, then clapped Shane on

the shoulder and nodded at Brit as he walked around the table to his own seat. "How's it going, guys?"

Brit answered, but Jake didn't really hear what she'd said. He was too preoccupied with the way Melina glowed. Most likely the result of three-hour-long-barely-had-time-to-shower sex, but Jake let himself imagine it was something else, just for tonight.

She almost looked content. As though he would ever be enough. He tried to ignore the thought, but it had his lips lifting into a hopeful grin every time he looked at her.

Maybe this time he would be.

"You need to work on getting your sister to come next time, Jake," Melina said before glancing at Shane. "I bet she would have loved it here."

Jake didn't miss the side-eye Brit tossed Melina's way.

"Yeah, Jake," agreed Shane. "You need to get her to come one of these times. I tried, but she shot me down again."

"Hmm. Sounds like someone is disappointed," said Melina before casually taking a sip of water and ignoring the glare coming from Brit's side of the table.

"Don't worry, Shane," replied Brit, "you've always got me."

Maybe Melina was right. Jake had always thought Shane asked Brit to come along on the mission because he was hoping she'd be more than just an employee. Judging by how instantly the man's face had flushed, and how quickly the awkward silence was currently growing . . .

"Thanks, Brit," Shane finally replied. "I do appreciate that." He picked up the menu lying on the table in front of him and opened it. "So, what are we all having tonight?"

Redirection at its finest. Okay, maybe Brit did only get asked to accompany them by default.

In the midst of wondering if it was possible Shane could have feelings for his sister, Jake noticed Medusa's eyes cut to a man sitting at the bar.

Jake couldn't tell how tall the man was since he was sitting, but he could see he wasn't a slouch. He was athletic and handsome, and this was the third time Melina had tried to hide her interest. Jake had ignored the first two times, but he drew the line at triple-takes.

His irritation fired up, quick and hot. Or was it jealousy? Or perhaps the fact that Asshole Jake had been right all along?

The the other shoe had dropped, just like he knew it would, and his subconscious was using it as the perfect excuse to prepare for the inevitable.

"Do you know that man?" he asked Melina, the roller-coaster ride of emotions getting the better of him. He leaned to the side, making it a point to move out of the way so she could get a better look.

Total Asshole Jake move, and an involuntary reflex.

"I think I do, actually," she said, setting down her menu. "Will you please excuse me?"

What the actual fuck? First of all, what were the chances that he'd take her to Greece and she'd just happen to know someone? Second, was she actually going to humiliate him like this?

A shot of adrenaline flooded his system, making his heart hammer in response. Warning bells rang loud inside his head, but he couldn't do anything but gape at her as she got up from the table and walked toward the man sitting at the bar.

Jake snapped his mouth shut. This couldn't—*shouldn't* —be happening. He liked Melina, might even be falling in love, but this intense possessiveness over her was too much.

Another reason why he needed to cut his losses and walk away. He'd just hoped he wouldn't have been forced to do it here, the first damn night.

Operation: Find the Loophole was officially back in progress.

Jake struggled to keep his emotions in check. Shane, being the friend that he was, tried to diffuse the ticking time bomb that was Jake Sullivan right now.

"So, guys, should we meet as a group tomorrow morning, so we can all take the bus to the city together?"

"Sure," agreed Jake. "Sounds good." His tight smile was fooling no one, but he was stuck. He'd told Shane bringing Melina had been nothing more than strategic, and he couldn't let on how big of a lie he'd told.

Nope. Jake had to sit there and pretend it didn't bother him.

Something that was proving extremely difficult to do since there was no conversation happening between Shane and Brit. Just rapidly growing awkward silence.

"I'll be back," said Jake, pushing his chair from the table. He needed some air.

For a split second, he thought about going over and introducing himself. But knowing Asshole Jake would not be able to resist introducing himself as her fiancé, just to drive home the point to Melina how hurt he was by her behavior, it was probably better to go with the original plan to step outside.

Jesus, it was like she had a split personality the way she flipped like that. Attentive and all eyes on him one minute, then leaving him sitting at the table like yesterday's news the next.

He made his way toward the front door, blowing out a breath as he exited into the crisp night. He inhaled deeply, letting the bracing sea air calm his nerves.

Slap him in the face and bring him back to reality.

His phone buzzed in his pocket. He looked to see who was calling and was relieved when he saw it was Kara. Thank God. He could really use some advice right now.

"Hey, sis. What's up?"

"Tell her to take it down, Jake. *Now!* Hailey is devastated!" How could she do something like this?"

Jake's stomach dropped.

"Kara, slow down," said Jake. She was talking so fast he could barely make sense of what she was saying. "Have who take what down?"

"The picture! The picture on Melina's Instagram, Jake!"

Jake pulled his phone away from his ear and put Kara on speaker before tapping through several screens. He didn't have the Instagram app on his phone, and that was because he hated that social media shit.

As he stood near the street, waiting for the app to download so he could see exactly what Kara was talking about when a screenshot popped up on his notifications.

A picture of Melina and Hailey at the costume gala a few months back.

His eyes scanned the image, stopping on the tag *#beautyandthebeast* before moving down to the comments. There were several hundred of them. All discussing Hailey's scars.

His mouth went dry. He tried to breathe, but it was difficult with how hard his heart was punching his ribs.

He'd just found his loophole.

CHAPTER TWENTY-FIVE

Medusa gave the messenger of the gods a sweet but totally fake smile as she tried not to slam her clutch on the bar top.

"Excuse my Greek, Hermes, but what the fuck?" Grabbing him by his collar and shaking the shit out of him might also prevent their chat from appearing friendly, so she refrained. "You couldn't have just texted me?"

Hermes cocked his head and thought about it. "Well, I suppose I could have."

He took his time sipping his martini as he pondered, and Medusa had to stop herself from reaching over and choking the immortal life out of him.

"I have a couple of urgent messages for you and I thought a face-to-face might be the best way to go." A grin broke out across his face. "And, as you already know, I was in the area and, I don't know, figured I'd just kill two birds with one—"

Medusa's hand flew up, and she shook her head in case he didn't get the message. Zeus's electric nut sack. That saying was so frigging *tired*.

She rolled her eyes before glancing over her shoulder to see how Jake was taking her rather abrupt departure. Her chest tightened. Only Shane and Brit occupied the table, and whatever they were talking about seemed painfully awkward.

Medusa made no attempt to hold back a nervous huff. Or was it a frustrated sigh?

It figured things would implode now. No social media, no fans, nothing to do and nowhere to be but spend every waking moment with Jake. To think, she'd just started truly enjoying herself on this damn vacation and now she sat next to Hermes, the bearer of news she had a feeling was going to be bad.

"Okay, let me have it."

Hermes chewed on an olive thoughtfully. "I'll give you the good news first. Ready?" He arched a brow at her until she nodded her head. "Hades wants the assessment early." He gulped down the rest of the olive so he could continue delivering his bad news.

"What?" Medusa whisper-screamed, gripping the edge of the bar and digging her nails into it. "Why? And how is this the *good* news?"

Hermes took a careful sip of his martini. "It is compared to the other message."

Medusa closed her eyes, pressing her lips together and trying to remain calm. *First circle of Hell . . . Second circle of Hell . . . Third circle of Hell . . .*

"All right. How early does he want it?" She would worry about the "bad" news later. Nothing could be worse than what she'd just received.

"Mmm. Yeah. Like, pretty much *now* early. You've got until the end of the week."

Her palm smacked the bar top. This was definitely not good news. "He can't be serious." *Fourth circle.* "I was just beginning to . . ." *Fifth circle.* She forced her grip on the bar top to loosen. "Relax."

She inhaled. *Six.* Exhaled. *Seven, eight.*

Zeus must have riled Hades up somehow. Honestly, she

shouldn't have expected anything less, but it figured it would be right when she was starting to get somewhere.

Medusa swallowed hard, collecting her panicked thoughts so she could think more clearly. All she needed to do was gently but firmly remind her boss that she had everything under control, which she totally did—not.

Ninth. Circle. Of. Hell.

Medusa raised her hand for the bartender, and when she had his attention, she pointed at Hermes' martini and then held up two fingers. The man nodded and set to work with a bottle of vodka and a shaker.

"Damn, girl," said Hermes. "Only two? You're taking the news well. I was a little scared to tell you, to be honest."

Medusa snatched the glass he was holding from his hands. "One, I'm really not okay. And two, you're going to need another one of these in about three seconds." With that, she downed the rest of his martini.

What else was there to do at the moment but drink heavily? Hades had decided he wanted the assessment early, which would have been fine under normal circumstances— the old her would probably have been bored and ready to leave by this point—but she was no longer her old self, now was she?

Her mind began to race again. No doubt Hades expected her back in the office next Monday, which only left the rest of this week and the weekend to get her affairs in order. Tie up loose ends.

Say goodbye.

The thought filled her with a strange sinking feeling. It would only be by a few months, but still, she dreaded going back into the office early.

Plus, it was a few months less she had to spend with Jake, before he . . .

Anger suddenly sparked, growing in intensity until it shot up and out of her. It was unfair. All of it. Jake's fate.

Hades forcing her to give her assessment before she was ready.

She'd been approved for 365 vacation days, and she was entitled to use every last one of them.

"You know what? No. Tell Hades he'll get his assessment when I'm good and damn well ready."

Hermes' hands shot up before his shit-eating grin returned. "Hey, I'm just the messenger."

"Ugh," groaned Medusa. "I like you, Hermes, but you have the worst comedic timing. Can you *please* tell Hades I need a couple more weeks?"

"Sure thing, but if his temper flares?"

"Smooth it over with one of your jokes." Medusa pursed her lips. "Speaking of jokes, do I need to put in a formal request to get a match made or—uh oh."

She'd caught a glimpse of movement in her peripheral vision. Someone was moving past the hostess station at a rather determined clip. When she realized that someone was Jake, with an equally single-minded expression on his face, she lost all train of thought.

She ripped her gaze away from Jake and looked at Hermes. "What's the other message?"

Hermes glanced over his shoulder to see what she'd uh-oh-ed about. Seeing Jake headed for them, he whipped his head toward her, his eyes wide. "Dylan messed up."

Medusa tilted her head when Hermes didn't elaborate. "Can you be a little more specific? Messed up how?"

"She kind of, sort of might have . . ."

"Out with it, messenger! I've apparently got the gods-damned Minotaur headed my way," ground out Medusa, her patience wearing dangerously thin.

"She posted something that's going to take you back a few steps with your dude." Hermes tipped his head, a quick half-nod to indicate the dude he was referring to was Jake.

Medusa's shoulders dropped. "Mother. Fucking. Zeus,"

she muttered. She thought she'd made it clear to Dylan that pictures of Jake were off limits. She'd promised him he'd stay off her timelines.

Hermes rapped his knuckles on the bar. "Well, it's been super fun, but I do believe that's my cue to leave." He plucked the olive out of her martini and slid off the barstool.

Medusa kept her gaze on Jake, who continued to make his way through the dining area, now with an utter calmness that gave her goosebumps. Her bottom lip found its way between her teeth. The only sensible thing to do was gnaw on it. It was that or run.

She knew it was too late, though. If looks could kill, she'd already be stone.

To her surprise Hermes hadn't left. He was still standing beside her, and when he clapped a hand on her shoulder she winced.

"Looks like one hell of a lover's quarrel is about to go down," he said. "You sure you don't need a little help from the matchmaker yourself?"

"What?" Medusa shifted, shrugging out from under the weight of his friendly gesture. It made her uncomfortable. "Don't be ridiculous. He's a *mortal*."

"Love is love, and it doesn't take a genius to see that you, my friend, are in—"

A growl vibrated low in her throat. "I'm not in love. Now, if you'll excuse me. I need to get back to work."

"Sure, whatever you say," laughed Hermes. "Oh, and Robbie Winger."

"What?"

"My name . . . So the lie you're about to tell sounds more legit."

CHAPTER TWENTY-SIX

nger carved hard lines into Jake's face. The sight of it made Medusa's stomach go from moderate churning to full-on roiling. She preferred a smiling Jake to this one, with affection lighting up his eyes instead of hostility darkening them.

She scrambled to think of something she could say to soften that hard glare, smooth out those sharply angled brows, but her brain refused to cooperate.

You should have known how leaving the table to go talk to another man would have looked, it kept telling her, *how it would have* felt *to someone with a wounded heart.*

She silently cursed Hermes for not waiting until she was alone, for not picking a better time to deliver his message. That is until her brain reminded her what *he'd* said, *"So the lie you're about to tell sounds legit . . ."*

Dammit. Curse retracted. It wasn't Hermes' fault Hades was impatient, or that she should have known better than to mix business with pleasure. Or that she was a giant fraud—lying to both herself and Jake this whole time, in more ways than one.

Poor Hermes, it had to suck being the patron of thieves

on top of the bearer of bad news. Thieves and liars, pretty much one in the same, and she was both. She'd selfishly inserted herself into Jake's life—into all their lives—and then had proceeded to steal their hearts. It wasn't just Jake's that would be broken when she left.

She could have stopped, *should* have. And now it was too late.

Despite marching toward her like he'd been on one hell of a mission, Jake now stood before her, peering down at her with a chilling calm, absolutely still save for the rapid rise and fall of his chest. Not a good sign. An obvious indicator that she had some explaining to do.

If only she could.

Instead, she would have to tell more lies.

Medusa commanded her heart to harden. It was almost too much to bear, because somewhere along the way, it had started beating again.

"I was just about to come find you," she said, which wasn't a lie, technically. Her next move would have been to go find him, that was true enough.

"I have good news." She stood, squeezing the clutch wedged into her armpit tighter than a boa constrictor. "The man I was just talking to owns a textiles company right here in Greece. Isn't that amazing? His name is Robbie Winger." Hermes had been right. Lie, indeed. They were flying out her mouth so fast her brain could barely keep up. "I was hoping I'd run into him, actually. He wants to partner with m—"

Jake held up his hand. "Just stop, Melina. You don't think I know a lie when I hear one? I'm a lawyer, remember? I expected you to get tired of me . . . eventually . . . let's not pretend you're in it for the long haul."

Not knowing what else to say, Medusa replied, "I don't understand what's going on here."

She most certainly did. She'd picked at the edges of his

still healing wound. She hadn't meant to open it back up, but she'd had no choice, and there was no turning back now.

"It was just a harmless conversation regarding business. Are you that insecure, Jake?"

He laughed, his gaze flicking to the side before his transformation into an ignorant asshole was complete. "Don't flatter yourself. I have a different bone to pick with you right now."

The shift had happened in an instant. He'd detached fully, and just like that, the man she'd met at the airport bar was back. Arrogant. Entitled. Detached.

Devoid.

Her downward slide was also quick.

"Really?" she ground out. "And what bone would that be?"

"I said no photos of me. I thought you were smart enough to assume that meant no photos of Hailey either. But that's par for the course for women like you, isn't it?"

Medusa jerked her head back. Not at the tone of his voice, which she'd expected to have some degree of chill to it, but at the way he sneered at her when he'd said it. Exactly like when he'd said something similar to Natasia. Except, now it was directed at her.

It stung worse than an actual slap to the face.

And there was that image of the Graces again, showing up to the party in her head uninvited.

Medusa pulled on a scowl. It was uncomfortably tight, like a pair of pants that were several sizes too small, and she felt like she couldn't breathe, but it had to be done. "What are you talking about?"

"Always thinking of yourself," he said, pulling his phone from his pocket and waking it up. "How *you* look."

That used to be true, yes, but it wasn't anymore. The way Jake stood before her, however, visibly grinding his teeth—

down to nothing if he kept it up much longer—suggested he didn't believe anything of the sort.

"I'm talking about this." He held up his phone, turning the screen toward her to reveal the source of his anger; a selfie of her and Hailey at the Halloween gala.

A grenade went off in Medusa's chest, sending shards of panic to embed themselves in her ribs and belly. She couldn't move, couldn't speak. Couldn't explain.

"I didn't post that." The words came out in a strangled whisper.

"Yeah, right," said Jake as he raked his fingers through his hair before pressing them into his scalp, like he was trying to keep his own head from exploding. The other hand gripped his phone so tightly his knuckles were white.

"I'm starting to wonder if there's nothing you won't do for attention." He stuffed his phone back into his pocket. "Hailey is a *light* in this world, Melina, and I'll be *goddamn* if I let anyone extinguish it. She means the world to me . . . and I thought she meant something to you, too . . . but, once again, I was wrong."

This wasn't about jealousy. It was about trust. He'd given what little of it he'd had left to her, and she'd been no better than Judy and Natasia at keeping it. She'd broken it.

And she didn't have time to fix it.

Medusa was fuming, at Hades, at herself, at Dylan for posting the damn thing. But Medusa couldn't be sure she'd actually said, *"Photos of Hailey are off limits,"* so she couldn't blame it all on Dylan.

Besides, it wasn't in Dylan's control—Medusa suspected fate had a little something to do with this.

Medusa did the only thing she could do under the current circumstances, which was clamp her mouth shut. Lock her feelings up tight. Throw away the key.

This was the beginning of the end. There was no getting

around the Fates' not so subtle way of speeding up her departure, probably so they could get on with their business.

Medusa's throat ached from holding back a sob. She wanted to let loose and wail. Bawl until all this wretched emotion had leaked out of her eyes and went away for good.

The only thing that kept her upright was knowing that he was going to Elysium. She would call Hermes to bring her the paperwork. She'd even fill it out while he was standing there.

Jake inhaled, then exhaled a long, suffering sigh as his hands slid into his pockets. "I can't do this anymore."

Medusa reached out to touch him, but he stepped back. She couldn't blame him. She still asked the question anyway. "Can't do what?"

"This. Us." Jake gestured between them before waving his hand at her dismissively. "You."

Her panic grew, and the sick feeling in Medusa's stomach crept upward, dangerously close to her throat. She flipped open her clutch and extracted her phone. Her fingers trembled, making it difficult to pull up her Instagram account, but she somehow managed.

"She's just a little girl," he said, shaking his head. "Did you think I wouldn't find out because I'm not on Instagram?"

She scrolled through the comments, her eyes catching on words like "mini monster" and "scar face." When she tore her gaze away to look at Jake, his jaw was set, eyes narrowed.

She tried going back to the comments, but the letters that formed sentences, which then gave life to unspeakable cruelty, blurred. She'd seen all she needed to see right there on Jake's face anyway.

Medusa deleted the photo from her feed.

"There, it's gone." She showed Jake her phone as proof. His gaze flicked toward the screen before landing back on her.

His jaw was still set, which seemed a good indication it

did little to stem the tide that was about to come in. The tidal wave about to take her out, more like it.

"I would never intentionally hurt Hailey," she said softly. "You know that."

He ground his teeth.

"You do know that don't you?" she said, almost as weakly as she felt.

She'd only just broken through Jake's walls—as well as some of her own—and made her way into his heart. It'd felt good there. She felt wanted, beautiful even, and she'd hoped to be able to stay as long as she could. Until the bitter end.

"Jake?"

"You know, Melina," he said. "I thought you were different." He locked her in his sights. "Turns out you're just like the rest of them . . ."

Please don't say it.

"A selfish monster."

All the fight drained out of her. Sadness welled in its place.

He hadn't said she was ugly, but she knew he'd wanted to, and he should have because she was, no matter what she looked like on the outside. Even though she could finally admit the truth—despite trying not to, she loved him—and that everything she'd done, at least in the beginning, had been done for selfish reasons.

And she wished she could take it all back, starting with listening to her heart that night out on the balcony. As cold as it had been, it had still tried to tell her. To warn her with those little twinges of sympathy.

She'd dragged him into a ruthless game of cat and mouse anyway, and she regretted it. The zoo and the gala, too. She shouldn't have gone. Then she wouldn't have met Hailey and Kara, never gotten attached to them.

She should have said no to Greece.

Jake knew how to twist the knife. She knew because she'd

seen him do it to Natasia, had even helped him. He hadn't called Medusa ugly because he knew that calling her selfish would hurt ten times worse.

And it did, more than she ever imagined it would.

"I never pretended to be anything else, Jake," she said, as evenly and calmly as she could manage. "I'm sorry if you thought I did."

He looked at her, shock widening his eyes, his mouth, before defeat overtook it. He had been hoping she'd fight, prove him wrong.

But she couldn't. He was right. She was a monster.

"Why don't we sit down and finish dinner." She glanced in the direction where they'd been sitting.

What else was there left to do but try and salvage the evening?

Jake followed her gaze to the empty table. He shook his head, his fight gone, too. "We have a long day ahead of us tomorrow. Why don't you order something, have them bring it up to the room? I'll be up in a bit."

It wasn't a bad idea, especially since their argument had left her drained, both mentally and physically. Perhaps a nice soak in the tub would do her some good.

"Okay. But promise me you won't be gone too long." She stepped closer to trail her fingers up the back of his arm. Her last-ditch effort to spend her remaining time together.

He stiffened and, just like that, Medusa knew it was over.

No.

She almost said it out loud, the urge to command him—the situation—into bending to her will.

No, no, no, no.

She released his arm, which she discovered she was desperately clutching instead of seductively caressing, and a wave of panic rolled through her, making her head spin. This was it, the end.

If he knew, would he feel differently? Would he change

his mind and let her wrap herself around him—crush him to her and never let go.

But she fought the urge to control him; demand he move past whatever doubt he was experiencing and go back up to the room with her. He needed space, and if she cared for him at all she would give it to him.

She prayed to every god and goddess she knew existed as she left him standing there, silently pleading with the Fates to be kind when they took him. Make it quick and painless.

The tears came when she stepped onto the elevator, which was blessedly empty, and she let them fall. It was the least she could do, as repentance for having been so vain to think she could make herself feel better—wanted and loved— at the expense of another.

In her defense, if she even had one, she'd set out to break hearts. She just hadn't expected it to be hers.

CHAPTER TWENTY-SEVEN

The waves pounded against the shore, but Jake barely heard them above the cacophony going on inside his head.

His demons were loud.

He wanted to believe the photo had been an accident, but the head demon, AKA Asshole Jake, wouldn't let him. In fact, he was insisting it was the perfect excuse to end it with Melina.

In the grand scheme of things, it wasn't necessarily a deal breaker, but it was still a loophole. Albeit a small one, but that didn't matter. He only needed it to be big enough to squeak through.

Melina had her whole career—her whole life—ahead of her. She should focus on that, not proving there wasn't an ulterior motive for everything she said . . . Everything she did. She'd be meeting all kinds of people. It was inevitable she'd come across a more interesting man, one who wasn't quite so broken. One who could give her what she needed.

He wasn't that guy. Couldn't be. He'd tried, and maybe walking away like this, for such a stupid reason, was a cop out, but . . .

Now was the perfect time as any to free her from the broken mess that was Jake Sullivan.

He drained the glass of whiskey he'd ordered at the bar before heading out to the resort's patio. The bracing night air had driven most of the guests inside, leaving only a handful of people to brave the chill. They congregated near the heat lamps, but Jake had opted for a far corner of the outdoor space to drown his sorrows alone.

The cold had seemed like a good way to help clear his head. The whiskey had seemed a good way to numb the pain.

He looked at his watch. It was late, and he was just intoxicated enough to go book his own room for the rest of the week. He'd sleep in the same room with Melina one last time, a goodbye of sorts. After tonight, though, Asshole Jake was back in charge.

Jake scrubbed his forehead with his fingers before raking them through his hair and pushing to his feet. He couldn't even blame it on Mort and Judy this time. This misery was his fault.

It was a wonder he heard the unmistakable sound of female tears over the methodic rumbling of the shoreline behind him. When he glanced in the direction of the sniffling, he saw Brit huddled under a heat lamp drinking wine from the bottle.

"Hey," he said, unable to continue walking by as if he didn't see her. Asshole Jake wasn't in charge quite yet. "You okay?"

"Just peachy," she said dryly, the words in stark contrast to her red-rimmed eyes.

"I hear you." Jake nodded at a chair. "Want some company?"

"Sure." She held the bottle out to him. "Want some wine?"

He shook his head as a piece of the does-Shane-have-a-thing-for-my-sister puzzle he had been pushing around the table finally fit into place. "Shane?"

Brit nodded as she held back another round of tears. "I feel like such an idiot. I don't know why I tortured myself for so long, thinking he was ever going to feel anything for me. He's in love with her, you know."

"Yeah," said Jake. "I do now."

He swallowed hard, feeling a bit dense for not putting two and two together sooner. Shane probably hadn't said anything because he knew Jake would have reacted poorly to the fact that his best friend was in love with his sister.

It seemed as though Kara hadn't put the pieces together, either. Or at least she'd pretended as though she hadn't. They were so alike, he and his sister. Self-sabotaging any chance at happiness that came their way. It was no wonder, either. They were all they had growing up. It was something they'd learned to do to protect themselves—and each other—from disappointment. An unwritten rule they abided by.

"Hearing him say it out loud was . . ." Brit failed to hold back her tears any longer and a fresh torrent broke loose. "It was awful, Jake. I tried so hard to make him want me. The Botox, the fillers, the boob job, all of it, and it didn't work."

"Well, of course not, Brit. If you don't think you're enough, then why would Shane?"

"Because we live in L.A., Jake. Looks are everything, and men like you and Shane want perfect barbie dolls. Do you actually think blonde is my natural hair color?" She unleashed a snort. "Melina and Kara are lucky enough to be gorgeous without trying. Some of us have to work at it."

"First of all, you're generalizing and that's not fair. Second, I'm sorry you feel you have to change everything about yourself just to be happy. For what it's worth, I think you're very attractive."

"So, *you'd* date me, then?" She tilted her head, and he

could tell her wheels were spinning. He just didn't know in which direction.

"Sure," he said, carefully.

"If you and Melina weren't a thing?"

"Melina and I aren't a thing . . ."

She pursed her lips at him.

"Anymore."

Brit sat up straighter at this information, leaning closer. "Oh really? What happened?"

Jake shook his head. He knew exactly where Brit was going with this line of questioning now. A last-ditch effort to make Shane jealous.

The thought piqued Asshole Jake's interest, he had to admit. It would be the perfect way to make the loophole with Melina bigger.

Much, much bigger.

Jake pushed the thought away. Sleeping with Brit would only backfire. There wasn't any scheme she could come up with to make Shane jealous enough to choose her over Kara, anyway.

And even though Melina had ruined other women for him, possibly forever, he couldn't be *that* asshole.

Jake shrugged. "I don't really know what happened, to tell you the truth."

He knew, he just didn't want to get into it. Not here, not now. Not ever again. If he did, he'd have to face the facts: He wasn't good enough, had never been good enough.

"I know you didn't ask for it, but I'm going to give you a piece of advice anyway," continued Jake. "Sometimes it's better to cut your losses and walk away, Brit."

"Is that what you're doing with Melina?" She was sincere this time. Almost apologetic, as if she thought it was a shame they were breaking up before they had really even gotten started.

"Yeah," replied Jake. There was no use denying it. He was

too exhausted. "Come on. It's late, and I'm not leaving you out here alone to become an episode of *Dateline Exclusive*." Jake held out his hand, offering to escort her safely back to her room.

Brit took his hand and let him pull her up out of the chair. "You're a good guy, Jake." She sent him a tired half-smile before unleashing a weary laugh. "For a lawyer."

Was he though? He'd done a lot of horrible things in his life, the least of which was using his niece as a way to end it with Melina. It was wrong, not to mention cowardly, and it was no wonder he had earned a reputation for being a snake. Coiled up in the grass, waiting to strike before slithering away.

Shutting it down and leaving before things got a chance to get real.

He pulled Brit into his side and gave her a friendly squeeze as they headed into the lobby. Even though he didn't feel like laughing, he did.

He guided them to the brushed metal elevators before releasing Brit to push the button. When the doors slid open, Jake came face-to-face with the man from the bar earlier. The textiles guy, that wanted to work with Melina.

Even though the anger and hurt and jealousy began to well up inside him again, Jake nodded to the man as he exited the elevator.

He got a good look at him this time. The man was tall—even taller than Jake—dark, and pretty goddamn good-looking.

He wanted nothing more than to punch the suave son-of-a-bitch in the face, knock out a couple of teeth from his chiseled jaw, but he kept his hands in his pockets as he entered the elevator.

He also ignored the thought the fucker had just come from his and Melina's room.

Doesn't matter now, anyway. It's over.

Jake shoved his emotions down deep. Stuffed them into tiny, dark cells in his mind and locked them up tight. If he was going to be able to move forward, he had to let go first, or at least compartmentalize.

The truth of the matter was it was that guy who could give Melina the opportunity she needed to achieve her dreams, not Jake.

CHAPTER TWENTY-EIGHT

edusa lay in the bed motionless, even though she was awake. She hadn't slept a wink, but she laid there, keeping her eyes closed on purpose. Part of it was to pretend she had indeed slumbered, but mostly it was so the tears wouldn't escape.

Turned out, Medusa was just as fragile as any other being, immortal or not. Also turned out, that wasn't ideal, especially right now.

She hadn't ordered room service last night. Instead, she'd booked a flight home, washed off her makeup, turned off her phone and the lights, and crawled into bed.

What else was she supposed to do? Wait up for him? There was nothing left to say. She was leaving, as soon as she could, so she wouldn't cause any more damage than she already had.

He had come in just after midnight, using the light from his phone to find his way around. She'd thought of saying something when he'd slipped into bed, but he'd turned his back to her.

She'd hoped to feel the warmth of his body curled up against hers when she had woken up this morning, that things weren't completely screwed up. That the hurt in his voice had been a figment of her imagination.

All she felt at the moment was the cold indifference of a mind made up.

She was relieved to hear the shower running. Resigned, she finally opened her eyes and slipped out of bed. Even though she hated it, she knew what needed to come next.

A tear slid down her cheek, and she quickly wiped it away. No, she would not cry anymore. She'd get up and go to the clinic, help out where she could, and then say farewell before leaving with her snakes held high.

It had been fun while it lasted, and now it was time to go. With all he'd taught her about how to be a decent human being, the least she could do was spare him from being abandoned without some form of goodbye.

He'd already experienced enough of that.

The bathroom door swung open just as Medusa contemplated bursting in while he showered and confessing everything. Hot steam billowed out, creating the perfect moment to coax Jake's towel from his hips. She actually thought about it for a second, but he was staring at her with such a tortured look on his face she couldn't bring herself to do it.

"Excuse me," he murmured, gripping the spot where the white hotel towel was tucked in on itself like a vice.

Medusa wanted to shrink into nothing. A part of her felt like screaming while she flipped furniture, but deep down she knew it would do no good. No amount of seduction could bring Jake back from that dark place in his head. She knew it and so did he. He was already long gone, and it was time for her to do the same.

"I really didn't post that picture." She folded her arms, to keep herself from reaching out for him. She'd intended to come here and wreak havoc, and, well, she'd certainly done that. Now it was time to go back to Hell where she belonged.

His back was to her. She looked away when he dropped his towel to get dressed. It seemed the respectful thing to do.

She inhaled deeply, resolved to do what needed to be done. "But you're right. We're trying to make something work when we both know it's going to eventually fall apart. You want someone who won't break your heart again . . . And I can't guarantee I won't. Not in this lifetime, at least."

She forced the words out to shred through the last of the threads she knew were barely holding his tattered heart together.

None of what she'd said was a lie, but it wasn't exactly the truth, either. She was lying by omission. He would never, not in a million years, comprehend the truth—an honest-to-gods monster had fallen in love with him.

The break had to be quick, the cut deep and clean. It was the only way he would be able to heal without another painful scar.

"I've booked a flight back home. I think it's best if I just go at this point," she said.

There was a sharp intake of air, followed by a slow, shaky release he tried to hide.

Gods, did she ever want to go to him.

Gods? Wasn't it their fault she was here right now, having to destroy the man she'd fallen in love with?

No. It was all hers.

Home meant the Underworld. The words would mean something else to Jake, but Medusa didn't want anymore lies leaving her lips. Not even tiny white ones.

"When?" he asked, paying an exorbitant amount of time and attention to buckling his belt.

That was fine. He was allowed.

Medusa stiffened, clenching every muscle in her body. It was the only way she could stop herself from rushing over to him. She wanted to full-on wail, to beg for his forgiveness in the worst way, but there was no other option but to continue to act like she didn't give a shit.

"Tonight. It's the last flight out, so I can still help out at the clinic during the day," she finally answered. "I could snap some selfies with the parents, take a few videos." Medusa's gaze dropped to the hands in her lap. "That's the real reason you asked me to come in the first place, isn't it?"

Jake snapped the clasp on his Rolex shut. He shoved his wallet and one of the two hotel keycards into his back pocket and strode over to the door, reaching for the handle, turning it, but then stopping.

He bent his head slightly as he said, "We both know it's not . . . but it would have never worked between us, Melina. It's better this way."

"Yes," whispered Medusa, letting him believe the lie he was telling himself in order to protect his heart. The one she wanted to protect now, too. "It is."

CHAPTER TWENTY-NINE

The morning at the clinic had been tough, and Medusa had been relieved when the caterers had arrived to set up. She'd grabbed anything that looked good and left to eat her lunch on the beach. Alone.

Good plan, except she'd attracted some rather annoying company.

Gods, Seagulls were nothing more than just better-looking vultures. She had to hand it to them, though. They were quite the enterprising scavengers. They went after their meal with a bravado not many birds possessed—except maybe pigeons, but those numbskulls excelled at shitting all over everything more than anything else.

She threw the rest of her lunch on the sand and let the bastards descend.

Surprisingly, the beach had been empty when she'd come out here to spend her lunch break alone. Now, as she trudged over to a bin to toss the empty container away, she noticed a man walking up from the shoreline, headed straight for her.

There was something about the way he sauntered . . . That swagger seemed familiar . . .

Medusa hurried and shoved her trash into the can so she could grind the heels of her hands into her eye sockets.

Please, for the love of Hades, let this bastard be a figment of my imagination.

She inhaled, blew out a breath, then opened her eyes.

Poseidon stood before her dressed in an off-white linen shirt and khakis rolled up past his ankles.

"Hello, gorgon."

He held a pair of leather sandals in one hand, while the other was casually tucked into a front pocket. To add insult to injury, his curling dark hair had the audacity to accentuate his smug good looks, blowing into a carefree mess in the sea breeze.

If Hades was the brooding black sheep, and Zeus the mighty golden lion, then Poseidon was the slippery rat bastard. He had balls showing up like this—especially here, now—after taking advantage of her in the worst way possible.

If anyone deserved to be turned to stone, it was this evil prick.

Her heart hammered in her chest with equal parts terror and rage. His presence infuriated her, but it also made her feel small.

Stop it. He can't hurt you anymore. You're a monster now.

She willed herself to stand taller, to square her shoulders and keep her gaze trained on him. She was done thinking she was to blame after all these years.

Like she had asked for it.

"Oh joy," she snarled. "What do *you* want?"

"To help you," he said simply.

A cynical laugh rocketed from her throat, her hand begging for permission to slap him across the face. "What is it with you people?"

She fixed an icy glare on him, wishing she could still turn a bitch to solid rock.

He tilted his head slightly, his gaze dropping for an instant. "I also wanted to apologize."

"You? Apologize?" Medusa laughed even harder.

"Look, I know you're far from delighted to see me, gorgon, but you're in a real pickle here. A complicated mess concerning love and morality, am I right?"

Medusa clamped her mouth shut, refusing to answer the ridiculous question. It was rhetorical, and she hated rhetorical. What the hell did he know about love? And did he actually think he was the authority on morality?

Her fist pleaded with her brain to land a punch.

"What if I told you there was a way you can have your cake and eat it, too."

"If you mean lie about the assessment, I've already thought of that. I can't do it. He's not going to the Underworld. He's going to Elysium. My mind is made up."

"Still so pious." Poseidon rolled his eyes. "I thought you'd have shaken that monkey off your back by now. I was talking about something more efficient than lying . . ." He shrugged and began to fade. "But I guess if your mind is made up."

"Wait!" It pained her to say it, but she couldn't resist. She and Jake could never be together, but if there was a way to prevent his untimely death, she had to know.

Poseidon smiled wider than a cat after having just eaten a canary. "Ask the Fates for an extension."

Medusa groaned. Here she thought he'd wanted to actually help her. When was she going to learn not to listen to anything that came out of his mouth?

"I've already thought of that, too. It won't work. You know how they feel about extensions."

"You'll never know if you never try."

As much as she hated to admit it, he had a point. She was sending him to Elysium, she at least had comfort in knowing that, but if she could convince the sisters to extend his time on Earth, she'd feel even better.

She regarded Poseidon carefully before answering. There was always an ulterior motive when it came to the gods. You'd have thought they were the damned monsters.

"I'll give you points for thinking out of the box, but you do know that option is more dangerous than it is feasible, right? Especially for me. I lost my head once, I'm not keen on losing it again. Also," she continued, "I'm not a gullible mortal anymore. What's your angle? How much of the cake would you get?"

His lips curled into a devious grin. "Well, I have to admit, getting Athena's armor tied into a knot by helping you finally find happiness is rather appealing."

Medusa folded her arms, her jaw setting. There it was. Pushing Athena's buttons. It wasn't about helping Medusa at all. She should have known.

"Do you two ever stop fighting?" snapped Medusa, not caring how defiant she sounded. She had no time and zero patience for this shit.

"Not if I can help it," sniffed Poseidon. "Why should she be Zeus's favorite? *I'm* his brother. She's just a spoiled brat."

For Fates' sake. Thousands of years old and he was still acting like a child.

"You mean to tell me I got turned into a monster because you were jealous that Athena is Almighty Douche's favorite?"

"Almighty Douche . . . Is that what you guys call him down there?" Poseidon threw his head back and laughed. "Holy shit, I love that for him."

"I'm glad you're amused." Medusa unfolded her arms in preparation to turn and walk away. Once again, Poseidon was talking out of his ass. Only this time, she wasn't falling for it. "Now, if you'll excuse me. I have more pressing shit to worry about than your cockamamie ideas."

"Can't fault me for trying." He arched a brow at her. "You look good, by the way. You want to get a drink or something, see what happens? I wouldn't mind helping you make that poor mortal bastard jealous."

Medusa curled her lip at him. "You're an absolute piece of shit, you know that?"

"So I've been told." A bottle of wine appeared in his hand —filled with nectar of the gods, no doubt—and he waggled his eyebrows at her as he shook it back and forth.

And that's when her fist slammed into his face.

The blow had enough force to almost knock him off balance. He took a step back, wine bottle vanishing immediately, and pressed on his jaw, testing it out to make sure it still worked.

Medusa prepared herself for the consequences of punching the king of the sea right in the mouth. He laughed, short and incredulous, as he dabbed at his split lip with the back of his hand. "I suppose I deserved that, but wow, I didn't know you had it in you, gorgon."

She glared at him as she first stretched, then shook out her sore knuckles. "There's more where that came from, trust me."

Taking her word for it, Poseidon bowed his head and vanished.

Relieved he was finally gone, Medusa sighed before trudging up the beach. It had felt good to finally unleash on the no-good son-of-a-titan—he deserved every ounce of her wrath and more—and she regretted nothing.

Although the cracks in her heart widened with each step, she forced herself to keep moving. There was no use prolonging the inevitable. It was time. She needed to go say goodbye, so she could get an earlier flight and get her ass back to Los Angeles to tie up loose ends. After that, it was back to the Underworld and possibly a meeting with the Fates.

Vacation was officially over.

CHAPTER THIRTY

The last time Jake had seen Melina, she'd been headed out of the clinic. After their argument, and subsequent break-up, she was doing precisely what he'd done —was doing—which was keeping as much distance between them as possible.

Seeing her this morning, eyes swollen and puffy from crying, even though she'd pretended she hadn't been, filled him with regret. When she'd told him she was leaving, it had taken all he had not to beg for forgiveness.

He considered skipping lunch and going after her. What would be the harm? They were both mature adults. He'd said some pretty hurtful things, but she knew he didn't really mean them. They could remain friends, right? They could both put aside their emotions for one day, couldn't they?

He inhaled deeply. No, they couldn't. He didn't deserve forgiveness. He *knew* calling her selfish would be a low blow. And he'd done it anyway.

Besides, going after her would make him seem desperate, and he was not going down that road. There was a reason he'd relinquished control to Asshole Jake this morning.

Nice Jake had to be stopped. There was no way around

the fact that pretending everything was okay, that it would work itself out in the long run, would lead to nowhere good. If he followed after Melina right now, he'd crack. Nice Jake would beg for her to take him back.

Jesus. He had problems. Big ones. Chief among them was that it was *him* with the split personalities, not Melina.

His thoughts warred with each other inside his brain, the pros so equally matched in strength with the cons their struggle to gain the upper hand made his temples throb.

He found a spot in the small dining area and sat down. After unwrapping his gyro, he took a bite and tried not to gag as he chewed. The spicy roasted meat and the sharp, salty feta paired with tangy tzatziki sauce should have had his tastebuds in heaven.

But his appetite had suddenly vanished, leaving his stomach churning in break-up hell.

His mind insisted on wandering again as he continued to force down his lunch. It was no surprise they headed straight back to Melina.

Going after her would only prolong the inevitable. Stick to his guns, that was what he needed to do. He'd gotten jealous on the first freaking day they'd arrived, for Christ's sake. The first damn time she talked to another man.

His behavior wasn't healthy, it was toxic. The last thing he wanted to do was get caught in that vicious circle again.

As guilty as he felt about it, Jake chucked his half-eaten lunch into the trash. He headed toward the bathroom to go wash his hands, pop a breath mint into his mouth, and prepare for another round of checking on parents waiting for their children to go into the operating room.

He didn't know how Shane did it, performing surgeries from dawn until dusk, for a week straight. The man was a machine. A good guy. And someone who'd probably make a really great brother-in-law.

Jake barely heard the water running, hardly felt it washing

over his hands, but he turned off the faucet and stared at himself in the restroom mirror.

Had Kara been ignoring the obvious? And if she had been, had she been doing it on purpose? A sinking feeling dropped into his stomach when he realized he'd never really stopped thinking about himself long enough to consider it.

He scrubbed a hand over his face, through his hair. That would be just like her. If he couldn't find love, then his twin wouldn't either, on principle, like sympathy pains or something.

A wave of regret crashed over him as he dried his hands. Instead of a mint, he took his phone from his pocket. It rang once before he remembered the time difference and ended the call. He set the ringer to vibrate and slipped his phone back into his pocket.

The next thing he knew, he was standing outside the restroom. Just standing there and staring. Thinking. About going out and finding Melina, telling her . . .

Damn. He needed to get it together. If he didn't, and soon, he might end up making a rash decision, one that could only end terribly.

He scanned the clinic, deciding the best way to reign in his thoughts was to banish them into solitary confinement and ignore them. There were quite a few parents waiting today. He owned it to them to stay out of his head, so he could focus on doing what he came here to do.

He was intent on doing just that, when, out of the corner of his eye, he saw Melina walk in through the front door. His heart pounded in his chest at the sight of her.

She looked flushed, and a bit bothered. His brows furrowed, and that merciless tumbling in his gut started again. The urge to go to her, ask her if anything was wrong, was overwhelming.

She's fine, dip shit. Keep it together. Play it cool.

Jake kept glancing at her while she talked to some of the

parents, calming their fears with kind and comforting words, like she had done with Hailey.

Sorrow stabbed at his heart. Hailey was going to be devastated when Medusa no longer came around.

Why had fate been so cruel? Sending Melina crashing into his world if he couldn't be with her? If he'd known he was going to end up here again, he would have never gone to that damn launch party. Unrequited love was a different brand of pain and suffering, but it was right up there with being cheated on.

The worst part is that he'd done this to himself. He *had* known there was a chance things would lead to exactly this, and he'd still decided to stay that night.

She went over to the area where they kept the bags filled with post-surgery gifts like homemade pillows, stuffed animals, and tubes of medical grade anti-bacterial and scar-reducing creams. He was halfway over to her before his brain caught on to where his feet were taking him.

His heart had never ached like this before. He wanted to be with her, in the worst way, but the timing was off. If he asked her to stay it would be a mistake. She would grow restless, and then eventually, resent him for wasting her youth on him.

Those were the cold, hard facts, and his heart could not be trusted in this particular case. He needed to keep counsel with his head. The big one.

So then why was he digging himself a bigger hole right now?

"Hey." He stuffed his hands into his pockets, insurance he wouldn't reach out and touch her. Tell her he'd made a mistake. "Are you all right?"

"Of course. Why?" she replied.

A lie, and he knew it. Could *feel* it.

Maybe there's a chance she does love you back.

"I don't know. You just look upset." His gaze dropped to

her hand, to where her knuckles were red and swollen, and his stomach flew into his throat.

"What happened? Did that textiles guy say something to you?" His hands came out of his pockets, and he leaned on the table so he could get a better look at her face. "Did he try anything funny?"

They might no longer be a thing, but he would find that son of a bitch and rip him apart if he'd so much as hurt a single hair on her head.

She stopped fiddling with the bags and took a deep breath. "No, he didn't do anything. I'm fine."

"Are you sure?" *I'm in love with you, Melina. Give me a sign you love me, too, and I'll try to make us work.*

It was Nice Jake talking, he knew, but he was safe as long as he didn't say those things out loud.

He watched as she resumed arranging the bags, handling each one a bit more aggressively. It must have made her mad, possibly creeped out, because she stopped all together and turned to him.

"Look. We had fun while it lasted. Yeah, I like you . . ." Her gaze darted to the side. "But what do you want me to do? Beg you to stick around until one of us gets bored?"

Well, then. If that wasn't an iron-clad argument.

And a proverbial punch to the gut.

"Fair enough." He stepped back, putting his hands up and hoping his voice wouldn't crack even though his heart had just landed on the floor. "Just wanted to make sure you're okay."

"I am." She smiled, and to his horror, it seemed genuine. More than that, even. It seemed patronizing.

Final.

"I'm going to go back to the resort and pack. If I don't see you before . . . " She stopped herself. They both knew she'd be gone by the time he got back to the hotel. "Goodbye, Jake."

Jake nodded. "Okay. Have a safe flight."

It was childish and insensitive and the wrong thing to say, but he couldn't bring himself to say that word—goodbye—out loud.

She was right. He'd found the loophole and had walked through. They both had. Now it was time to close the door. All the way. She was in agreement it was for the best.

What more of a sign did he need?

CHAPTER THIRTY-ONE

I'm sorry! I'm sorry! I'm sorry!

Those were the two words Medusa said over and over in her mind as she'd watched Jake walk away. She had wanted to scream, hide, run—tear this gods-forsaken world apart—all those things, but she couldn't, so she had stayed calm, had pretended he didn't matter, because there would have been no use causing a scene.

What would it have changed?

It would have changed nothing, certainly not her fate or his, so she'd opted to let Jake keep walking. Forcing herself to act as though she hadn't been dying inside as she left the clinic and headed back to the hotel had been the worst thing she'd had to endure in centuries.

She still had the puffy, red eyes and frigging awful migraine to prove it.

"Beverage?" asked a flight attendant.

"No thanks," she replied softly.

The woman offered her a sympathetic smile, whispering, "They didn't deserve you anyway, honey," before moving on to the rows further back.

Medusa squeezed her eyes shut, so a fresh round of tears

wouldn't fall. The woman had meant well, but she'd gotten it backwards.

Medusa inhaled several deep breaths while repeating a new mantra to herself. *Don't cry. Don't cry. Don't cry.*

Waterworks crisis averted, she bent down to dig through her carry-on for her ear buds. Hopefully, she would fall asleep for the majority of the flight. Damn. She was really feeling it if she didn't even want a drink. She hadn't even booked first-class.

As she rummaged through her bag, she noticed a pair of expensive leather shoes walk down the aisle. When they stopped beside her, she looked up.

"Scoot over, will you?" said Hermes.

Medusa sighed but unbuckled the lap belt and slid into the window seat. She wasn't particularly glad to see him, but she wasn't unhappy about it, either. She supposed she could use the company right now.

"You got more bad news or something?" she asked as he settled himself into the seat next to her.

"Nah. Just checking on you." He elbowed her in the arm. "I know it's been a rotten couple of days."

"You can say that again. So much for a nice, relaxing end to my vacation."

"Everything happens for a reason."

"Good Lord. I thought you were the god of bad puns, not clichés."

"The good Lord ain't got nothing to do with it, sister. I come up with my own material. In fact, it's copyrighted."

"Not the clichés, though, because they're public domain," snorted Medusa, a giggle escaping. "You're so extra, you know that?"

"Oh, I know, but I made you laugh, didn't I?"

"I guess you did."

"Now, as I was saying . . . everything happens for a reason. Trust me on this, it will all work out in the end."

"And everything happens for a reason? Things like your boss forcing you to come back to work early because he's impatient, and fate cutting short the only thing that's made you happy in a couple millennia? You mean those things?"

He lifted an arm toward her. "You need a hug, don't you?"

"Nope," she said, turning to stare out the window. "What I need is my heart of stone back," she muttered under her breath.

"Come on, now." Hermes dropped his arm and leaned his head on the back of the seat, directing his gaze out toward the clouds. "Don't think like that. You learned some pretty important things about yourself, stuff you would have never known had you not gone on this vacation. The biggest being that you *are* capable, of loving and being loved. You also learned that heart of yours isn't as hard as you think it is. You did the right thing."

Medusa turned to look at him, the friend that had been under her nose the whole time, but she'd been too angry and closed-off to notice.

"Did I? I always knew I'd have to go back to the Underworld. So why didn't I just leave him alone? Why didn't I just make the assessment and move on. I was there to have fun, not to . . ." Her gaze dropped as she trailed off.

"What? Fall in love?" asked Hermes.

Medusa nodded, tears springing into her eyes again.

"Well, I'm here to tell you no one can help falling in love, or stop it, for that matter. I'm besties with a guy who has it on good authority, you know, and he'll back me up on that."

"Yeah?" said Medusa. "Then why hasn't the matchmaker hooked *you* up yet?"

"Because I'm a thief, girl. I steal the hearts, not the other way around."

Medusa rolled her eyes, but she was thankful she had the god of thieves to pry open her heart with laughter, then rob it of the sadness that hardened it.

For the duration of the flight, at least.

Three hours and twenty-seven minutes.

That's how long Jake lasted without her, and it had been three hours and twenty-seven minutes too long.

He'd known, from the second he'd put one foot in front of the other and walked away it had been a mistake.

He couldn't do it. Could not let her go.

Because he loved her.

He loved her, and he'd run after her, to the ends of the Earth and back, because he couldn't live with himself if he didn't at least try to make it work.

"Would you like a beverage, sir?" the flight attendant asked.

"No thank you," he replied before turning to look out the window and into the darkness.

He'd been lucky to get the last flight out of Athens, and when he landed in L.A., he was going to find her. He was going to find Melina and he was going to tell her how much he needed her.

CHAPTER THIRTY-TWO

Medusa had barely gotten through the door before Dylan crashed into her, hugging her so hard she had to drop her bags and pull her off before the girl choked her to death.

"Oh, Melina, I was so worried. I called and called, but it just kept going into voicemail and, holy shit, I'm so glad you weren't on that flight!"

"Dylan, slow down," said Medusa, grasping her shoulders to stop her from latching on again. "What are you talking about?"

"You didn't hear? An airliner en route from Greece to Los Angeles went down earlier this morning. I thought you were on it!"

Bile rose in Medusa's throat. It must have been the last flight out of Athens, the one she was supposed to be on before she'd switched to an earlier departure. Not that it would have mattered for her, but for the others onboard . . .

Her heart fell. All those human lives lost. What an absolute tragedy.

"I switched to an earlier flight last minute," she said, a wave of nausea roiling her belly. "I should have called . . . I'm sorry I didn't let you know I got an earlier flight, Dylan. I should have turned my phone back on when I land—"

Dylan pounced on her again, but this time Medusa hugged her back. After 30 seconds of hugging it out, which was about 29 seconds too long, Medusa patted her on the back.

"Okay. I'm safe and sound, alright?" She pulled out of Dylan's embrace. It had felt good, but baby steps. "And I have something I need to discuss with you, sooner rather than later."

Dylan gnawed on her lip. "I'm sorry about the Instagram post. I honestly don't know what happened, but I promise I didn't do it on purpose."

Medusa had plenty of time on the 16-hour flight to decide how to handle the situation. In the end, she'd decided that Hermes had probably orchestrated it, at the behest of the Fates, in order to speed things up.

He hadn't brought it up, and she hadn't asked.

"I know you didn't, and it's fine. I just came from Kara's apartment. Hailey knows it was a misunderstanding, and that neither of us would intentionally do anything to hurt her."

Medusa had wanted to apologize to Hailey in-person, and let Kara know about her and Jake. She had also wanted to see them both one last time.

"That's not what I wanted to talk to you about, though," continued Medusa. "I'm giving you Snake Head."

Dylan's eyes went wide. "Wait. Did you just say what I think you said?

"Yes. I'm giving you Snake Head. Is there an issue?"

"No, no. It's just that you've worked so hard to get it off the ground," replied Dylan. "Why would you just give it to me?"

"I didn't do the work, you did," said Medusa. "All I did was bark orders and act like a royal bitch."

"Not the whole time . . ." said Dylan, her cheeks pinking up.

Dylan wasn't just an assistant, she was a friend, and Medusa appreciated all she had done for her, more than she would ever know. She'd miss this hard-working, kind-hearted mortal terribly.

"There's another reason," confessed Medusa. "Jake and I broke up."

Dylan's mouth dropped open. "Shut up. You guys seemed so happy. What happened?"

"The timing wasn't right. But it's okay." Medusa gestured around the room, at the high ceilings, breathtaking view, and expensive furniture. "I'm tired of obsessing over this . . . stuff. It's exhausting. I'm giving you Snake Head because I know it's your passion. Creating beautiful things is your end game, not fame or fortune. Take it in whatever direction you want. I know you'll do great."

Dylan hugged her, again, and this time Medusa leaned into it. "Thank you," she whispered. "For seeing past what's on the outside and looking inside and seeing the real me."

Without meaning to, Medusa stiffened when a man in boxers sauntered into the kitchen

"I can explain," whispered Dylan.

"Morning ladies," said Derrek, Medusa's former boy toy.

Medusa released Dylan, her mouth dropping open playfully. That's how she'd meant it, at least, but Dylan's expression was still wide-eyed and stricken when Derrek came up from behind and wrapped an arm around her.

He kissed her shoulder. "You want some breakfast, babe? I'll make waffles."

Dylan nodded, and he rested his chin on the top of her head while giving her another hug. "Oh hey, Medusa. Still take your coffee iced?"

"Um . . . yes?" replied Medusa, feeling a bit awkward.

After how she'd treated him, it seemed as though the man wasn't holding a grudge.

"M'kay. I'll make you one."

"Thank you, Derrek."

Medusa had gotten mortals being useless meat bags wrong. They were so much more, capable of the things her hardened heart had forgotten. Sympathy. Kindness. Humility.

Forgiveness.

Medusa cocked her head and lifted a brow at Dylan after Derrek headed over to the fancy coffee machine.

"I . . . We . . ." struggled Dylan. "You didn't seem to be into him . . . He was so upset and the more we talked, well, it just kind of happened."

Derrek had found someone better. Someone who appreciated all he had to offer, and Medusa was truly happy.

"It does just kind of happen, doesn't it?" she said, thinking of Jake. "No harm, no foul."

Dylan sighed with relief. "I thought you were going to be pissed."

Medusa had to laugh at the irony. In fact, she almost cackled hysterically. Oh, how far she'd come. How much she'd learned from these mortals.

Her vacation had indeed been epic.

"I know I'm a self-centered monster, but I'm not *that* selfish."

"I'd say you're not selfish at all," replied Dylan. "You just gave me your brand."

"And my house."

Dylan shook her head. "No. No, I'm not taking your house, too."

"Oh, yes you are. I don't need it. I'm going back home for a while."

More like forever.

"You'll come back, though, right? To visit?" asked Dylan,

hoisting some of the bags onto her person and heading toward Medusa's bedroom.

"Perhaps," said Medusa, picking up the rest of her bags. "If I'm desperate for a vacation."

Medusa extended the handle of her suitcase, no less than three bags in the crook of her arm and several more hooked around her shoulders.

"Are you sure you don't want us to drive you to the airport?" asked Dylan as she gave Medusa one last hug.

"I'm sure," she replied, returning Dylan's embrace as best as she could. How she was going to fit all this luggage into the trunk, she hadn't a clue. "My Uber is already waiting outside."

Dylan and Derrek followed Medusa as she wheeled her suitcase down the drive. "Guys. Stop. It's not like you'll never . . ." Her words trailed off because she didn't want another lie to come out of her mouth.

They probably wouldn't ever see her again. If Jake wasn't on this earth, she highly doubted she'd ever come back.

"Well, you're going to be too busy building your fashion empire to think about me, okay?"

The driver got out of the car to help Medusa with her bags, and she chuckled when she saw it was Hermes. Of course, it was Hermes, and of course he'd insisted on picking her up in an Uber because he thought it would be hilarious.

She'd humored him this time.

In fact, she'd actually thought it had been a brilliant idea. There was no way she could carry all her crap into the Underworld herself. She'd have her hands full with the staggering amount of emotional baggage alone.

"Damn, girl," commented Hermes under his breath as he loaded bag after bag into the opened trunk.

"Make it work, messenger," Medusa said through a smile as she opened the door and climbed into the back of the car.

A manila folder lay on the backseat next to her, a pen neatly placed on top. She picked it up, inhaling deeply as she clicked open the pen.

She had just finished signing the Final Assessment form when Hermes slipped behind the wheel and shifted the vehicle into gear.

"Ready?"

Medusa sighed.

"No, but I guess I'll just have to deal with it." She smiled and waved at her friends one last time as the car drove away. "I can't believe I'm actually going to miss this place."

CHAPTER THIRTY-THREE

The elevator doors opened, and this time, when the brilliant rays of Olympus flooded the rickety contraption, Medusa didn't flinch. Go figure. She'd finally gotten used to hanging out in the light.

The girls were none too pleased, however.

She inhaled the crisp mountain air before slithering her way across the flagstone, past the dry cleaner and the hair salon, the gym and the cafe where minor deities sat and drank coffee, thin wisps of smoke curling from their cigarettes as though they were at a Parisian street cafe.

Her snakes hissed in disapproval, but her thin lips tipped up into a smile. Let Olympus go about their business of pretty much doing nothing, the anger and indignation she once felt, constantly using her self-worth as a punching bag, was no longer there. She'd adopted a new attitude since returning to Hades Realm. Live and let live. Let go of things that no longer make you happy.

Also? Looks weren't everything. The girls would come around eventually. Besides, she wasn't there to scrutinized how the other half spent their days. She was on a mission.

The heavy gilded door swung open as Medusa climbed the

steps, and a goddess dressed in gleaming armor stepped through the door.

Medusa's heart nearly leaped out of her chest when their eyes met. She began to sway like a cobra, her snakes standing on end and following suit. She swallowed hard, discovering that not giving in to her urge to hiss made the back of her throat ache something fierce.

Likewise, Athena stopped in her tracks, fixing a pale, narrow-eyed glare on Medusa and gripping her spear so tightly her knuckles went white.

"What are you doing here, gorgon?" said Athena. "Shouldn't you be down with the other monsters where you belong?"

The pressure in Medusa's clenched jaw grew, and she could feel her razor-sharp nails puncturing through the rapidly crumpling manila folder she held in her hand. When they bit through the paper and into her palm, she inhaled, telling herself to relax. She needed that paperwork intact. It was the whole reason she was up here in the first place.

"Hello, Athena," said Medusa, straightening up from the crouching—fighting—position she'd automatically assumed. "Beautiful day, isn't it? Nice armor. Did Hephaestus make it for you? It's gorgeous."

Athena touched her helmet, her mouth dropping open but no words coming out. It was obvious she was shocked Medusa had, one, actually had the nerve to respond, and two, did so in such a complimentary manner.

It was a move she never saw coming, and it had disarmed her.

"Thank you." Athena looked down at her breast plate before lifting her elbow so she could also inspect her shield. "The blacksmith's work is top-notch."

Medusa leaned in to take a look, and Athena let her . . . Until she didn't.

"Why was it you said you were here?" said Athena, suspiciously, which was better than aggressively, but it still made the scales on the back of Medusa's neck rise.

Athena wasn't known for her ability to let bygones be bygones.

"I have a meeting with Eros." Medusa held up the folder but didn't explain beyond that. She may be ready to bury the hatchet, but she didn't exactly want to stand here and have a conversation about it. "Not to be rude or anything, but I need to go or else I'm going to be late."

Athena's head jerked back. "Oh." She lifted her chin. "Well, I must be going as well." A hard edge crept back into her voice. "Now, if you'll excuse me."

They stared at each other for a moment, an understanding passing between them. Athena was trying to hold on to control over Medusa, but there was nothing there to wrangle back. Athena could go on with her miserable pissing contest to prove who was right and who had been wrong. Medusa wasn't playing that game anymore.

"Cool." Medusa tapped Athena's arm with the folder, hardly believing what she had just done. "Have a great day, then."

Athena looked down at her arm, gob smacked. Medusa didn't wait around, and she grinned when a shocked gasp from the goddess of mind games came from behind her as she made her way into Life Industries.

The psychological warfare between them had finally been won, and not by Athena.

Medusa's sigh of relief at not having been pierced through the spine by the goddess's spear as she slipped through the doors came out in a long huff. After smoothing down her still wriggling snakes, she headed for Leto's desk.

"Medusa, darling. It's so nice to see you. How was your vacation?"

"It was great." Yeah, at the beginning. Not so much toward the end. "Thanks for asking."

Leto picked up the phone, fishing for more details as she dialed. "Anything interesting happen?"

Medusa almost laughed out loud. Only that she'd grown fond of the people who'd taught her not to judge a book by its cover, and that she'd actually fallen in love with one of them.

Oh, and she'd ended up having to let fate run its course, and now she was back in Hell.

"Good morning, Eros," Leto murmured into the phone. "Medusa is here. Shall I send her back?" Leto took a sip of coffee while she waited for the answer. Nodding, she replied, "Very good. I'll get her signed in."

Medusa took the visitor's badge Leto handed to her and clipped it to the black sweater she was wearing. She'd been excited to put it on this morning, knowing she'd need it to ward off the chill from the bracing mountain air. She didn't get to wear cute sweaters down in the Underworld, on account of the heat.

"Ooh, I love your sweater. Where did you get it?"

"I know, right? I brought it back with me from Los Angeles."

Who was she right now?

A changed gorgon, that was who. Less angry at the world. Less caught up with what she looked like on the outside because she'd learned it was what was on the inside that showed who you really were.

A gorgon who was finally comfortable in her own monstrous skin.

Even though she didn't have to Leto got up and motioned for Medusa to follow her. "Come with me, darling. I'll show you to the Hall's entrance. From there you can just walk on through to Eros's office. Their names are on the doors. They're in alphabetical order."

"It's a flower shop, right?"

"That's right, you've been here before. Oh, good gods, my memory is getting worse. Can I conjure you a water?"

Medusa shook her head, and Leto continued with her random acts of chatter as they walked down a carpeted corridor lined on either side with enormous white marble statues of the Olympians.

Medusa lifted a brow at the thirteenth one, which stood apart from the others not only physically, but because it was made of black marble. A strong and brooding god driving a chariot drawn by four wild and dangerous-looking horses.

So, they hadn't forgotten about Hades, after all.

When they came to two Spartan guards standing stoically on either side of an enormous arched entrance, Leto stopped and showed them the work badge she'd pulled from the pocket of her skirt.

"All set, darling. Just drop off your visitor's pass when you leave."

Medusa nodded her thanks as she entered the Hall and headed toward the door that looked like the outside of a flower shop.

As she did, she heard Leto ask one of the guards, *"So, Leonidas, you're still single, right? Have you met my daughter Artemis?"*

Medusa tapped lightly on the glass door. Normally she would barge right in, hissing and growling like she had something to prove, but she was a changed gorgon.

Also, considering she needed to get the Emergency Match Request tucked inside the mangled folder in her hand approved, she decided proper office etiquette might be the better option.

Her stomached dipped when Eros waved her in, and her breathing went a bit shallow. Well, she'd be gods-damned. She was nervous.

Don't insult him. Don't insult him. Don't insult him.

"Hello, matchmaker."

"Hey, Medusa. Back already? How did that illusion of beauty hold up?"

Be cool. Be cool. Be cool.

"It held up great."

"What have you got there?" asked Eros.

"I filled out an Emergency Match Request," she replied.

"Oh? For whom?"

"Karalynn Judith Sullivan and Shane Robert Williams. No disrespect, but I think they may have fallen through the cracks and I'd like to see to it that they be matched immediately."

"What makes you say they've fallen through the cracks?"

Eros's expression was one of immense concern as he wheeled his chair over to a credenza and opened one of the drawers. He hoisted the thickest binder Medusa had ever laid eyes on out of the filing cabinet and dragged it over to his desk.

"It's kind of a long story," she began, "and they might be on your list for a match down the road, but I kind of need them together now."

"What do you mean *you* need them together now?"

He dropped the binder onto the top of his desk with a *thud*. Not maliciously, or because he was mad, but because, by the looks of it, the sucker was *heavy*.

"Okay. So, you know the job I was down there for? It was an assessment of this guy named Jake Sullivan."

"An assessment?" Eros flipped through the pages of the binder. "S . . . S . . . Where are the S's."

"Hades and Zeus were fighting—"

Eros snorted. "You don't say."

"Right?" Medusa rolled her eyes. "Anyway, they were fighting about whether he belonged up here or down there. I was sent to assess his soul, which I did.

"Is this where the story gets juicy? Like, it turns into a love story. Because I'm a romantic, you know."

Medusa pressed her lips shut. She didn't know how to respond, except maybe that she better set the record straight.

"I guess, but it's not *my* love story," she explained. "It's Kara and Shane's. They're on your list, right?"

Medusa leaned in, hoping to get a glimpse of the names in Cupid's binder.

Too bad the M's were nowhere near the S's.

"Ah, here we go. Sullivan, Karalynn," said Eros. "Looks like they are scheduled for a match, but not for another ten years."

"Ten years is too late. They need to be together now. Kara and Hailey are going to need someone after Jake is gone, or else Kara will fall apart . . ." Medusa twisted the end of a snake around a finger and tugged. "And Hailey will be even more scarred." The snake hissed, forcing her to focus enough to shove the tattered folder toward him. "Here's the EMR."

Eros took it. When he opened the folder, he held up the sheet of paper and stared at her through five ragged slashes.

"What in a satyr's hairy ass happened here?"

"Another long story. Here's the deal. I kind of grew attached to . . ."

Eros, who was all ears, tilted his head.

"The whole lot of them."

"Not just this Jake guy, then?"

Medusa's lips stretched into a tight smile. Hades' wrath, could she be any more obvious?

"No."

"Gotcha." Eros set the paperwork aside and consulted his list once more. "Who did you say Kara's match was again?"

"Shane Williams."

Eros flipped the pages backward. "Mm hm."

"And you need them together because her twin, Jake, the mortal man who you are *not* in love with," Eros's gaze flicked up at her, "his life is ending soon?"

Medusa nodded, keeping her mouth shut while Eros refocused on flipping through the pages again until he came to what he was looking for.

When his eyebrow slid up, so did one corner of his mouth. "You're right. Looks like a match is in order much sooner. I'll get on that ASAP."

CHAPTER THIRTY-FOUR

edusa stuck a mug under the spout of the office coffee machine. She was surprised the ancient piece of junk still worked, to tell the truth. She was used to the one she'd had in L.A., which had done practically everything except pick up her dry-cleaning.

Oh, what she wouldn't give for one of those frosty coffee concoctions right now. There were tons of processed sugar and plenty of sin to gorge one's self on down here, but ice cubes? Not so much.

Speaking of something she missed, what was Jake Sullivan doing right now? She wondered if he was on Olympus already, running around Elysium happy as a harpy tearing out eyeballs, or if he was still on Earth, grappling with their break-up.

She hoped it would be quick and painless whenever the Fates cashed in his chips.

Medusa almost felt bad for also hoping that it would be sooner rather than later. She could hardly wait for him to go to Elysium. He wouldn't remember much if anything about his time on Earth, which, thankfully, was the deal. He'd remember he was a good person, as far as mortals went, and that was exactly what she wanted for him.

If people remembered every detail of their bad sides, and what their basest human instincts, like jealousy and anger and fear, had made them do in life, they'd never be able to enjoy their ideal form of paradise.

Now, if she would have actually gone through with it and lied about Jake belonging down here, she would have had him with her forever, sure, but he would have remembered every bad thing he'd ever done. It was essential for the eternal damnation and never-ending torture of living in the Underworld.

Jake remembering the unsavory parts of his life wouldn't have presented a problem, necessarily, but the thing was, in addition to remembering being an asshole to others, he'd remember every horrible thing that had been done to *him*.

And that was the part Medusa couldn't have lived the rest of her immortal life knowing; he would remember how she'd been no better than the rest of the manipulative monsters he'd known when he was alive.

Catching feelings and actually caring what Jake Sullivan thought had not been part of the original plan. She'd hoped to bring a mortal back with her from vacation, so it could do her bidding, but somewhere along the way, she'd realized how wrong . . .

"Have to press START button."

The deep, gravelly voice made Medusa jump. Her surroundings snapped into focus, and, sure enough, the READY light was blinking.

Yep. The machine was ready. Just like her. Ready as she would ever be to get back to her lonely life in Hell.

She pressed the START button. "Hey, Clops." She leaned against the granite countertop while she waited for her coffee. "How's it going?"

"Clops still cause madness and mayhem. How Medusa vacation?"

"It was nice. Just what I needed."

"That good." He leaned back to examine her more closely, the skin around his one brow-less eye raising. "You different. Not so angry."

Medusa chuckled. That was an understatement of the century, now wasn't it?

"Is that so? Well, you can rest assured knowing I am still a monster. In fact, I'll probably rip someone's head off before the end of the day."

Clops took a sip of his coffee, then selected a lady's finger from the pastry box sitting on the counter and took a bite.

"Mmm. Hear that crunch? Nothing better than fresh lady finger with Clops's wakey juice." He grunted. "Mmm. You meet new guy yet?"

"What new guy?" She blew on her coffee. Hades hadn't said anything about hiring anyone, or having to train someone on her first day back. "From what circle? Six or seven?"

"Clops don't know. Demon nobody heard of named Lakobus. Real nasty, so maybe ninth? Boss man create new position for him." Clops popped the last of the severed finger into his mouth. "Anyway. Good to have Medusa back."

"Thanks. Later, Clops," said Medusa, turning right as she headed out of the break room. She couldn't honestly say it was good to be back, but it was definitely time to get caught up on everything she'd missed while she was out. Apparently, it was a lot.

So much for coming back refreshed.

Medusa made her way to Hades' throne room. When she arrived, she saw a pair of leathery wings draped over the old bone chair she always sat in. She was just about to give the new guy hell for sitting in her chair when Hades looked up.

"Ah, there she is! Medusa, our very own Head Monster."

Hades held out an arm toward her, welcoming her back to Hell. The new demon shifted, his wings rasping along the back of the chair as he turned.

Hades went on. "I'd like you to meet the Underworld's new Assess—"

Medusa dropped her coffee, the mug shattering on the stone. The new guy's eyes. Even though they were glowing like two pools of radium, she wouldn't have mistaken them for anyone else's. Ever.

They were Jake's.

Medusa's scaly hackles raised, a scream clawing its way up her throat. "What's he doing here?"

Hades stood, raising his hands defensively. "Before you rip my head off, I scrubbed the emotional stuff from his hard drive." He turned both palms up and shrugged. "Well, Mnemosyne did, but he should have no recollection of—"

"What is he doing here, Hades?" she asked through gritted teeth, to prevent herself from screaming the question at him.

So the Fates *had* wanted her back in the Underworld for a reason.

She swallowed hard, appreciating not being on Earth when they'd taken him from it, or even standing next to him. But why was he *here*, not on Olympus or in Elysium where he should be?

On the surface, it looked like the perfect opportunity to start over, so they could be together forever. Yes, under any other circumstances it seemed like a dream come true for a cursed gorgon who had accidentally gone and fallen in love with a mortal.

But deep down, Medusa knew it would only be a nightmare, even if Hades had taken it upon himself to have his memories of what she'd done wiped clear. *She* would still remember. Seeing Jake every day for an eternity, knowing full well how much pain she'd caused him, would be torture.

A curse worse than the one she already had.

More simple than that, she'd wanted Jake to be carefree and happy, to feel the comfort and security that comes with being blissfully ignorant thinking he'd been loved beyond words in his human life, by everyone. Even Judy.

The trade-off to make that happen had been to live the rest of her life without him, and she paid for his ticket to Elysium by setting aside her own wants and needs. By sacrificing her happiness for his.

And she'd do it again in a heartbeat.

"I know you said he belonged elsewhere . . ." Hades hesitated, his face softening. "But I thought we could use him down here. He was a damn good lawyer, you know . . ." Hades grinned. "I guess I should say *damned* now, eh?"

Hades arched his brows in jest. He was trying to lighten the mood, but Medusa was having none of it. There was nothing funny about Jake being a demon, not in her snake eyes.

"You should have discussed it with me first," said Medusa, folding her arms. Not to be petulant, but to press on her ribs, in order to keep her heart from busting through them.

Jake—she couldn't get on board with this Lakobus nonsense—stood up, adjusting his skull-shaped cufflinks. "Are you suggesting I can't handle my new role as Assessor of Souls?" He lifted his chin, spread his black wings, and flapped them once.

"Yes," said Medusa, directing a hard look at Hades.

"No," Hades said at the same time.

Medusa switched her gaze to Jake. "What I'm saying is you don't belong here," she said, cold as ice, before fixing a chilly glare on Hades again. "I told you that."

"I'm sorry, Duce, but we needed a permanent Assessor. You know Zeus is going to keep pulling his crap. I thought giving Lakobus, here, the job would make you happy because, you know, it would be a win-win."

Medusa looked at Jake. His features, though reminiscent of the man she once knew, were now contorted into a demonic version of the old Jake. The good Jake. Her Jake.

Horns growing out of one's forehead tended to do that to a person.

She shuttered, but not because his appearance scared her, or she found him any less attractive. It was because it was all wrong.

"Undo it," said Medusa.

"Can't." replied Hades. "Besides, we're going to need him. Pretty sure Zeus would have used him against us if I hadn't stepped in and snatched him away."

"And I'm happy to be of service, sir," cut in Jake. "Despite this lukewarm reception from your Head Monster."

Medusa wanted to howl with rage. This guy wasn't Jake. He possessed none of what had made him good. This demon displayed only the unappealing qualities, which made him— it—a shadow of the former man it'd been.

Sense of humor? Gone. Compassion? Gone. Jake's loving, protective, beautifully flawed human nature? That was gone, too. It seemed all that was left was arrogance and entitlement.

Hades addressed Medusa with finality. "It's done. So please just accept it and give our new Assessor of Souls an extra warm welcome, all right?"

Medusa's blood ran cold when Jake peered at her, his eyes narrowing as he looked her up and down. He seemed to be hitting the ground running in his new role as Assessor of Souls. Or was he on the verge of remembering something?

Medusa tilted her head at Hades.

"Don't worry," he assured her again. "He's got a brand-new lease on life and he's going to do a great job in his role down here, aren't you Lakobus?"

"Yes, sir."

Medusa didn't know why she was even arguing. It was out of her hands now. She'd tried to do the right thing, but Hades was right. What was done was done.

Or was it?

Hades' heart had been in the right place, and she appreciated the chance to start over with Jake, but she wasn't even going to try. It wouldn't be the same. The demon standing in front of her was no longer the man she'd fallen in love with, and she didn't have the power to change his fate.

Unless, of course, she managed to get him transferred.

CHAPTER THIRTY-FIVE

*O*ther than the fact that she was absolutely hideous, which, to a fellow abomination like himself was rather attractive, there was something very familiar about this monster.

She was the infamous gorgon of myth, Medusa, but it wasn't that. There was something else dancing around the edges of his memory.

A strange fluttering took flight in his chest when he surmised that, yes, something must have gone down between them. It felt like perhaps it had been romantic, but whatever it had been, it didn't matter.

He had one goal, and he wasn't going to let emotions—feelings he couldn't even remember—get in the way of his climb up the ladder down here.

"I appreciate your concern regarding my past, Medusa," he began, "but I assure you, my former self will not hinder my performance." Lakobus held out his hand. "Despite getting off on the wrong foot, it's a pleasure to meet you."

A zap of electricity passed between them when she begrudgingly shook his pro-offered hand, making him suddenly unsure of anything he'd just said.

Medusa jerked her hand from his grasp, as if she'd just touched a cute and cuddly puppy.

If he'd had an eyebrow, it would have been arched. "Is there something wrong?"

"No," replied Medusa curtly. Her eyes softened for a split second before dismissing the moment they'd just had with a scathing sneer.

And there *had* been a moment, Lakobus was sure of it. He swallowed hard. Shit. Maybe this weirdness between them *would* get in the way.

Hades cleared his throat. "Why don't you two get further acquainted by grabbing lunch together?"

Medusa glared at Hades. "We've already got one match-maker in this pantheon, thanks."

Lakobus glanced at Medusa just in time to catch her lip curl. She looked like she wanted to smack Hades upside the head, but she opted for a safer option—an eye roll.

His gaze cut to Hades so he wouldn't miss the big guy's reaction. Hades only pursed his lips and took her insubordination on the chin.

Damn. This monster had some serious clout down here.

Vicious. Rude. Giant chip on her shoulder. *Powerful.* Everything he could ever hope for in an opponent.

Lakobus had been skeptical he could learn much more about having less scruples when Hades had informed him that, along with assessing souls, doing Medusa's bidding was included in his job description.

If she was as ruthless as she seemed, Lakobus would have zero problem working under her. He would have no qualms exacting whatever kind of punishment she ordered, warranted or not. His end goal was to take the Underworld by storm, and to do that, he needed to align himself with the right people—schmooze the ones with influence.

And Medusa definitely had that.

According to the video he'd watched during his Welcome

to Hades' Realm orientation, although he could recall every shady deal he'd ever made, every unscrupulous thing he'd ever done, he didn't remember much about his personal relationships. Other than some basic knowledge that he'd been one of two children to a pair of deplorable parents, they were gone forever, so there was no point in remembering.

He cocked his head and tried calling up some memories, just for funsies, but it was no use. He recalled being an entertainment lawyer living in L.A. and that he'd recently handed over a couple of coins to a gaunt fellow in a boat, but that was about it. He barely even remembered the ride over.

All he knew was he'd woken up a few days ago a full-on demon. The whole nine yards, with jagged fangs and leathery wings and everything.

"Fine," said Hades. "Why don't you just show him around then, hmm? Can you at least do that?"

"No," said Medusa.

Hades rubbed his forehead. "Come on, Duce." He stopped to wave a hand at her. "I was trying to do you a solid. Work with me here."

"I'd love a tour, actually," offered Lakobus. He gave her the best innocent face he could muster under the circumstances, which were that he was a rotten lying bastard now.

Well, a bigger lying bastard . . . who was even *more* rotten.

She inhaled deeply before shaking her head while glaring at Hades. "Fine. I'll give him a tour, but after that he's on his own. Seems like he's already got the relentless torment part down."

Lakobus grinned, even though his nerves were flailing around like a live wire. He would have thought monsters like her appreciated a persistent, overly confident demon, but perhaps he'd come on a little too strong.

That uneasy fluttering in his chest was back, wiping the smile from his face. He swallowed hard when she narrowed her slitted eyes at him. Maybe accepting this Assessor gig hadn't been the best decision. It was his first day, and he was already failing as a demon. Perhaps he should have taken the lawyer job on Olympus.

Of course Hades and Zeus had been fighting over him. In fact, both openings had been created specifically with him in mind, and apparently, both had needed filling immediately.

When he'd interviewed with Zeus, Jake had gotten the feeling there wouldn't be much opportunity for growth at Life Industries. The way Zeus had rambled on and on, mostly about himself, all Jake pictured was being chained to his desk, at the king of the gods' beck and call century after century.

When he'd met with Hades about the Assessor of Souls position, the working environment had seemed like a better fit. It's not that the Underworld was lawless, but with a little grit, Jake felt he could realize his plans for domination relatively easy. Plus, he'd get a set of company wings.

It had been the opportunity to travel that had sealed the deal, though.

Lakobus had accepted the job in the Underworld, and now he was here, in the presence of this gorgeous creature hissing and growling at his new boss as if she owned the place. She would be a fine mentor, indeed, someone to show him the ropes and how things were done around here.

And it was going to be so satisfying taking her place as Head Monster one day.

CHAPTER THIRTY-SIX

*M*edusa barged into Fates Incorporated as if she wouldn't regret it in about ten seconds. Themis, their mother, who also served as their administrative assistant, looked up from doing a crossword puzzle at her desk.

"Medusa?" She tucked the pen she'd been using behind her ear for safekeeping. "What brings you here?"

Medusa's gaze skimmed over the goddess's bouffant, which was higher than Mount Olympus and redder than Mars, before taking in the way her green collared box dress made her look sort of like a 1960s Christmas tree come to life. Not exactly how she pictured the goddess of justice.

Medusa cleared her throat. "I need to talk to the Fates, the sooner the better."

For her throat being as dry as it was, the words managed to tumble out fairly quickly.

"You seem distressed, my dear." Themis took off the cat-eye reading glasses perched on the end of her nose and let them dangle around her neck by their chain. "Has Athena been giving you grief again?" She made a disappointed clicking noise. "That girl. If I've told her once to stop being such a hard-headed bully, I've told her a thousand times."

"It's not about Athena," said Medusa. "It's about a demon."

That got her attention.

Themis made another clicking noise, sounding even more disappointed than the first, if that was even possible. "Medusa. You know Atropos doesn't make very many mistakes. Lachesis makes even less. If it was their time, it was their time. And if they wanted to be a demon, well, that was their prerogative, so I would tread lightly if I were you."

Medusa began to sweat, suddenly realizing what a harebrained idea it had been to waltz into Fates Inc. unannounced, without an appointment.

Had she really thought their very protective mother was going to just grant her instant access to fate?

"I'm not saying they made a mistake . . . Not exactly."

"Then whatever are you implying?" said Themis, leaning back in her chair with her arms folded.

"Look, I'm not implying anything. I'm here to ask them to reverse the demonization of Jake Sullivan."

"Well," said Themis, lifting an eyebrow before turning her attention to tidying the paperwork on her desk. "Seems more like a demand to me," she murmured. "And you know how the girls respond to demands."

"Please, Themis. I'm begging you. Let me talk to them."

"You're putting me in a terrible position, my dear. I'm the gatekeeper. It's my job to weed out the—"

Time to put her silver forked tongue to good use.

"I was turned into a monster for no good reason," began Medusa. "And what did I do?" She paused, but not because she expected an answer. It was for dramatic effect. "That's right. I took it, and I never asked for my fate to be changed, not even once. How many gods come through here on a daily basis, huh? Asking for this and demanding that?"

Themis nodded her head, weighing Medusa's argument against the truth. She was the goddess of fairness, and Medusa had her claws crossed she'd sparked Themis's passion for equality.

"Okay. You've convinced me. Have a seat in the conference cave and I'll call them down." She picked up the phone and began to dial.

Medusa's heart pounded, and her legs felt like jelly. If she didn't move now, she might pass out. She hurried over to the conference room and pushed through the heavy wooden door, shuddering at the ominous scraping sound the bottom made as it skimmed across the stone floor.

She closed the door and looked around. The room essentially amounted to a cave. Her surroundings looked like they hadn't changed since the dawn of time. To say they were sorely outdated was an understatement. Not surprising, since the Fates didn't exactly have the time to renovate their workspace. They were some busy gals.

Medusa jolted when the door burst open and in stomped Atropos. Her jet-black hair was pulled into a tight bun and her jaw was set, but it was her eyes that gave away her extreme displeasure at having to attend a last-minute and wholly unexpected meeting. They glowed like two red-hot embers; lasers ready to burn through the offending party.

Medusa steeled herself for an attack, not just physically, but mentally. She'd heard stories about those eyes, and how Atropos used them as weapons to manipulate emotions to get her way during meetings. If Medusa was going to have to fight tooth and nail with fate to get Jake transferred out of the Underworld, she would be ready.

He deserved it.

Bring it on, you red-eyed b—

The door opened again, cutting off her thought, and she blew out a breath as Lachesis and Clotho entered the conference cave. A blessing, probably from Hermes, since Medusa wasn't sure Atropos could also read minds as well as manipulate them.

Easy. You don't know what kind of century Atropos is having.

Perhaps it hadn't been Hermes who'd saved her from falling back into her old ways. Maybe she'd saved herself, by learning a thing or two about thinking of others.

Atropos had one mean resting bitch face, though.

Once they were all seated, Clotho smiled sweetly at Medusa, her violet eyes sparkling brightly despite the dark circles under them. She weaved the threads of destiny, and by the look of it, the Head of Production at Fates Incorporated worked a hell of a lot of hours.

"Mother tells us you are here to ask us to reverse . . ." She consulted the paperwork she'd brought in with her. "Jake Sullivan's demon status and turn him back into a regular old human soul. Is that right?"

Medusa nodded, keeping her gaze on Clotho. She could already feel the heat of Atropos's glare. "Yes. I'd also like to request he be transferred to Elysium, like I had originally intended."

She wanted to say more, explain how she appreciated that they had seen fit to work with Hades to get Jake into the Underworld for her sake, but that it hadn't been necessary because he didn't belong there.

But she couldn't make her mouth form the words. To this, her heart promptly began screaming at her.

Open up. If you want to save him, you're going to have to tell them the whole story . . . that you love him.

Medusa opened her mouth, to lay her feelings bare, but Fate Inc.'s Account Executive spoke before she could get anything out.

"Well that's not happening." Atropos propped her arms on the table and clasped her hands, steam beginning to rise off of her dark skin.

"What my sister means to say is that Mr. Sullivan chose

to become a demon," interjected Lachesis, the fate responsible for measuring the threads of life.

"Exactly. And, honestly, I couldn't wait to cut his threads, which I believe was just as recently as last week." Atropos rolled her eyes flippantly. "I can't recall, they're all the same to me."

Medusa made the mistake of meeting Atropos's gaze. The rage welled inside her at an alarming rate, and that was saying something.

All she wanted to do right now was lunge across the table and swipe the smirk off Atropos's face before turning all the gods and goddesses on Olympus to stone. She was seriously contemplating it when the heavy wooden door creaked open yet again.

"Knock, knock," Hermes stepped into the chilly conference cave. "Hello, ladies. I don't mean to interrupt . . ."

"What is the meaning of this, messenger?" Atropos pushed away from the table, looking ready to stab him with her ink pen.

"Just got a couple announcements to deliver really quick."

The god of love entered the cavernous room next, holding a box of donuts.

"Well, I wouldn't exactly call them announcements so much as *requests*." Eros widened his eyes at Hermes as he walked past him, emphasizing there was definitely a difference.

"As the king of the sea," announced Poseidon, sauntering through the door with his chest puffed out and chin held high. "I would have to agree with Cupid. We have a request."

He reached inside the pastry box Eros had deposited in the center of the conference cave table.

Medusa swayed in her chair. She felt lightheaded, and like she was about to pass out.

"On behalf of Olympus." Poseidon selected an eclair. "We ask that you consider reversing the demonization of the mortal who's soul means a great deal to Medusa. As a unit, and not just you, Atropos." He tipped the custard-filled pastry toward the fate of death before taking a bite.

Medusa nearly fell out of her chair. Poseidon was *here*, acting every inch the arrogant ass he was, but he was at Fates Incorporated, helping *her* plead her case to get Jake changed back, so that he could be transferred to the right place.

That fact was absolutely mind-boggling in and of itself, but the real shocker was Poseidon hadn't referred to her as "the gorgon."

He had actually used her name.

Clotho smiled sweetly, and Lachesis remained expression-less. Medusa noticed they weren't breathing—just sitting there waiting—and realized they were both holding their breath, preparing for their sister to lose her shit.

Atropos did not disappoint. She slammed her fist on the table so hard Medusa felt it vibrate, amazed the ancient wood hadn't split clean in half.

Something else rocked her, too. She had friends on Olym-pus, and even if the Fates said no, those friends had shown up, in a big way.

Medusa looked at each of them. At Hermes, then over at Eros, who was eyeing the box of donuts lovingly. At Posei-don, the god who didn't possess a selfless bone in his body, but somehow had found it within himself to at least try.

Atropos's eyes blazed, the temperature rising to an uncomfortable level. Not for Medusa, she was used to it, but the gods had to have been sweating their balls off.

A loud click sounded, so unexpected it made them all jump, and a commanding voice filled the stifling air.

"My vote is for a reversal . . . and then a transfer to Olym-pus. You ladies can do an old pal a favor, can't you? I mean, you have to admit, Medusa's assessment that he belong on the mountain was pretty spot on."

The crack of lightning accompanied by a faint roll of

thunder heard through the intercom was all Medusa needed to hear to know that even The Douche was rooting for her.

CHAPTER THIRTY-SEVEN

*L*akobus took a sip of coffee before exiting the break room. The bats were squeaking from where they clung to the rocky walls, and the eternal doom and gloom was glowing dimly outside.

He smiled. Today was going to be an excellent day.

There was one thing, however, that had the potential to take his good mood down a notch. Hades had sent him an email late last night. All it had said was *Throne room, first thing,* which, he had to admit, did make him a bit nervous.

But he'd just started this gig, and Lakobus couldn't imagine whatever it was Hades needed to discuss with him would be anything to be concerned about.

Nonetheless, he was a little surprised to see the messenger, Hermes, in attendance when he walked in.

Lakobus told himself not to worry. He'd be crossing more than a few boundaries, as well as dimensions, in his new job. Perhaps that was the reason for the meeting, so the god of travel could bestow to him some sort of special passport.

"Good morning, fellas," said Lakobus, trying not to frown at the fact Hermes had already claimed the bone chair.

Hades waved a hand and a crappy Herman Miller office chair appeared.

"Good morning," he said, his tone serious. "Please, have a seat."

Well, shit, maybe Lakobus had been wrong about not being concerned.

He sat and, without preamble, Hermes held out a folded piece of paper to him. Lakobus took it, unfolding it with one hand so he didn't have to put down his cup of coffee.

"What's this?"

Neither god answered.

Nope. Not looking good at all.

Lakobus set the letter into his lap, not bothering to read it. He'd bet his wings Zeus was still trying to get him to step toward the light, so to speak, and quite frankly, he was over it.

"Look, if it's a transfer, tell Zeus I appreciate the enthusiasm," he said, glancing at Hermes before taking another sip of coffee, "I'm flattered, really, but I just don't think I'm a good fit for Olympus."

"It's not a transfer to Olympus," replied Hermes.

"Okay, then what is it?" Lakobus tilted his head and blinked.

Hades' gaze cut to Hermes, and Lakobus's stomach dropped. It seemed as though things were going from Not Good to How Much Worse is This Going to Get? in a rather hot hurry.

Then a terrible thought hit him, and he whipped his head toward Hades.

"Are you sending me to Tartarus?" Lakobus unleashed a panicked huff. "Because, with all due respect, sir, I haven't even gotten a chance to show you how truly evil I can be."

Hades shook his head. "You're not going to Tartarus, either."

Lakobus relaxed, but not for long because now he was

confused. "Well, if I'm not going to Olympus, and I'm not going to the tar pits, then where in the hell am I going?"

Hades remained silent, which made Lakobus nervous again.

He swallowed hard. "Is somebody going to tell me what's going on?"

"Why don't you just read the letter," said Hermes.

Lakobus snatched the piece of paper from his lap.

Dear Mr. Lakobus, The Unscrupulous One,
Due to recent events that are beyond your control, your status
as Demon of the Underworld has been revoked. Please contact
our office to schedule a reversal ASAP.

Regards,
The Fates

"Revoked?" said Lakobus, leaning over so he could set his coffee on the edge of the dais. Can they even do that?"

His heart hammered as he folded the letter into quarters and stuck it into the front pocket of his black button down.

"They're the Fates," replied Hades, peering down at him. "They can pretty much do whatever they want."

Lakobus folded his arms, mostly in an attempt to keep his composure. He'd been a demon for less than a week. He hadn't even been given his first project yet, and his demon status was being revoked by the Fates? Something wasn't adding up.

Was Medusa trying to sabotage him already? He'd expected her to do something cut-throat like this, eventually, but he hadn't imagined it would be so soon.

"I'm not sure I understand what's going on here," said Lakobus, determined to get to the bottom of whatever shit Medusa was pulling. "I could have gone to Olympus or come here, and I picked here. I *chose* to become a demon. I've barely even gotten my feet wet, and now the Fates want to revoke my demon status?"

"That's . . . partially correct," answered Hermes. "You did choose demonization, but I'm afraid you didn't have the full story, my friend."

Lakobus's gaze went straight up to Hades, who, he discovered, was chewing on his bottom lip.

After a few agonizing seconds more of silence from the King of the Underworld, Hermes finally piped up.

"Are you going to explain it to him, or do you want me to?"

Hades sighed. "Fine, if you insist on divulging such trivial details." He rested an elbow on each of the ornate arms of his solid gold throne and clasped is hands over his stomach. "I suppose it should come from me, anyway, since I'm the one who lured you to the dark side."

"Lured me? But I thought . . ."

"Medusa wanted a vacation," said Hades. "And I wanted to best my brother. So, I approved her request for time off and away to Earth she went."

An image of a beautiful woman, out on a balcony, lights from a big city twinkling in the background, flashed through Lakobus's mind, and that unsettling feeling that something had happened between him and Medusa began to dance around the edge of his memory again.

"But she's a monster . . . how did she . . .?"

"Eros hooked her up with some Illusion of Beauty," replied Hermes.

"Okay, but I still don't see how her taking a vacation has anything to do with me," snapped Lakobus, realizing the moment the words left his mouth the woman he was remembering must be Medusa in disguise.

Silence.

Hermes cleared his throat, urging Hades to continue.

"She was also tasked with assessing your soul."

"*My* soul? Why?"

Hades rolled his eyes and he gestured dismissively with a hand. "Oh, it was rumored to be questionable, and Zeus was trying to pawn you off on us . . ."

"But it was, right? That's why you offered me the job. Because I was a despicable human being. I was already corrupt."

"No," cut in Hermes. "You were a good guy, flawed, but good, and Medusa determined that you belonged in Elysium."

Another image, this time the woman—Medusa—smiling and laughing at him from the passenger side of a Range Rover, windows down, sunroof open, dark curls blowing in the wind, infiltrated his brain.

"So she wanted to sent me to Elysium, not the Underworld?"

"Yes," said Hades. "And it broke her heart. Really tore her up, but, of course, Medusa being Medusa, thinking monsters aren't worthy of love, she refused to admit it. Gods above, I couldn't bear to see her in so much pain, you know? So I created the position and offered you the job, so you two could be together. But it made her even more unhappy because she thought you were perfect the way you were."

Hades inhaled a breath, but didn't continue.

"And?" prompted Hermes.

"And I had you turned into a demon so I could give you the job and apparently I fucked up and now here we are."

Hades glared at Hermes.

Lakobus rubbed at the base of a horn. "But why would that break her heart? Why would she even care?" He dropped his head into his hands, trying desperately to remember and simultaneously forget his human life.

Lakobus was vaguely aware Hermes was digging something out of his pocket when he heard the messenger say, "I think it's best to just reinstate his memories, don't you? I can call Mnemosyne right now."

His head snapped up, just in time to see Hades nodding at Hermes . . . And Hermes wasting no time dialing.

Lakobus's heart hammered in his chest, and his gut churned now, too. He knew Hades had asked the goddess of memory to give him a clean slate as far as loving and being loved was concerned.

He'd thought it had been a good idea when he'd been informed of what had gone down, even appreciated the Collector being onboard with not letting things like feelings get in the way of being the best demon he could be.

But now he wanted—needed—to know. Because it was like a part of his soul was missing, and he felt incomplete without it.

"Hey, Mnemmy. Can you unblock the memories for Jacob Sullivan?" Hermes nodded. "Yep. Judith and Mortimer. Thanks, girl."

Lakobus switched his gaze between the two gods, wondering what in the hell else had been wiped clean, when suddenly, a flood of memories came crashing back all at once.

How the sight of Medusa at the airport bar the day they'd met, clad in her stunning disguise, had taken his breath away.

Kissing her out on the balcony, relishing the thrill of it even though he already knew he was risking his still broken heart again.

The Halloween gala, and how he'd hoped she wouldn't show up . . . and then realizing how much he'd actually wanted her to when she had.

The constant butterflies during the entire trip to the zoo with his niece Hailey.

Hailey, his beautiful little Comet and, oh, how he miss her. And Kara. And Shane. And even his parents.

The images kept pouring in, wave after wave of emotion

rolling over him. Drowning him in an ocean of love and longing and regret.

He thought about making love to her night after night, waking up next to her in the morning, and how much hope it had given him.

These memories, these feelings, they explained so much. He'd suspected something had happened between them, but it hadn't mattered a few days ago; he hadn't cared one way or the other because he hadn't known.

And now that he did know, everything was different. Much different. He didn't belong here.

Wherever she was, that's where he belonged.

"She loved me," said Lakobus.

Another memory came to him, a woman with the most striking hazel eyes, with the orange and pink glow of a sunset catching the gold flecks and making them shine.

"And I loved her back," he said, knowing beyond a shadow of a doubt that he still did, and he always would, no matter what time or space lay between them.

"You did," confirmed Hermes. "But she knew it was impossible for you to be together, so she had to let you go."

"And I was too afraid of loving her, so I let her." Lakobus swallowed down his emotion. He no longer wanted to best her at anything. He wanted to be with her, and wherever she was right now, he wanted to be there, too.

"Is there still a chance for us?"

"That's up to fate," said Hades, his lips tipping into a small, knowing smile, "but I'd say there's a pretty good chance they're on your side."

Hermes stood, and after sliding his hands into his pockets and nodding, he said, "Come on, man. I'll give you a lift to Fates Incorporated."

Lakobus was standing now as well, ready to finally be with his soulmate no matter what she—what either of them —looked like on the outside.

CHAPTER THIRTY-EIGHT

Medusa stared at the television screen not seeing much, and when her eyes began to burn, she finally blinked. Chloe and Lucifer suddenly came back into focus, and Medusa realized that she had spaced through the entire third season.

She'd missed the moment when Chloe saw the real Lucifer. It was one of her favorite parts because you just knew that, even though she didn't want to believe it, she still loved him.

And if Chloe Decker could still love someone even though their face was uglier than sin . . .

It's a freaking television show, Medusa. That wouldn't have happened in real life. If Jake would have seen the real you, you'd have had zero chance.

She reached for the glass of whiskey on the coffee table. She was supposed to be rested and relaxed. That's what the Rs in R&R stood for, right?

Instead, here she was, thinking about the what-ifs like there had truly been a chance her and Jake could have been together. The only reality right now was that she was alone and in the dark.

Had she mentioned she was alone in the dark? How about that she was right back where she had started? Lonely. Had she mentioned *that?*

Except, this time, instead of feeling sorry for herself with a nice bottle of wine she was numbing the pain with shots of whiskey. Several so far, to be exact, because where a once impervious heart of stone used to be was now a cavernous empty space, and filling that void needed lots and lots of grain alcohol.

Disappointed with her tasteless raw steak dinner, she'd decided the only reasonable thing left to do was to put on her pajamas and watch Lucifer until she fell asleep on the couch.

Now she sipped her whiskey, bleary-eyed and half-heartedly laughing at the cheeky fallen angel's antics while solving crimes in . . . Oh gods . . . Los Angeles.

Great. Even binge-watching her favorite show was a painful reminder of her time on Earth.

Her brush with true happiness.

She stifled a groan, which, if she was being honest, was really a sob, so when her phone buzzed it was a blessing from above. Actor Tom Ellis might be a mortal with one killer set of abs, but even that wasn't enough to save her from her misery.

Jake's were better, anyway.

She glanced at the caller ID, saw it was Hermes, and contemplated letting it go into voicemail. She didn't particularly want to talk to anyone right now, let alone fend off a litany of stupid jokes.

But, however remote the possibility, it might be regarding Jake's fate, so she answered it.

"Hey."

"Hey," responded Hermes, a tentativeness in his voice. "How are you doing?"

"Oh, you know us monsters . . ." Medusa's thought

trailed off as she rubbed her forehead, failing at her attempt to look on the bright side. "I'm fine."

She was glad Hermes had called versus just showing up in her living room. That way, he couldn't see how huge the lie written all over her face was.

His silence told her he knew anyway.

"Fine," she said. "I feel like shit. Happy?"

"Of course I'm not happy you're sad," he replied. "Contrary to popular belief, not all gods are selfish assholes, you know. Just Apollo."

Medusa couldn't stop herself from chuckling. Wasn't that the truth. Apollo was the worst.

"So, the reason I'm calling—besides checking up on my favorite Head Monster—is because I have some good news to share. Kara and Shane's EMR went through. Eros should be shooting them as we speak."

Medusa nodded, smiling faintly. "That's great. I'm glad to hear it." She inhaled a shaky breath, not knowing whether she wanted to know the answer to the question she was about to ask. "And Jake? Any word on him?"

"Yeah, about that. Still no word. I'm sorry."

Medusa sighed heavily, despite her resolve not to sound disappointed. "It's all good. I should just accept his soul's been corrupted. I'm sure I'll get over it. Eventually. Thanks for keeping me posted."

"Of course," said Hermes.

She'd detected a hint of mirth in those two words. The way he'd said it made it seem like he knew more than what he was telling her.

Even though she was curious, she didn't have the energy to get it out of him. So she remained silent, not taking the bait. She was too mentally drained to process anything else right now, anyway.

"Aaaand," continued Hermes. "Even though you probably don't want to be seen hanging around downtown with a god, you know we can grab coffee any time, right? All you have to do is call and I'll be there in a flash, girl."

Cheesy but sincere, Hermes' words finally succeeded in making her crack a smile. A wide one, too, since he'd just presented proof that he would be there for her through thick and thin, just like the thieves they were, and even when her temper got ugly.

"I appreciate that, messenger. I mean, as far as gods go, I guess you're not so bad."

They shared a laugh, and Medusa had to dab at her eyes. She told herself they were only watering because she was tired, and she was about to bid Hermes a good night when he spoke.

"Don't give up hope, Medusa," he said with a seriousness that made her squirm a bit. "There still might be a chance he'll get transferred. Atropos and Lachesis hold pretty firm, but Clotho . . . Let's just say she's been known to throw in a little twist of fate into the mix every now and again."

She appreciated what Hermes was trying to do. He was trying to give her hope. Hermes was good like that.

"Yeah, well, I'm not holding my breath," she murmured. Then, done with wallowing in her self-pity for the night, she cleared her throat. "Okay, messenger, it's past my beastly bedtime."

"Sleep well, Medusa. Tomorrow's a brand new start. Who knows? You might wake up feeling like a new person."

"No, I'll still be a monster," she said softly. "And I'm totally okay with that. What do they say? It's better to have loved and lost than never to have loved at all."

"Alfred Tennyson. Sometimes they do know what they're talking about, don't they?"

Medusa pushed a small huff through her snout as she grabbed the remote and switched off the television. "If you say so, bro." She tossed it on the coffee table before stretching out, a couple of her snakes pulling down an afghan from the back of the couch. "Good night, Hermes."

She closed her eyes, utterly exhausted from all the feels currently plaguing her. *Still* plaguing her. She burrowed deeper into the blanket as she imagined the happiness on Jake's face walking into Elysium.

As she sank into unconsciousness, the last thought that floated through her mind was that if, by some twist of fate, *she* ever got a do-over, she would make damn sure she'd do things differently.

She'd focus less on what others thought of her and more on what mattered. Peace. Joy. Kindness. Loving someone with your whole heart.

And not one made of stone, either.

If she ever got another life to live, she'd do everything in her power to make sure no one ever cowered in fear when they heard the name Medusa.

CHAPTER THIRTY-NINE

*S*nap.

Medusa stirred awake.

Snap.

She could have sworn she'd turned off the television, but maybe she hadn't.

Snap.

Annoyed, and unwilling to open her eyes just yet, she reached for the coffee table to grab the remote.

Where the hell was the coffee table?

And was someone *blowing* on something?

Her eyes flew open, and to her utter shock and amazement, she discovered she wasn't on her couch.

Heart pounding, she took in her surroundings. The room was small, the floor hard-packed dirt, and rays of golden morning sun beamed through the cracks in the shuttered window.

What in Hades' Realm was going on? She definitely wasn't in her condo anymore. Living in the Underworld, she'd come across some weird shit, but never waking up in a *hut*.

That's what this was, wasn't it? A hut, as in a hut like the hut she used to live in when she was a . . .

Medusa gasped.

No, it couldn't be.

She looked at her hands, not claws, and her mouth went dry. She felt silky hair, not hissing snakes, and could scarcely breathe.

What had Hermes said last night?

"Tomorrow's a brand-new start."

"Hermes, you shit!" she whispered. "Did you know about this?

No answer. But if she really was a mortal again, there wouldn't be.

Medusa heard blowing once more and realized that, even though she hadn't heard it in centuries, it was the sound of someone trying to bring dying embers back to life.

The snapping had been the kindling, and the person who'd always been in charge of breaking up twigs to get the fire going in the morning had been her sister Sthenno.

Medusa clapped a hand over her mouth.

Her sisters!

Medusa threw off her sleeping covers and bolted out of bed, rushing into the common room of the wood and sun-dried mud hut of her youth. When she laid eyes on Euryale and Sthenno for the first time in centuries, she skidded to a halt, barely believing what she was seeing.

They were here, alive and breathing, and not just vague, fading memories.

Her sisters stopped what they were doing to both eye her as though she were mad.

Euryale was the first to speak. "Are you alright?"

Rapid-fire blinking commenced in order to keep the tears welling in Medusa's eyes from falling.

Medusa didn't answer, only went over to Euryale and hugged her. "I've missed you so much."

"What has gotten into you?" asked Euryale, returning Medusa's embrace.

She'd been given a do-over, that's what had gotten into her. A chance to make different choices . . . experience another outcome.

Euryale had always derived such pleasure in the domestic side of things. Sthenno had found joy elsewhere, with tending to the plants and animals.

And Medusa? She had been a devoted priestess to the temple of Athena. Some might have even said she'd been a zealot.

Her sisters had been—and still were, it seemed—ordinary women content with everyday things while leading a normal life. That had been all well and good, but it hadn't been enough for Medusa.

Medusa had needed more back then. She had wanted to be *seen*. Euryale had her weaving, Sthenno her husbandry. An oath of sacrifice to the goddess Athena at such a young age had been what Medusa was known for. It was what had made her stand out. What made the citizens of Athens *notice* her.

She'd been noticed alright, by Poseidon, and it had turned out horribly. Notoriety would not be top priority this go-around.

Nope. Not in this lifetime.

What about Jake? The thought of him pierced her heart. Had he gotten a do-over, too? She hoped he wasn't still a demon.

Sthenno's voice scattered her thoughts. "Has cleaning the temple until the small hours of the night finally driven you mad?" She grunted as she set the heavy iron pot over the now lively fire. "You would think Pallas Athena wouldn't mind if you got some sleep for once."

Medusa smiled as she patiently waited for Sthenno to finish situating the pot over the flames before hugging her. "You would think."

Even though it made her want to sob wondering what had become of Jake, she was grateful to have been granted this new lease on life. She loved her sisters, dearly, and being here with them, receiving another chance to avoid being cursed, was everything.

Her first life had been lived. *That* story would still be told, and the infamous gorgon of myth would still exist to mortals not yet born. That hadn't changed.

But existing alongside *that* Medusa's life would be *this* Medusa's life. One that would be lived with gratitude, and then quietly fade into the vast expanse of time with the rest of the forgotten tales of ordinary lives lived.

Medusa smiled as she strapped on a pair of worn leather sandals.

"My dearest." Sthenno had come over to lay a staying hand on her shoulder. "The candles and incense can wait. Besides, breakfast will be ready shortly." Her sister absently combed her fingers through the luxurious strands of Medusa's long hair. She did it lovingly, as a mother would do to a daughter. "See to Athena's temple with a full stomach, yes?"

Medusa nodded. "No temple today. I thought I would go to the market and tell everyone there of all the colorful yarns my sister Euryale makes, and the potent and healing medicines by my sister Sthenno. Have either of you any samples I can take?"

She'd learned a thing or two about marketing, and she was going to boost the shit out of her sisters' talents.

It had only been the three of them for as long as Medusa remembered, even in this lifetime. If it wasn't for the profits from Eurayle's weaving and Sthenno's herb gardening, Medusa would not have been able to dedicate herself to such pious worship.

Medusa tried remembering her parents, and if her sisters had ever told her what had happened to their mother and father. Not only was there an empty space in her heart there was a a blank spot in her memory.

Had he been handsome and brave? Had she been beautiful and kind? It was hard to imagine a reason why they would abandon their children. If they were not dead, they must have been forced to leave them behind. Surely, it hadn't been on purpose.

And apparently it was part of her destiny to never know.

Medusa patiently sat as the oats finished cooking. Euryale had gone to her weaving, and Medusa had decided to make herself useful and comb through the wool waiting to be spindled and dyed into colorful threads.

Euryale smiled absently as she sat at her loom, and Sthenno hummed cheerfully as she scooped their breakfast into bowls.

Medusa hadn't ever known her parents—she often pictured a woman who looked like Euryale at the hearth, a man who'd passed on his angular features to Sthenno out in the garden.

In their absence, Medusa had thrown herself into the only thing she felt could keep her mind occupied. That would set her apart.

Sacrifice. Dedication. Veneration.

She had been determined to be admired for her ability to take her suffering to the utmost extreme. It hadn't hurt that she had the face for that kind of thing, or that it was made even more fair by being surrounded with locks of golden-brown waves so lustrous they were envied throughout all of Athens.

Despite her penchant for going over the top, the biggest reason Medusa had promised to dedicate her life to Athena—who she knew even back then, before she was privy to the fact that, yes, gods and goddesses indeed existed, held great sway with Zeus—was much simpler than being known for vows and hair.

Her dedication to the goddess, her singularly focused energy, had started out as something innocent enough: A way to bring her parents back.

In an attempt to do so, she had decided not to marry or have children. If she suffered and sacrificed for whatever sins her parents had committed, perhaps Athena would have found it in her heart to reunite her and her sisters with them.

That's what she'd thought, anyway.

"You look vexed," said Euryale. "Is that man still bothering you? The one who visits the temple in the hopes of catching a glimpse of Athena's most ardent devotee?"

Ah, she must be talking about Poseidon.

He popped into her mind. His blue-green eyes, as bright and sparkling as the Aegean Sea, were pretty, she'd give him that. Still didn't excuse what he'd done, and it most definitely didn't mean all was forgiven between them.

It's not like she would never step foot into Athena's temple again, she would still worship on occasion, just nothing compared to the degree in which she'd previously centered her life around the goddess.

But if not the temple, he'll probably show up somewhere else.

She'd have to always be on guard.

Medusa tipped her bowl, showing both sisters that it had been scraped clean. "There, belly full." She wiped the vessel with a cloth and set it inside a small cupboard. "I'll be back in a few hours."

Medusa gasped when she saw the old woman fall in the street up ahead. Except, she hadn't exactly fallen. The woman had been talking to two young boys, or rather, they had been shouting at her.

Medusa's heart had seethed with anger when one of them, pudgy and red-faced, had reached for the woman's satchel and violently ripped it from her waist.

"You! Stop that!" Medusa cried as she broke out into a run.

The awful brats dashed away, ducking into a side street and out of sight. Who does that? Bullies an old woman minding her own damn business.

The boys didn't look like they were starving, especially the portly one, so were they stealing from an old woman for thrills? The thought made Medusa even more angry.

"Are you okay?" she said as she guided the old woman to her feet. "Are you hurt?"

"Oh, I'm fine." The old woman wiped the dirt from her chiton. "But what a surprise they will have, those hooligans. Old Magdathena never carries coins."

The woman cackled with delight and Medusa couldn't help but smile. "What was in your purse, if not coins?"

"Dried beans!" The woman tapped a finger to her temple. "Strategy. Old Magdathena knows how to outsmart those little thieves. Yes, they will get what they deserve. The gods will make sure of that."

"They shouldn't be stealing at all, and certainly not from a kind old woman such as yourself. Do you know who they are? I have a mind to put a stop to their thieving with a good thrashing."

"Old Magdathena has never seen them before. Then again, her and her grandson have just moved to Athens. You sound exactly like him, girl." The old woman lifted an arm and pointed a withered finger over Medusa's shoulder. "In fact, here he comes now."

When a man with tousled dark hair rushed up, Medusa's heart leapt in her chest like a frightened rabbit. He glanced at her, and she noticed his eyes were the most beautiful shade of green she'd ever seen before . . .

Jake?

"Grandmother?" said the man. "What's happened? Did

those brats steal from you? I have a mind to stop their thieving with a good thrashing."

The old woman looked at Medusa, a twinkle dancing in her pale-blue eyes. Medusa had seen those eyes before, too.

Athena?

"Ha! If you would have been out of bed early, like your sister and niece, Old Magdathena would not have had to leave for the temple without you."

Medusa's mouth hung open. Even if she could speak, she had no idea what to say.

"This nice young woman came to Old Magdathena's aid . . ." continued the goddess in disguise. "And a selfless deed like that should not go unrewarded."

According to outward appearances, it would seemed as though Athena was talking to the man. But Medusa knew the words were meant for her.

She swallowed around the lump in her throat.

"Thank you," said the man. "How can I repay you for your kindness?"

Medusa swayed on her feet, disappointment spiraling through her. He didn't remember.

Maybe it wasn't Jake.

"There is no need to repay me," said Medusa, finding her composure and quickly regaining her balance. "I was happy to help your grandmother."

"I'm grateful you did." The man smiled, and then his brows furrowed, as if he knew he'd seen her face somewhere but couldn't place it. "Have we met before?"

All the air in Athens seemed to vanish. What could Medusa even say? Well, whatever she managed, it wasn't going to be another lie.

"It sure feels like we have, doesn't it?" she replied. "Perhaps it was in another lifetime."

The moment he looked deep into Medusa's eyes, peering

straight into her soul, an expression of familiarity smoothed his face.

Medusa had no doubt the same tingling sensation she was currently experiencing raised the flesh of his arms just the same as it did hers.

He smiled wide when he finally recognized her.

Good gods in heaven. It is you. And you remember!

It was just as dazzling as ever, that smile, and it still had the power to make her lightheaded.

"Yes," he said, grinning. "Another lifetime. I think that must be it."

She may have a different face, and he may be a smidge shorter, but they'd know each other's souls anywhere.

"Were you on your way to the temple?" he asked.

Medusa shook her head. "No, I was on my way to the market."

"May I accompany you? And perhaps afterward we can share a drink . . . Or take in a beautiful Mediterranean sunset."

"I'd love that."

"Me too."

"Oh, for the love of the gods, get it over with and tell her your name!" barked Athena.

"Jacob," he said, laughing. "But you can call me Jake."

"Hello, Jake." said Medusa, laughing now, too.

"Hello, Medusa." He reached out for her, cupping her face and brushing a thumb over her cheek. "It's nice to see you again."

She hadn't told him who she was, or her name. He'd just known.

Exactly how Clotho had planned it.

Medusa took a moment to catch her breath. It didn't matter what they looked like on the outside, their souls were finally one. She knew it and so did he, and she was grateful when he steadied her with strong hands when her legs nearly gave out.

"I promise I won't walk away this time," he murmured as he took her into his arms.

She nodded, slowly but surely, before looking up into those beautiful green eyes of his, the ones she'd know anywhere, in any lifetime. The ones she knew she was going to spend the rest of her second mortal life gazing into.

"Good," she whispered. "Because I don't plan on ever letting you go."

Hands on hips, wings silently maneuvering him in front of the old woman, Eros peered down at her. "And Poseidon has agreed to keep his hands to himself this time around?"

"Yes, yes." Athena cocked an eyebrow up at him.

It must have killed her to have to parade as a grand-mother, keeping her true form, in all its lady-warrior glory, under wraps.

"Now get on with it," she murmured before resuming the walk toward the temple Athens had erected in her honor.

Eros held in a laugh as he watched both Medusa and Jacob give Athena a look. No doubt it would have appeared as though she'd been talking to herself, and that delighted Eros more than he could safely let on.

Athena might be tempted to aim a few choice spears at him when they were back on the mountain if she knew just how funny he found it.

Jake shrugged, widening his eyes at Medusa and blowing off Athena's rudeness. Medusa laughed, the sound high and melodious, and Eros grinned.

"She's justified," said Medusa, a bit breathlessly. "She did just wave the white flag, after all."

If Eros had been in the middle of taking a sip of coffee, it would have sprayed all over the place.

He watched as Medusa and Jake rushed off towards the market, his heart nearly bursting at the sight. Something sweet and pure—and so powerful nothing and no one could live without it—was growing inside them.

Today was the day worshiping a goddess became second fiddle to falling in love.

Athena knew it, too, and it made him positively giddy she had finally found it in her hardened warrior's heart to end Medusa's suffering. She had finally agreed that making peace and not continuing to wage war was the best strategy when it came to Medusa's fate.

Eros whistled absently, flapping his wings double-time in order to catch up to the fated couple. Getting on with their new lives took major precedence over prayers. And that was the way it was intended to be in this do-over.

Oh, he'd have to come back and shoot them properly, with his great golden bow and arrows and all that jazz. This initial dusting was just the love-at-first-sight portion of the long and beautiful life together program. He'd come down to make sure Athena held true to her word of being present for the meet cute.

This day would go down in the books, indeed. In fact, he was still on a love high from when Hermes had delivered the good news earlier this morning. The Fates had refused Medusa's request for a transfer, but when Athena had gone to them yesterday, asking that a matter of her own regarding destiny be addressed, surprisingly, they'd been open to meeting with her without protest.

Even more surprising, the Fates had stayed late so the meeting could take place ASAP.

What was discussed during the after-hours meeting is

hearsay, but Themis often lunched with Leto, Olympus's goddess of gossip, and the rumor was the most stubborn, proud, and hard-headed goddess on the mountain had asked for, quote, "A second chance for both souls, Medusa and her love, which is richly and most honorably deserved."

Unsubstantiated, of course, but all that really mattered to Eros at this point was the sisters had heard Athena out.

He knew they hadn't made their decision on the spot from Hermes, but that they had sent a letter to the Underworld relatively quickly afterward. They were kind of cruel and unusual like that, but they were quite literally the end all, be all, so everyone, including Athena, had to roll with their punches.

And, well, while fate was going to be fate and take its time, Eros was just happy he still had his wings, he had the best friend a god could have, and that Athena had finally made the right move.

But the best part? It looked like Medusa finally had the love—and life—she had always deserved.

ABOUT THE AUTHOR

Kerri lives in Michigan with her husband, son, and cat they lovingly but aptly refer to as The Maleficence. When she's not writing, she's probably raking leaves, shoveling snow, or looking into where science is on that human cloning thing. For news and updates, visit kerrikeberly.com to subscribe to her mailing list.